BROTHERHOOD

As Franc and Verdon rode off side by side, they chatted.

'A fine lad, that Hal,' said Verdon.

'Yes. A good valet.'

'And pretty. Almost like a girl in disguise.'

'Ah, but for all his girlish ways, he's got a fine cock between his thighs,' said Franc, and then he blushed, as he realised he'd given the game away.

'And a pert arse too, I'll warrant,' smiled Verdon. 'Just right for plugging.'

Franc made no reply, and they rode on a little further without comment.

'Your grandmother told me you were a virgin, but I see now she misinformed me,' continued Verdon a little later.

'My grandmother knows nothing of my sex life . . .' spat Franc.

BROTHERHOOD

Guy Edenbridge

First published in Great Britain in 2001 by
Idol
Thames Wharf Studios,
Rainville Road, London W6 9HA

ISBN 0 352 33633 1

Typeset by SetSystems Ltd, Saffron Walden, Essex
Printed and bound in Great Britain by
Mackays of Chatham PLC

The Terrence Higgins Trust

SAFER SEX GUIDELINES

We include safer sex guidelines in every Idol book. However, while our policy is always to show safer sex in contemporary stories, we don't insist on safer sex practices in stories with historical settings – as this would be anachronistic. These books are sexual fantasies – in real life, everyone needs to think about safe sex.

While there have been major advances in the drug treatments for people with HIV and AIDS, there is still no cure for AIDS or a vaccine against HIV. Safe sex is still the only way of being sure of avoiding HIV sexually.

HIV can only be transmitted through blood, come and vaginal fluids (but no other body fluids) passing from one person (with HIV) into another person's bloodstream. It cannot get through healthy, undamaged skin. The only real risk of HIV is through anal sex without a condom – this accounts for almost all HIV transmissions between men.

Being safe
Even if you don't come inside someone, there is still a risk to both partners from blood (tiny cuts in the arse) and pre-come. Using strong condoms and water-based lubricant greatly reduces the risk of HIV. However, condoms can break or slip off, so:
* Make sure that condoms are stored away from hot or damp places.
* Check the expiry date – condoms have a limited life.
* Gently squeeze the air out of the tip.
* Check the condom is put on the right way up and unroll it down the erect cock.
* Use plenty of water-based lubricant (lube), up the arse and on the condom.
* While fucking, check occasionally to see the condom is still in one piece (you could also add more lube).

* When you withdraw, hold the condom tight to your cock as you pull out.
* Never re-use a condom or use the same condom with more than one person.
* If you're not used to condoms you might practise putting them on.
* Sex toys like dildos and plugs are safe. But if you're sharing them use a new condom each time or wash the toys well.

For the safest sex, make sure you use the strongest condoms, such as Durex Ultra Strong, Mates Super Strong, HT Specials and Rubberstuffers packs. Condoms are free in many STD (Sexually Transmitted Disease) clinics (sometimes called GUM clinics) and from many gay bars. It's also essential to use lots of water-based lube such as KY, Wet Stuff, Slik or Liquid Silk. Never use come as a lubricant.

Oral sex
Compared with fucking, sucking someone's cock is far safer. Swallowing come does not necessarily mean that HIV gets absorbed into the bloodstream. While a tiny fraction of cases of HIV infection have been linked to sucking, we know the risk is minimal. But certain factors increase the risk:
* Letting someone come in your mouth
* Throat infections such as gonorrhoea
* If you have cuts, sores or infections in your mouth and throat

So what is safe?
There are so many things you can do which are absolutely safe: wanking each other; rubbing your cocks against one another; kissing, sucking and licking all over the body; rimming – to name but a few.

If you're finding safe sex difficult, call a helpline or speak to someone you feel you can trust for support. The Terrence Higgins Trust Helpline, which is open from noon to 10pm every day, can be reached on 020 7242 1010.

Or, if you're in the United States, you can ring the Center for Disease Control toll free on 1 800 458 5231.

One

Frank du Bois pushed a stray lock of hair out of his grey eyes and gazed with interest through the undergrowth at the handsome young man who was chopping logs in the forest clearing before him. The fellow paused in his work, stood up and wiped his sweaty forehead with the back of his shirtsleeve. Frank recognised his tanned face at once. It was Rob Oakley, only son of the late Will Oakley, woodcutter.

'What a handsome lad you've turned out,' murmured Frank to himself. He gasped with delight as Rob stripped off his shirt to reveal a well-muscled, broad torso that tapered into the slender waistband of his coarse leggings. For a moment, as the boy paused in his labours, Frank drank in his manly beauty. He admired the deep chest with its faintest sprinkling of dark hair, the well-defined arms, the firm pectorals tipped with pert nipples. Then Rob resumed his work, and Frank marvelled at the delicious way the muscles in his upper body rippled with power as he threw the whole of his athletic frame behind each swing of his axe.

Half of Frank loved this young peasant; the other half recognised that he was only one of the many subservient bonded men who belonged to his aristocratic family. But in the end it was love that welled up in his heart now, and this overwhelmed the arrogance of his grandmother's cold training.

He and the woodcutter's son, who was only some nine months older than he was, had lived for the first few years of their lives as brothers. Frank grinned as he remembered that he and Rob had often jokingly called each other 'milk brother' throughout their childhood years. The man's milk swelled in his bollocks at the thought. He shivered with desire to think of how as children he and Rob had been fast friends. How in secret they had measured their growing pricks against a home-made 'pintle-gauge' to see whose was bigger.

Frank licked his lips and stared at Rob's bulging crotch. The hefty contours of the young woodcutter's cock strained the tight-stretched cloth of his breeches. How Frank longed to touch that bulge, to pat it, to stroke it. But how?

What a shame we've grown apart as we've grown up, he thought. If only they hadn't forced you to learn your father's trade, Robbie. If only they hadn't forced me to study all those knightly virtues. Why did it all go sour? Frank reached up and stroked the horn ring and the silver locket that hung on the silver chain round his neck. He opened the locket and gazed at the portrait of his dead father. His father's painted eyes stared up at his – grey reflecting grey. But there was something sensual about the mouth that reminded Frank of Rob – masculine, yet at the same time somehow soft and vulnerable at the edges. In a sudden rush, tears filled Frank's eyes at the thought of that last boar hunt of his father's, and the double tragedy that was its bloody end. That was when it all went bad, and when the subtle wedges drove the milk brothers apart. Frank sighed, snapped the locket shut, and dropped it back inside his fine cambric shirt. And in his head he locked away his grief, and turned his hungry gaze back to watch Rob cutting wood.

As he looked on at his former playmate, now a strapping man, he felt strong physical desire well up in him in warm waves. With each chop of the axe that Rob wielded, Frank's cock throbbed and swelled inside his tight leggings, and his bollocks ached.

Frank hitched up the tunic he wore, and unlaced his waistband. He slipped his hand inside his leggings and curled it around his stiffening prick. As he watched Rob at work, he began to stroke the hot, hard rod of his manhood. It felt good. He drew back the soft foreskin to reveal the smooth dome of the glans underneath. A glistening teardrop of pre-come nestled in his cock's eye.

Frank stared transfixed as Rob laid down his axe and sat down on the ground to rest. More pre-come welled out of the tip of his tool. He massaged the oily liquid over his smooth cockhead and down the length of the gnarled shaft. His pleasure mounted.

Then Molly, Rob's buxom girlfriend, came barefoot into the clearing. Perched on her hip she carried a basket of bread and cheese, and a flask of beer. Frank stopped caressing himself, intrigued to see what would happen next. Rob slaked his thirst with the beer, and bolted down the cheese and bread. Then he wiped his mouth dry with the back of his hand and looked at his girl. She sat on the ground next to him. Her freckled face smiled. She twined a long curl of her wild red hair around her fingers, then looked away with mock modesty. The young woodcutter reached over and unlaced her bodice. Her round white breasts sprang free, and Rob fondled them. He tweaked and pinched her nipples, then cupped and squeezed her fleshy pears in both hands. Frank still watched from his hidden spot in the undergrowth. His prick reared up at the sight of Rob and Molly's intimacy. He imagined Rob's rough tanned hands stroking his smooth hard chest instead of Molly's large breasts. How good that would feel.

Frank took himself in hand again, and began to masturbate with rapid strokes. He watched as Molly lay back against a tree stump, hitched up her skirts high about her wide hips, and splayed her bare legs wide. She wore no undergarments, and the red bush of her pubic hair stood out – a triangular tuft of red moss – against the milk-white, soft skin of her belly and inner thighs. Frank's excitement mounted when Rob kicked off his shoes, unlaced his waistband, and eased off his coarse leggings.

When Rob's dick sprang into view, Frank stroked his own organ faster and faster. The young woodcutter's long, thick penis pointed up to the sky, with a graceful curve, like a swan's neck. His bollocks hung down between his sturdy thighs like two ripe plums.

Frank moaned as he wanked. Rob looked so beautiful, the

perfect example of a sturdy peasant, as he sat, stark-naked and aroused, in the forest clearing. Frank found it such a turn-on to look at Rob's masculine beauty from afar, but to be unable to touch it, unable to taste it, unable to possess it. His moans became deeper and more throaty, and he began to tilt his pelvis forward and back, as he thrust his prick in and out of his hollow fist. He revelled in the waves of tingling pleasure that spiralled out from his cock root and rippled over his taut abdomen.

Before his eyes, Molly rubbed her fingertips over her love cleft. Then she parted her cunt lips, reached in and began to caress her large and lust-swollen clit with light feathery strokes. Her head lolled back and she moaned as her sexual arousal grew. Frank looked on and stroked his cock in time with Molly's deft fingerwork. Shivers of excitement coursed through his body as he saw Rob crouch between his girl's splayed legs. But the peasant boy didn't stuff his hard cock into her soft cunt mouth right away. Instead he bent his head down and started to lap like a thirsty bear cub at her pussy, which now glistened with love juice, sticky as honey.

Thrilled, Frank watched Molly roll over, crouch on hands and knees, and tilt her pert arse up in the air to expose her gaping cunt like an aroused she-wolf. The young aristocrat wanked himself with renewed vigour as he saw his peasant friend at last kneel close behind that ripe full arse and thrust his superb tool deep into her cunt and start to fuck her doggy-fashion. She stroked her clit all the while to heighten her pleasure, moaned with desire at every thrust, and called out for more.

Frank saw the muscles of Rob's brawny arse flex as he tupped his she-mate, and he thought how gorgeous it would be to take Molly's place right now. He longed to be crammed to bursting with dick, to have Rob's colossal phallus rammed up his arse to its bushy hilt, to feel that hard rod shoved deep inside him, to sense it bite deeper and deeper into his innards with every thrust.

Frank closed his eyes for an instant and imagined what it would feel like to have this young peasant lad, his beloved 'milk brother', fuck him. To be the woodcutter's he-mate in a rough and manly sexual coupling was a delicious image. Suddenly Frank reached pure ecstasy, his aching balls contracted, and a fierce jet of man's milk streamed up inside him. Powerful, urgent, it sought release. Unable to restrain himself, he let the warm liquid rise up and spray out from his cock mouth in a sticky, silvery fountain. Again and again his throbbing organ pumped out great gobbets of the precious fluid – the tangible sign of his great love for Rob. Then he fell back on the grass, drained.

In the glade Rob and Molly continued with their lovemaking for a while longer. Molly now gasped and whimpered, as she reached the peak of her sexual pleasure and then, suddenly, Rob uttered a deep bestial growl as he shot spurt after spurt of his creamy load inside her. After that, all fell silent, except for the usual country sounds – the sparrows twittering in the nearby hedgerows, sheep bleating in the distant fields.

Frank sat up and peered through the undergrowth into the glade. He saw that Rob still knelt behind Molly, still hung inside her, his fine strong back arched up, his hands still on her hips, and a look of utter bliss on his handsome face.

Frank smiled.

Then the moment of postcoital quiet passed. Rob patted Molly on the rump, withdrew from her, stood up, and stretched. His cock and balls were still impressive even in their softened state, thought Frank, and his well-knit body was as attractive when relaxed as when tense with effort or in the throes of sex.

Molly, too, stood up, straightened her skirts, and laced up her bodice. She planted a saucy kiss on Rob's cheek, picked up the empty picnic basket and the drained beer flask, and left the glade. She swung her hips and sang to herself as she marched off along the path that led to her parents' cottage.

Alone now, Frank faced the object of his desire. The afternoon wore on, warm and autumnal, and Rob – now he had cast off shirt, leggings and shoes – seemed to have no wish to put them on again. He stood unclothed in the glade, and posed and flexed his muscles, like a superb young pagan forest god – Herne the hunter, maybe, Frank decided.

Rob now started to walk around the glade in the nude like a proud stag – lusty, restless, untamable. He oozed strong male sexuality from every pore. He strutted like a glorious wild beast, unaware of its own natural beauty, and the seductive effect that it had on others. Frank longed to belong to him, to become one with him, to *be* him. He yearned to rush into the glade, to kneel before this young god and to worship him, body and soul.

Rob now took hold of his limp prick and pissed against the tree stump in the centre of the glade, and Frank stared, fascinated. This small act reminded him of their shared childhood wintertime competitions – when they dared each other to piss in the snow, so that they could measure who pissed further. Now it was autumn, but Frank still cherished what he saw. The arc of Rob's yellow piss glinted in the slanting afternoon sunlight, like a stream of liquid amber. Strange how love could elevate even the most sordid, the most mundane detail, and make it precious, Frank thought. The young woodcutter's piss went on and on, and Frank shuddered with delight as a wicked idea formed in his brain. How glorious it would be to kneel naked before this warm fountain of Rob's piss and to let the golden droplets rain down on his hands, his chest, his neck, his face, his lips.

Even as he imagined Rob like a living colossus towering over him, and peeing down on him, the doubts and the feelings of melancholy began to crowd into Frank's mind. Would he ever be able to achieve his heart's desire and not have someone snatch it from him?

A cheery robin alighted on a twig just above Frank's head and looked down at him with one beady eye as if to say, 'Why so sad, fond lover?' With a flick of its wing the bird flew off, but the question stuck in Frank's mind, like deep-etched piss tracks in the snow. It was not the fact that he had fallen in love with a man that was the problem.

Frank had known strong feelings for his own sex from an early age. It began with the tapestry that hung in the great hall at Woodmere – the country home of the du Bois family. This showed a huge black eagle which soared skywards with a well-built naked young lad clasped in its talons. In later years Frank learned as a matter of course that this tapestry depicted the rape of Ganymede – the young Trojan boy whom Zeus carried off to

Mount Olympus to serve him by day as his cupbearer, and by night as his bedmate.

As a young child, however, the tapestry simply fascinated Frank for the sheer beauty of the naked youth at its centre. He would gaze for hours at the lad's deep, defined chest, the outflung muscular arms, the taut belly, the well-knit outspread thighs and calves. What most intrigued him, however, was Ganymede's hairless pubic mound and the boyish cock and scrotum.

He knew from self-examination, and from looking at older boys when they swam together in the castle moat, or visited the communal castle jakes for a shared shit, that naked genitalia were a thing of youth, and that around the base of older lads' organs a thatch of wiry hairs sprouted. How was it, then, that in this tapestry Ganymede had such a manly body, such developed sexual tackle, and yet was so hairless?

Later, of course, Frank learned that the hairlessness was probably a mere artistic convention of the tapestry weaver. But as a boy he became convinced that Ganymede was more than old enough to have pubic hair, but had shaved it off to increase his youthful allure.

These days, as an adult, Frank wondered a little too at the smiling figure of the goddess Hera, who looked at the rape indulgently from the corner of the tapestry. In the normal recounting of the tale, Hera was jealous and far from tolerant of her husband Zeus's young catamite, but, in the tapestry at Woodmere Hall, the queen of heaven seemed to look with pleasure on the seductive lad, as if she knew of her husband's proclivities for younger men but indulged him in them, and perhaps even hoped to share in them herself. At any rate, when Frank was a child, this tapestry fed and fanned the flame of his love for others of his own sex.

As an 'innocent' young boy, while his sexuality budded and flourished, Frank would often sit in the castle library gazing for hours at his father's books. There, too, he found many images of naked male bodies that titillated and excited him. There were strange alchemical texts with weird symbolic illustrations of homunculi that sprang fully formed, but in miniature, from a man's shed seed. But Frank favoured above all the illuminated prayer-book images of half-naked, muscular young saints like Sebastian, Cosmas, Damian, Florus and Laurus. This unholy ogling came to an end one day, however, when his mother entered the castle library and confiscated his fine prayer book with a stern look on her face. Had the servants told on him? Had his rotten older brother Philippe sneaked? After that, Frank always found the library door locked, and servants barred him from entering.

As a gangling youth, Frank nourished his maturing sexual fantasies with the songs of the troubadours which told of doomed love triangles – of two comrades who loved the same woman, of sworn friendships between males that lasted until death. Wryly, Frank recalled his teenage dreams of swearing eternal friendship with Gaston Charpentier, the handsome young fencing master who taught him sword and rapier fighting. However, before he'd had a chance to turn dream into reality, his grandmother, Yolanda de la Forge, had dismissed Gaston from their service.

Always the pattern repeated itself. Frank fancied someone. He yearned for them silently and at a distance. He was about to express that yearning, but then, before he could act, he invariably lost the object of his desire.

Frank stared hard now at Rob. He was still naked, but now he hung and swung from a low tree branch in the clearing. Like Adam in the garden of Paradise, thought the young lord, with no Eve and no Lilith in the picture to distract him. It made a tempting scene. Rob's cock and balls – like succulent, ripe, forbidden fruit – cried out for Frank to lick them, chew them, suck them and drain them of their potent juices.

The church bell tolled the hour in the distance. Frank crossed himself out of force of habit. He'd learned to do so from Edwin Burchet – the slender young curate who arrived at Woodmere Hall soon after dashing Gaston Charpentier's unexpected departure. During those days Burchet came to the great house to take confession, and by soft persuasive words he encouraged Frank to invent graphic descriptions of his impure thoughts about sex with serving wenches, sex with women old enough to be his mother, and sex with dashing fencing masters. After Frank's lengthy confessions, Burchet would direct the young lord – together with his milk brother Rob – into the small chapel vestry. Rob acted as Frank's whipping boy throughout their childhood, taking the punishments on his thick peasant hide that Burchet believed Frank's aristocratic flesh was too delicate to bear.

Rob now hauled himself naked up into the tree, like a muscular wildcat. It was hard for Frank to believe – as he looked at the strapping fellow Rob had become – that he had once borne the brunt of systematic floggings. Shuddering, Frank closed his eyes. He recalled the great delight Burchet had taken in getting the young woodcutter's boy to drop his leggings and to bend over. Once he was in position, the cleric whipped his nut-brown arse with a cane till the cheeks turned bright red. Rob braved this punishment by proxy, strengthened by his brotherly love for Frank, while Frank in a secret and inexplicable way actually liked to watch Rob suffer for him in such an erotic fashion. Rob's pain was mingled so clearly with the pleasure of brother love and of doing good. Even the strange excitement of watching these clandestine beatings was not to last, however. Yolanda dismissed Edwin Burchet from Woodmere after a couple of years, again without explanation, though it seemed to Frank to be part of a plot to rob his life of one pleasure after another.

In the glade Frank saw Rob jump from the tree and land on the forest floor. He finally began to get dressed, and Frank too tucked his own prick away, hitched up his leggings and laced them up at the waist.

He felt no shame at all about being head over heels in love with another man, but other concerns troubled him. Although he harboured intense sexual feelings for Rob, it was possible, even probable, that Rob felt no wild lust for Frank in his heart. If this was so, the lad would find it difficult, perhaps even impossible, to reciprocate any sexual advances, even if Frank did try to start something. From Rob's performance with Molly, it was clear where the young woodcutter's preferences lay, and, though Frank and he had shared many of their childhood years together, those days were past now, and beyond recall. Yet even this was not the whole story behind Frank's reticence.

Rob shouldered his axe and left the clearing to go home, unaware that he had been the object of Frank du Bois's scrutiny and the focal point of his desire for the past couple of hours. Seeing Rob leave, Frank got up. He intended to walk off smartly in the other direction, back towards Woodmere Hall.

As he turned round, however, he realised with a start that Mad Quentin Holly stood close by, and was looking at him strangely. How long had the old fellow been there? Frank wondered. What had he seen?

'Young sir,' said Quentin, 'take care.'

Frank looked at the man – once a trusted servant at the Hall, now a hermit who lived in the woods, and survived on nuts, berries, and on people's charity. The old addle-brained fellow now dressed in rags and would have nothing to do with Frank's grandmother, Yolanda, nor Frank's older brother, Philippe.

'What do you mean, Quentin?' asked Frank.

'It isn't right, Master Frank. That young stripling, Rob Oakley, means trouble. Only grief will come of it, mark my words, young sir. I knew your father, and old Will Oakley, the woodcutter that was. They were like brothers sir, but their friendship ended on that last wild-boar hunt they went on. What's more, it led your poor lady mother to do away with herself, and you and your half-brother have suffered for it all these years since. Take care.'

With that, Quentin Holly shuffled off back to his hermit's cave, and left Frank to ponder on what he'd said.

'Why did he have to bring my "half-brother" into this?' snarled Frank to himself, as he kicked a crop of toadstools that stood in his path into oblivion. He stomped back towards the hall. Mad Quentin's tirade had put him in a foul mood.

Frank and his older brother Philippe appeared in the church register as the true sons of their father, Sir Oliver du Bois, and his wife Lady Isolde. However, if a visitor from foreign parts asked anyone in the local tavern for the village gossip, the barmaid was sure to let slip sooner or later that Frank was illegitimate – a bastard by-blow Sir Oliver had fathered on the woodcutter's wife, Ursula Oakley, and then forced Lady Isolde to adopt.

With a knowing nod the girl would assure the visitor that Sir Oliver had been a frequent visitor to the woodcutter's cottage, and that it was a known fact that Ursula had nursed young Frank as a babe. She would leave the visitor to draw his own conclusions.

Frank, however, did not believe these wild tales. He felt sure that his father and Will Oakley had simply been close friends, and he had it on oath from Ursula herself that she agreed to act as his wet nurse only when her second pregnancy ended in a stillbirth.

Frank clung fiercely to these counter-arguments in his mind. If these rumours of his illegitimacy ever proved to be true, he stood to lose all his du Bois inheritance – or at least what remained after his brother Philippe had got his hands on the first-born's share. Also, if Frank turned out to be Ursula Oakley's son, then he was also Rob Oakley's half-brother.

That was a fate too horrible to contemplate, for then Frank would be guilty of lusting after his own flesh, and the penalties for incest – as he recalled them outlined one day by Edwin Burchet – were terrible indeed. He certainly had no desire to fester in one of the circles of hell, mired in pitch and with fiends pulling out his fingernails with tweezers one by one and shoving red-hot pokers up his backside for all eternity. This was why he bridled at Mad Quentin's use of the term 'half-brother'. This was why the rumours of his illegitimacy irked him. This was why, when he thought about it, he hesitated before he declared his passion to Rob, why he hung back from propositioning or seducing the lad. The nagging doubt in his head that he and the young woodcutter might be brothers prevented him from following where his heart – and his cock – wanted to lead him.

As Frank neared the kissing gate that led to the kitchen garden at Woodmere, he saw his page, Hal Ashe, come running towards him. Hal was a little younger than his master, and full of energy, like an enthusiastic puppy. He was a cute thing, with his green eyes, his mop of ginger curls, and his round freckled face. That face lit up into a smile as Hal spotted Frank.

'Sir, sir, your grandmother has sent for you,' panted Hal as he neared the kissing gate and came to a halt.

'Why?' Frank only half listened. He admired Hal's impossibly long eyelashes, his tip-tilted nose, the curve of his sensual lips. Really the lad looked exactly like a mischievous cherub, or an angel. A fallen angel, thought Frank, as he remembered how adept Hal's soft lips were at kissing and sucking.

The page continued with breathy earnestness, 'There is a gentleman come to see you, sir, and he awaits you in the banqueting hall. Lady Yolanda has invited him to sup and stop here tonight, and we must make haste to dress you for dinner.'

Frank smiled.

'What's the hurry?'

He looked at Hal – so trim in his tight orange leggings and the close-fitting green livery tunic that bore the du Bois crest: an oak tree split in two by a lightning bolt on a shield surmounted by a wild boar's head.

'Come here, boy,' he said, and he indicated the spot inside the kissing gate where someone could stand and swing the gate past them.

The pageboy obeyed and entered the gate.

'Do you know what we call this kind of gate, Hal, my lad?'

'Yes, sir, a kissing gate, sir,' replied Hal, and his eyes twinkled with mischief.

Frank drew closer.

'And how must I get through it, dear Hal?'

'You must pay the toll, sir. Like anyone else,' replied the servant, and he grinned.

'Very well,' said Frank, and he swung the gate forward, squeezed into the passing place, and pressed himself up against his all-too-willing serving lad.

He stroked Hal's cheek with one hand, and with the other he reached down and patted him between the legs. Through the tight leggings he felt the servant's cock. It was bone-hard and it throbbed fiercely.

'My, my, Hal. You are happy to see me, aren't you?'

Without another word Frank planted his lips upon Hal's half-open mouth, and kissed him, at first tender and dainty, but then more and more hungry and insistent. The page melted within his arms and their two bodies moved closer. Frank ran one hand through the lad's hair, and stroked the nape of his neck and his shoulder. With the other hand he first squeezed Hal's round buttocks, firm as ripe peaches. Then he placed his hand in the small of Hal's back and pressed the lad even closer against him. Their stiff cocks – as they strained to be free of the codpieces that encased them – rubbed together. Frank's long strong tongue thrust in past Hal's red lips, past his pearly teeth, and lashed around in the warm moistness of Hal's kittenish mouth. How Frank longed to have Hal kneel before him so that he could thrust his cock into that pert mouth instead of just his tongue.

Frank changed his point of attack, and he started to nibble and kiss the page's ear. At this point, Hal drew away from him, and pulled a long face.

'Please, sir, please. Someone may see us.'

'And what if they do?'

'But your grandmother . . . I could lose my job.'

Hal was right. The old witch would do anything to spite him. Discretion was the better part of amour.

'All right. Let's go to my room, and you can dress me for dinner.'

Hal kept a respectful distance, and preceded his master by four paces as they made their way towards the uneven spiral staircase that led to Frank's room – up the half-ruined turret.

An air of neglect hung over the whole of Woodmere Hall. Sir Oliver and Lady Isolde now mouldered in the du Bois crypt, below the castle chapel. In their absence, Lady Isolde's mother – Yolanda de la Forge – had run the hall for over a decade. She let it go to ruin, and spent her money instead on rings for her gnarled fingers, fine necklaces for her wrinkled throat, and costly gowns to sheathe her wizened frame. In a corner of her room she kept a large chest that contained her extensive collection of jewels and trinkets under lock and key, and all the riches that could have gone to repair Woodmere Hall poured instead like a shower of gold into that treasure chest. She would sometimes invite Frank's

GUY EDENBRIDGE

elder brother, Philippe, to her room, and to amuse herself she would deck him out in her jewelled collars, bangles and diadems like some young Byzantine prince. She cosseted Philippe as she cosseted herself, but to Frank and to Woodmere she showed no love or care.

As new stone was expensive to quarry and work, Yolanda's workmen avoided it. Instead they patched the cracks in the old walls with wooden planks, and, when old ceilings threatened to fall, they erected makeshift timber scaffolding to prop them up. Frank considered this use of wood a false economy, for it turned a once safe fortress into a tinderbox which enemy saboteurs could easily set alight during a siege.

Frank was relieved not to meet his grandmother as he followed Hal up to his bedchamber. If the old woman had the slightest inkling of the sexual antics her younger grandson planned with his eager page, Hal would have been dismissed that instant.

Once they reached the safety of Frank's bedroom, Hal bolted the door behind them. Frank stripped off his clothes and sat on the bedside chair with his legs splayed wide. The maroon tunic and leggings he was to wear lay in readiness upon the bed. Since Lady Yolanda would be praying in the chapel until eight, there was time enough to have some fun with young Hal.

'Come and sit at my feet,' he ordered.

The young page obeyed, and crouched between his master's legs.

His gaze was fixed firmly upon Frank's cock. It lay limply to one side on his thigh, but it now began to pulse with life, to swell, to writhe and to grow.

'Do you like the look of my family jewels?' asked Frank.

Hal nodded, and swallowed his excitement.

'Would you like to touch them?'

'Oh, yes, sir.'

'Then take my cock in your hand,' commanded Frank. 'Feel it stiffen in your grasp. Stroke it. It's a soft snake now, but you can make it into a hard wand, a powerful rod, by the magic of your touch.'

The red-headed lad followed his orders to the letter. He took hold of Frank's prick and stroked it with reverential fingers. His caresses started at the tip and moved to the root. The thing reared up now, no longer a snake, but a rod, a pole, a pillar of hard, hot manhood.

'Go on. That feels good,' murmured Frank, as he reclined against the chair back and closed his eyes. 'Now peel it.'

Deftly Hal reached up to the tip of his master's dick. He eased back the soft fleshy foreskin, and brought the smooth purple head into view.

Frank gasped with pleasure as his exposed cock head met cool air.

'Oh, yes, Hal. Kiss the rod.'

The boy's soft lips pressed against the mouth of his glans, where a copious pool of sticky pre-come welled up.

'Lick me.'

Hal bent his head forward again and licked Frank's cock shaft with small darting strokes of his tongue. He behaved like a cat licking a naughty kitten into shape. He licked up and down the whole length of the pulsing rod. Then he licked Frank's testicles, which nestled, heavy and swollen with desire, in the fleshy sac that sprawled between his thighs. Now Hal moved lower, and darted the tip of his pointed tongue into the puckered mouth of his master's arse. Frank moaned and writhed with pleasure under the sweet assault.

The pre-come now dribbled down the gnarled shaft of Frank's tool. He revelled in the pleasure Hal gave with his tongue.

'Now suck me.'

Hal took the whole of Frank's sticky cock head into his mouth. He licked and sucked it like some warm soft exotic fruit, and his saliva mingled with the salty pre-come that now oozed out in abundance.

While he sucked, he ran his fingers up and down Frank's torso. He stroked the firm pectorals, caressed the taut muscles of his abdomen, and pinched and twisted his master's nipples until they stood out stiff and proud from his chest.

'Oh, yes,' moaned Frank.

Hal's licking became stronger, rougher. He sucked like a lamb

GUY EDENBRIDGE

fastened on a ewe's teat. Soon Frank would nourish him. Soon
Frank's cock would rear up and spit out its precious load. Soon
Hal's hungry mouth would fill with copious draughts of the salty
man's milk that he so craved, that he so yearned for.

'Harder, harder.'

Frank now began to buck in the chair. He pushed his cock up
and fucked the young page's face. He thrust his cock into that
sweet moist mouth as far as it would go, and all the while Hal
slurped and guzzled.

At last Frank teetered on the brink of orgasm and then – with
a rush and a roar – he let go, and ejaculated. Several strong jets of
spunk spurted like a series of immense tidal waves out of his cock
and into Hal's mouth, and the boy swallowed, swallowed and
swallowed again, as he drank down the warm salty sea foam,
satisfied and content.

They sat for a while and held hands, Frank in his chair, and
Hal at his feet on the floor, while the sea storm of passion that
throbbed in their ears died down. Then, suddenly, there came a
knock on the bedroom door that broke them out of their pleasant
reverie.

'Who is it?' asked Frank.

He heard Philippe's whining voice. 'Your brother, Philippe.
We are back from the chapel. You are called for in the banqueting
hall.'

'By and by, I come.'

'Do not make Grandmamma wait. Oh, and have you seen
young Hal? He is wanted to serve at table.'

Hal shot Frank a pleading glance.

'No, he called me in from the garden earlier, and helped me to
dress, but where he is now, I can't say. Perhaps he's down in the
cellar preparing a flagon of wine to accompany our supper.'

'As like as not,' grumbled Philippe. His heavy tread got fainter
as he trudged away down the spiral stair. At lightning speed Hal
dressed Frank in the maroon tunic and leggings.

Just as the young page was about to leave, Frank beckoned him
over to the panelled wall and pressed a catch hidden behind a

16

carved boar's head. A concealed door in the panelling swung inwards to reveal a secret spiral staircase within.

'The quickest and safest way for you to go down to the wine cellar, I think,' said Frank, and he grinned as he handed Hal a taper to light his way. 'Just follow the stair right down and you'll find the door that leads into the cellar at the bottom.'

'Thank you, my lord,' said Hal, and he disappeared down the stair with alacrity.

Thank heavens that Woodmere was full of secret passages, thought Frank. He and his 'milk brother' Rob had discovered most of them in their youth. They made good places to hide in when you wanted to eavesdrop on others, good ways to move unseen from one place in the castle to another in case of emergency, and good private refuges for a solitary or a shared wank.

While Hal Ashe scurried down the secret stair to the cellar, Frank closed the door in the panelling, left his room by the usual door, and sauntered very publicly down to the banqueting hall to meet the mystery guest.

His grandmother and elder brother stood before the large baronial fireplace, below the Ganymede tapestry, as Frank entered the room. They were deep in conversation with a stranger. Frank saw the fellow's back first, but even this rear view told him something of their visitor. His long blond hair, his turquoise tunic and blue leggings indicated someone who took pains with his appearance – a peacock. His broad shoulders and muscular legs showed he was either a fine sportsman or a splendid fighter, or both.

Yolanda's hooded eyes opened wide, her nostrils flared, and she glared at her youngest grandson as he approached. Her angular frame looked splendid, swathed in a close-fitting lilac gown and wimple, but the face and the hands were weathered, wrinkled, like the beaked head and talons of a bird of prey.

'Vincent de la Tour, you must meet my other grandson, Frank.'

The stranger turned and looked Frank full in the face. He had a handsome face, with a close-cropped beard, and startlingly blue eyes. As the man looked him up and down, Frank blushed. In some strange way the fellow appeared to undress him with his piercing eyes, and to judge the youthful muscles that he saw underneath with a professional eye, like a horse trader who gauges the quality of a young stallion he is about to buy.

After his silent appraisal, Vincent smiled at Frank.

'Your grandmother tells me things about you that make me keen to know you better.'

'Indeed, sir,' replied Frank. He blushed, and he felt his cock stir.

'And, now that I have seen you, I find I wish to see more of you,' replied Vincent.

'That can be arranged,' snapped Yolanda. For once Frank appreciated his grandmother's directness. This handsome young stranger attracted him, and he wished to spend time in Vincent's company, to get closer to him.

'You see, Frank,' blurted out Philippe, 'as I am the elder and the heir to the family fortunes, Grandmamma thought that you should be the one to go.'

Frank looked at him. He was amazed at how Philippe was a near miss at practically everything. He was not quite good-looking, not exactly clever, and not entirely straightforward.

'What do you mean "go"? Explain yourself, Philippe.'

'No, let me explain,' Vincent intervened. His voice was calm, soothing. 'I am a knight of an order based some two days' ride from here, in the castle of Nonpareil at Castleford. I come to find a young man to be my squire. My requirements are that he be presentable, able to wield his weapon well in close fighting, fit to mount and ride the fiercest steed, skilled at hitting the mark in target practice, and of good family.'

Frank fantasised about lying naked in bed with Vincent, even as they talked. He imagined wielding his stiff cock well, wanking himself as the two of them kissed. He imagined Vincent face down on the bed, inviting Frank to mount and ride him. He imagined aiming his cock between Vincent's muscular buttocks, driving the tip and shaft of it through the centre of the young knight's anal sphincter, and plunging deep inside his target. He imagined fucking him long and hard until he reached orgasm.

'Will you come with me?' asked Vincent.

Frank started, jolted back to the present.

'I . . . I . . .' he stammered.

'I think it would be for the best,' snapped Yolanda at Frank. Then, as she turned to Vincent, she allowed charm to suffuse her voice like honey. 'He is a good swordsman, a good rider, and a good archer. In the matter of his presentability, that you can see for yourself. As for his being of good family, well, he bears the name of "du Bois", does he not?'

Yolanda had skilfully not mentioned the scandal of his illegitimacy in public, though Frank felt sure by the way she treated him that she was convinced of it, and that this was one of her reasons for wanting him out of the way.

'What do you say? I will give you a few moments to reflect before you give your answer,' urged Vincent.

Frank looked at him. Here was a man who combined the manners of his own class, the virile beauty that he so worshipped in Rob and the sexual availability he appreciated in Hal. He weighed things up in his mind, and felt sure that he and Vincent could get close, and become lovers, without complications. Rob was an unattainable dream, and had better remain so. Hal was a temporary pastime that led nowhere. He decided to take the adventure that fate offered him, and to throw in his lot with Vincent.

He turned to the young knight, took a deep breath, grinned at him and said, 'Yes, I will come with you.'

After that they sat down to dinner. Hal served the platters and cleared them away. He was the very model of an invisible servant – graceful and pleasant to look at, but inscrutable. He betrayed nothing of his emotions, and revealed nothing of the secret relationship he enjoyed with Frank.

Halfway through the meal, Yolanda complained of the cold, and summoned Rob Oakley to bring in an armful of logs to place on the fire. Philippe sulked shamefully. Vincent's attention was rooted in his new squire, and the two laughed and chatted together. Philippe seethed because he was not the centre of things. When Rob arrived and crossed the room with the logs, Philippe stuck his leg out and tripped the poor lad up. The logs went flying.

Rob rounded on Philippe, and the two stared and snarled at each other for a moment, almost like mirror images. Philippe's face, however, was like a warped reflection of Rob's handsome countenance viewed in a mirror that cruelly distorted whatever stared into it.

Yolanda sprang up.

'You clumsy oaf!' she shrieked at Rob. 'Here we have an important guest for dinner and you cannot refuel the fire without disgracing us.'

'I'm sorry, my lady,' murmured Rob as he bowed his head and picked up the fallen logs. 'It was an accident.'

Frank had seen how the 'accident' had happened, and his blood boiled. He turned to Philippe.

'An accident that you caused, my clumsy brother, by sticking your foot in Rob's path just as he walked by, his arms so loaded with logs that he fell right into your trap.'

Yolanda blinked, then turned to Rob and said, 'Lay the logs on the fire and go.'

Frank noticed with a thrill that Rob shot a meaningful glance of silent thanks to him as he left the room. His heart was still in love with the lad even if his head told him that the situation was hopeless.

'Philippe is sometimes not very co-ordinated in his movements,' continued Yolanda. 'He cannot help it.'

'I see,' replied Vincent. He saw all too well the grandmother's need to cover up her grandson's petty spitefulness.

That night Hal came to Frank's bed with some mulled wine. Frank's departure with Vincent was set for the following morning and Hal felt sad.

'Cheer up,' said Frank. 'Stay with me tonight.'

While Frank supped the warming spiced wine, Hal stripped off his livery and slipped into bed. Frank then threw off his clothes and joined the lad.

Their mouths met in a long kiss. Their tongues rubbed and writhed together like two lively eels. Frank reached down and grasped hold of Hal's pulsating cock. Hal's hand closed round Frank's stiff prick. Each of them pulled at the other's rod with growing excitement. Now Frank lay on top of Hal and gave soft sucking bites to the young lad's lips, his ear lobes, his neck. He took hold of both their sticky cocks together, wrapped his hand round the double thickness and wanked for all he was worth.

It was not long before a double-voiced cry of pleasure heralded a double explosion of creamy white spunk. After wiping themselves clean and dry, Frank and Hal kissed each other goodnight, snuggled together, and drifted off to sleep in each other's arms.

Two

The next day Frank awoke at dawn with an irrepressible hard-on. He nudged Hal awake.

'Master?' asked Hal, yawning.

'Hal, I want you to service me as only you know how,' Frank murmured in his ear.

Soon the young page's lips pressed against Frank's mouth and his fingers caressed the rigid shaft of Frank's cock, and stroked his aching balls.

Frank writhed and moaned on the bed under the onslaught. He loved it when Hal fingered his prick and bollocks in this way. He lay back as Hal kissed him on the lips, the cheeks, the throat. After months of sexual obedience, Hal knew the various little ploys that excited Frank, and on this farewell morning he used them all, to make this a lovemaking that Frank would remember.

First Hal licked, sucked and chewed his master's nipples, until they stood out proud and stiff from his muscular chest. Then, lower down, he ran his lips over his young lord's taut abdomen, and tongued his navel, sending him crazy with desire.

Then Hal grasped his master's iron-hard dick and eased back the foreskin fully. He licked the smooth cock head, and mixed his saliva with the juices that oozed from the hole in its tip.

Frank's moans doubled in intensity.

Hal stopped licking. He shifted position, straddled his master and brought his own stiff cock close to Frank's. He grasped their two pricks together. The oily pre-come now dripped like thick syrup from Frank's prick hole. Hal anointed the heads and shafts of both their organs with this natural lubrication and began to wank them both together.

When Frank teetered on the point of shooting his load, Hal stopped masturbating, and shifted position again. For a moment there was a lull in the sexual storm, a pause in the erotic siege that Hal waged against him. Frank's urge to ejaculate quieted and the battle recommenced in a new guise.

Now Hal lay next to Frank on the bed, top to tail.

'Come on top of me, Master Frank. Fill my humble mouth with your dick.'

Frank needed no further urging. He crouched on all fours, and arched over the servant boy, who lay face up on the bed underneath him.

Hal's fingers guided his cock tip towards his spunk-hungry mouth, and Frank rammed his turgid tool between those sweet coral-red lips. At first he penetrated Hal's mouth gently and slowly, but then, after a while, he increased both the speed and intensity of his pelvic movements. And, as he thrust, he felt Hal's fingers caress and squeeze his bollocks to heighten his satisfaction.

As he face-fucked Hal, he eyed the page's sexual equipment, which lay inches away from his own mouth. Hal's long and slender penis pulsed with desire. His purple-veined testicles swelled with passion. The bush of his pubic hair shone bright ginger. Pausing mid-thrust, Frank bent his head down and smelled the musky aroma that rose from Hal's crotch. He drew back Hal's foreskin and ran his tongue over the tip of his tool. Hal sucked and slurped on Frank's tumescent organ and now Frank took Hal's prick head into his mouth. He ran his tongue over the smooth dome, probed the dimpled cock mouth with his tongue tip, and ran the flat of his tongue around the rough flange at the base of the young man's glans.

These manoeuvres aroused Hal, too. He thrust his hard dick up into his young master's mouth. Frank pushed his circling lips down Hal's shaft every time there was an upward thrust, and drew his lips up the fleshy pole at every downward pull.

To be joined at cock and mouth like this felt glorious to Frank. He experienced sheer bliss as Hal's mouth and fingers teased his prick and balls, and as his own tongue simultaneously flickered eagerly over the young man's penis.

Mid-suck, Frank felt, with a rush of joy, the spunk rise like the sap of pleasure within his cock root. He teetered on the brink and then, unable to hold back any more, he let go and gave himself to pleasure. At once his hot seed spurted in rivers of bliss from his tool, and Hal gulped down the nourishing silvery liquid. Then, a split second later, Hal's organ reared up and disgorged its own precious cargo into Frank's mouth. Like a connoisseur of wine, Frank rolled the warm, salty liquid round his palate. He savoured its creamy flavour and texture before it trickled down the back of his throat.

How wonderful, Frank thought, to be caught up in this circle of masculine desire – sucked and sucking, penetrated and penetrating, the sower of seed and the receiving furrow, the thirster and the thirst quencher.

After Hal left, to get Frank's horse ready for travel, Frank dressed, and then went downstairs for breakfast.

His grandmother and brother had already breakfasted and Frank was left alone in the banqueting room to break his fast with Vincent de la Tour.

'Did you have a rough night?' asked Vincent.

Frank blushed as he replied, 'No, not really.'

'I thought young Hal looked a bit the worse for wear this morning.'

Frank looked at Vincent. The young knight's eyes twinkled. Did he know about Frank's clandestine relationship with Hal, or was it just by chance that he mentioned the tired look of the two of them so close to each other?

Perhaps he was simply making conversation, Frank figured.

'I think my young valet is upset that I am leaving,' he said, to keep the conversation going.

'I have no doubt of it,' replied Vincent. 'You leave a gap that will be hard for another to fill. Your firm yet sweet presence will be sorely missed, I warrant.'

Frank wondered a little at Vincent's turn of phrase as he supped up his milky porridge.

After breakfast Frank and Vincent said farewell to Lady Yolanda and Philippe. Frank could not bear to kiss either his grandmother or elder brother goodbye, but, as the two of them stood stony-faced before him, he knew that they hardly expected a physical display of affection from him.

Frank looked round for Hal at this point. He had gone to pack Frank's saddlebags, and had not yet reappeared.

After some time waiting in vain, Frank and Vincent went to the stables, and there they found Hal. Red-eyed and sniffing, he was fastening the saddlebags in place. At Frank's approach, he fell on one knee and raised his master's hand to his lips.

'I shall never forget your kindness to me, sir,' he murmured.

Frank reached down and raised the young man to his feet. He threw his arms around him in a warm embrace, and gave him a kiss full on the lips. Hal drew back. His eyes darted towards Vincent, but Frank patted the lad on the arm. He had worked out his new travelling companion well enough to know that he was pretty broad-minded. Frank felt sure that he was sympathetic to intimate friendships between men.

'Look after yourself, Hal,' Frank smiled, and he chucked the youth under the chin.

Frank mounted his horse – a fine bay gelding named Cinnabar. Vincent climbed astride his mount – a splendid white stallion named Milken. Then they laughed and joked as they rode out of Woodmere Hall together.

Hal clung to the castle gate, waved with false cheerfulness, and then wept at his master's going. Frank's brother and grandmother, haughty and aloof, stood high on the battlements of Woodmere. Without comment they watched Frank depart with his new mentor along the winding road that led to Castleford. They were dry-eyed, and inwardly they rejoiced as they turned at last from the vision of Frank's dwindling back and went indoors to toy with Lady Yolanda's treasure.

As Frank and Vincent rode off side by side, they chatted.

'A fine young lad, that Hal,' said Vincent.

'Yes. A good valet.'

'And pretty. Almost like a girl in disguise.'

'Ah, but for all his girlish looks and ways, he's got a fine cock between his young thighs,' said Frank, and then he blushed as he realised he'd given the game away.

'And a pert arse, too, I warrant,' smiled Vincent. 'Just ripe for plugging.'

Frank made no reply.

They rode on a little further without comment.

'Your grandmother told me you were a virgin, but I see now that she misinformed me,' continued Vincent, a little later.

'My grandmother knows nothing of my sex life,' spat Frank.

'So I see,' continued Vincent. 'And yet I must ask you a little more about your sexual experiences. The Order of the Tree of Life, to which I belong, is a secret brotherhood of knights with strict requirements of its members.'

'Such as?'

'Such as . . . we admit no one to the order who has had sexual congress with a woman. We consider that a woman's vagina defiles the male organ and weakens its magical powers. For this reason our master forbids us sexual intercourse with females.'

'Ah, well, then,' laughed Frank, 'you may rest easy on that score. My sexual experiences have all been to date only with men of my own age.'

'And what experiences exactly have you had?' continued Vincent. Frank noticed that one of Vincent's hands – the one that held the reins of his steed – rested on the pommel of his saddle, and rubbed against his crotch.

'Where should I begin?' Frank played for time.

'Self-exploration?' Vincent continued.

'Wanking, you mean. Yes, I've done that – alone and with my accomplice, Hal. I enjoyed it a lot. I love the way my cock transforms itself under a chafing hand from a soft snake to a hard rod, and I love how – when I reach the height of my pleasure – the liquid spunk spurts out, like a silvery fountain that springs from a cleft in a mountain top.'

'Good. The image of the phallus is central to our sacred rites. We worship it above all other body parts. The phallus is our sacred tree. Now, what about oral sex? Have you tried that?'

'Sucking and being sucked off? Yes, I've tried those, too.'

'With Hal?'

'Yes, with Hal.'

'And was it good?'

'Yes, very good. I like the taste of freshly spilled sperm as it fills my mouth, and I enjoy the sensation when I ejaculate into another man's mouth.'

'That's good,' murmured Vincent. 'Next to blood, semen is the most magical liquid that the male body contains. We often use it in our rituals. The blood is the life of a man, they say, but semen is even more powerful than blood since it gives life, and so we count ourselves as Brothers of the Living Seed. And have you experienced the mysteries of anal penetration?'

Frank coloured. He thought of the times he had daydreamed about penetrative sex with Rob Oakley.

'No, sir. Not yet. Though I have sometimes dreamed that another man's cock pierced me to the core, and rode me to ecstasy. Or that I was the rider and ran my prick into another man's arse to the hilt, and plunged away within him until I filled his soft innards to the brim with my liquid desires.'

'My prick grows stiff to hear you talk so, my young squire. But what you tell me is good. At least you will have something to learn at the castle of Nonpareil.'

They now reached the outer limits of the village of Woodmere, and the track they trotted along passed close by the woodcutter's cottage. Frank was surprised to see Rob Oakley standing by the roadside, waiting for them.

'Hullo there, young master, and fine sir,' came the peasant lad's warm greeting as the two riders drew near him.

'Rob, why are you here?' asked Frank. He gazed down at his

GUY EDENBRIDGE

former childhood companion and felt a tingle begin in his scrotum and spread to his penis at the sight of him.

'I came to say goodbye to you, Master Frank, and to thank you for your kind words and deeds yesterday at dinner.'

Frank coloured. He remembered Philippe's cruel trick of tripping up the lad as he bore in logs to the hearth.

'It was nothing,' he mumbled.

'It meant a lot to me, Frank,' went on the woodcutter. 'It reminded me of our childhood, of our milk-brotherhood. And to show my gratitude I thought to make you a gift to recall me by.'

Here he took an oak rod out of his haversack and handed it to Frank. The young squire examined it. It was beautifully carved, oiled and polished. At its lower end the rod bore an acorn as its decoration, at its upper end it split into two acorn leaves, spread wide like angels' wings.

'It's beautiful,' murmured Frank, 'but what is it?'

'Well, Frank . . . young sir I mean, it's an oak wand from the forest here. Seeing as how I heard that you were leaving to join a magical confraternity –' here he nodded in the direction of Vincent – 'I thought as how you might be in need of a wand. And, as for its being oak, well, I figured that would remind you always of your brother-in-spirit Rob Oakley, or the forest hereabouts, and of the tree on your family crest, sir.'

Frank's heart melted with sweet anguish. Had he been wrong to give up thinking of Rob in a sexual way for ever? Vincent was charming enough, and as virile as Rob was. But Rob's near unavailability somehow made him much more attractive.

Frank tucked the wand into his saddlebag. Then, on impulse, he jumped down from his horse, took the young woodcutter in his arms, and kissed him full on the unresisting lips.

'Thank you, Rob. Thank you indeed. I am touched by your gift, and even more by your words. Let me give you something in return.'

He reached up and undid the silver chain that circled his neck. Threaded on the chain was his father's locket and also a finger ring carved out of horn. Frank removed the ring and then fixed the locket back on its chain around his neck once more.

'Take this,' said Frank and he handed the ring to Rob. Tears welled in his eyes and blurred his vision. 'This ring was my father's and bears the boar's-head crest,' he said. 'Now I want you to have it. Wear it always, and think of me as your brother – as more than a brother. And, if you ever need my help, send the ring, and I will return to Woodmere immediately.'

'I shall wear it on my ring finger with pride,' said Rob, and he grinned. 'As the thrusting of a boar's tusk united our fathers in death, so this boar's-head ring binds us two together in life.'

Frank mounted his steed again, and waved goodbye to Rob. Then, as they set their spurs to their horses' flanks, he and Vincent galloped off towards the village of Millhaven, which lay on the road to Castleford.

At Millhaven, after just over an hour's ride, the two dismounted and feasted upon pasties and a flask of mead which Hal had packed in Frank's saddlebag.

Frank blessed his young page for his care in provisioning them so well for the journey.

The two horses cropped the grass in the field where Vincent and Frank ate. Although both animals were male, the fact that Frank's steed, Cinnabar, was gelded as a colt seemed to confuse matters. Vincent's white stallion, Milken, snuffled around Cinnabar's rear, and, with no scent of a male aroma, his cock lengthened, and he reared up, ready to penetrate the other horse.

Vincent smiled.

'Look, even our horses wish to become more intimate.'

The horses' tethers stood too far apart for them to couple, but Cinnabar did not seem inclined to shy away from sexual contact with another male horse. Far from it. His cock too ballooned with excitement.

Frank looked on with interest.

'That young Rob Oakley is a comely fellow,' said Vincent.

'Do you think so?' replied Frank.

'Indeed I do. But what was he like in the sack? Well hung I warrant.'

Frank blushed.

'I regret to say I've never had the pleasure,' he snapped.

'I'm sorry. I assumed . . . the way he talked of milk brothers . . . I concluded that you had exchanged man's milk together.'

'Well, I'm afraid you jumped to the wrong conclusion, Vincent. The milk he talked of was mother's milk. We sucked from the same pap when we were infants. Rumour has it that Rob and I may be half-brothers, though we're not recognised as such by law. But that, I hasten to say, is the extent of our relationship.'

While Vincent packed up the saddlebags and tried to soothe the horses, Frank went off for a solitary walk along the banks of the River Werry, to calm his thoughts. Why did he feel so jealous, so defensive and so protective of Rob? Why was he so keen to declare their relationship an innocent one? Why did he bristle when another man looked at his milk brother with sexual thoughts? If Rob was interested only in women, then Frank need have no fear that the young woodcutter might go with another man. And yet . . . perhaps that was the nub of the matter. Could Frank be sure that Rob was beyond his reach as he thought? Sharing Rob with Molly was one thing, but having to share him with another man was out of the question. Even if Frank couldn't have him at all, he was damned if he was going to let another man get a chance.

Just round the bend, and out of sight of Vincent, Frank stumbled upon three Millhaven youths as they swam bollock-naked in the river. He watched them in secret from behind a thicket of thorn bushes and soon realised that they were all young men he recognised by face and knew by name.

Jack Hawthorne, the young blacksmith's swarthy apprentice, was there; and Martin Sycamore, the miller's sandy-haired son, and Dickon Pine, the carroty-haired merchant's son. While Frank watched, they splashed about in the water for a time, and then ran out. As they lay panting and laughing on the riverbank, the water ran off their smooth bodies, which glistened in the autumn sunlight. Their cocks, Frank noted, were, all three, standing hard to attention. He watched with interest.

Martin now knelt between Jack's thighs. He raised the young man's legs in the air, so that the crack of his arse faced his own cock. With a few well-aimed thrusts, the chunky miller's son penetrated his friend to the hilt with his huge tool, ramming it into place time after time. Frank thrilled then to see Dickon line the head of his prick up against the crack of Martin's rump. Soon – counterpointing the ins and outs of the young miller's love-making – Dickon started to fuck Martin's arse as Martin fucked Jack. Frank's cock throbbed and strained skywards. He was sorely tempted to rip off his leggings, and go and join in the fun, to make the threesome into a foursome, to position himself behind Dickon, and to ram his own cock into place between the cute merchant's flexing buttocks.

However, just at that moment, a familiar wizened face appeared further along the riverbank path, beyond the trio of intertwined fucking youths. It was Mad Quentin Holly.

'Stop your fornicating ways,' he yelled at the copulating three-some, 'or a wild boar'll get you and gore you, just as you're ready to shoot your load of white-hot spunk into your fuck-brother. Remember Sir Oliver and Will.'

The three boys disengaged. Disturbed by Holly's doomladen interruption, they grabbed their clothes, scattered into the bushes and ran off.

It was clearly well known even here in Millhaven that Quentin Holly was half crazed, and someone to steer clear of.

Frank didn't wait to see more, but hurried back to where Vincent waited. Knight and squire mounted their horses – which were calmer now – and rode onward to Castleford. Had Vincent let Milken fuck Cinnabar, Frank wondered, in order to tranquilise them?

Vincent kept silent and left Frank to his own thoughts.

He found himself remembering his farewell hug and kiss with Rob. Was it a mistake to leave the handsome young woodcutter behind and throw in his lot with Vincent de la Tour and the Brothers of the Tree of Life? Rob's gift of the oak wand, and his affectionate words as they parted, encouraged Frank to feel that perhaps he had misread the situation. Maybe he could seduce Rob after all, if he only dared to press the point and woo him.

Mad Quentin's words about a boar that gored two male lovers

– two brothers – to death sent a shiver down his spine. Was that really how his father and Will Oakley had met their end, pierced by an enraged wild pig's tusk as they fucked in a thicket? Or was this simply another example of Quentin Holly's madness – as he mixed up things in strange new ways to concoct something that never existed?

As if he could read Frank's thoughts, Vincent steered the conversation round to Sir Oliver du Bois's death while they trotted onwards.

'The leader of our order is Salim du Court,' he began.

'Salim. That sounds a foreign name.'

'His father was a French baron, his mother an Arabic princess. He is a great lord from the kingdom of Outremer. I believe he knew your father in his youth. Perhaps he can shed some more light on your father's death. I understand from your grandmother that only the vaguest details of it were reported to her.'

Frank's heart filled with hope. This journey he was undertaking might yet have some bearing on his understanding of his father, and on his relationship with Rob Oakley.

Frank felt his loyalty to Rob waver a little. Vincent was so kindly, so sensitive and so handsome. But maybe Frank was jumping to conclusions about his new lord's desires. At any rate, whatever happened, he felt sure that, with Vincent to look after him, he was in safe hands.

As they rode through the forest of Sombredell, an autumn storm suddenly blew up. The wind whistled round them and buffeted them nearly out of their saddles, and the rain bucketed down. It was folly to ride on in such weather, so they dismounted and sought refuge in a large hollow oak tree that Vincent knew.

Leaving the horses outside, covered in thick blankets to keep off the worst of the rain, knight and squire crept into the tree, stripped off their cold wet clothes, and lit a small fire in the very centre of the tree root to dry out.

At first, in the flickering orange firelight, they lay down under separate woollen travelling rugs. Then Vincent moved closer to Frank, and soon squire slipped together with knight and the two of them lay together under their two combined layers of blanket.

Frank was ecstatic when he felt Vincent's hand close round his stiff dick as if he grasped the pommel of a sword.

'Frank, my sweet young squire, I want to make love with you,' murmured the knight.

He guided Frank's hand to touch his own pulsing cock and balls.

'Take my weapon in your mouth, Frank. Show me your skill at lovemaking. Suck the very marrow out of my love bone.'

Impressed by the sheer size and weight of the erect tool in his grip, and also by the note of quiet command in Vincent's voice, Frank shuffled down under the bedcovers and took the massive prick into his mouth. He lapped and sucked at it. As the pre-come trickled out of Vincent's cock hole and dribbled down, it glazed the smooth purple dome of his cock head with a viscous coating.

Frank was pleased and honoured to serve Vincent in this way. With his lips and his tongue he worked away with enthusiasm and skill at the huge organ. Now Vincent cried out and clasped Frank's ears as if they were handles on a cooking pot. Vincent held Frank's head in place in a vicelike grip, and forced him to swallow every last drop of knightly jism as it spurted out of his wildly ejaculating cock. What a superbly sensual communion of man's milk it was! However, at the back of Frank's mind, even as he drank mouthfuls of Vincent's rich liquid seed, he was left unsatisfied. In his heart of hearts he realised that he still longed to milk Rob's sturdy penis and to quaff down the young woodcutter's warm fresh-spilled spunk.

Three

The next morning Frank drifted into consciousness at dawn. The storm was over now, and the sharp early-morning light lanced through the entrance of the hollow tree where Frank and Vincent lay on their makeshift bed. Vincent's warm body lay naked by Frank's side, facing away from him. Frank reached over and caressed his lover's dormant cock and bollocks. Vincent stirred and muttered something in his sleep, at which Frank withdrew his hand and lay back, still and quiet. He slowed and deepened his breath and pretended to be asleep. Through slitted eyes he watched Vincent blink and open his eyes, and then sit up and stretch like a great cat.

Frank revelled in the special sensation of spying in secret. He marvelled at Vincent's muscular back, which faced him. And, when Vincent stood up and stretched, catlike, once more, Frank felt a shiver of delight course through his body and melt his bowels. He gazed at the full glory of his lover's broad shoulders, and the rippling musculature that tapered into a neat waist, and then forked into taut buttocks, sculpted thighs and chiselled calves. He delighted in the sight of that rear view!

And then the gorgeous vision disappeared. With a cheerful whistle, Vincent slipped stark-bollock-naked, out of their tree refuge into the fresh morning air!

Frank opened his eyes wide and stood up in haste. He threw on his coarse linen shirt for modesty's sake, and stepped out of the hollow tree and looked around him. The bright morning light made him blink as he sought Vincent.

Then he glimpsed him, striding away between the dew-moist forest ferns and the overhanging trees. The sun gilded the bare skin of Vincent's handsome body and transformed him, as if by alchemical magic, into a beautiful golden statue on the move.

Frank followed him at a discreet distance. Soon a rushing sound filled his ears as if a great wind were blowing once more, like the storm of the night before – and yet there was not a breath of wind to kiss cheek or chin. The air hung balmy and still on that sunny morning. Then, as he rounded a turn in the forest path, Frank realised what caused the insistent sound.

There, at the path's end, sprawled a fern-fringed pool, and beyond it chattered a high rocky waterfall down which white-churned water gushed in perpetual motion, ever feeding the expanse of water beneath. And Vincent stood motionless at the very brink of these troubled waters.

Frank took all this in at a glance. Suddenly, before him, Vincent raised his hands and dived forwards into the pool. Where the older lover led, he compelled the younger to follow. Frank walked to the pool's grassy margin. The white water called to him, cool and inviting. Yet, as Vincent splashed about in it like a playful porpoise, Frank stood at the brink and hesitated.

Now Vincent caught sight of him.

'Come on in!' he shouted, and he swam on his back now. 'The water's gorgeous.'

'Like you, then!' replied Frank, and he laughed. Then he cast off his shirt and dived in to join his lover.

For some while they frisked together in the water like two dolphins. They chased each other, and nuzzled up against each other underwater. Then Vincent led Frank towards a shallow part of the pool. There they stood, waist-deep in the water, face to face. The fresh pool water dripped in glistening beads down Vincent's face and neck, and Frank's heart split with pleasure as he gazed deep into Vincent's eyes. Now Vincent wrapped his arms around Frank's waist and craned his neck forward. His lips met Frank's in a deep and prolonged kiss. Frank opened his mouth a little and he thrilled as Vincent's long tongue probed between his teeth and lashed within his mouth. The cool water had startled them both awake by now, and Frank's cock reared up hard in the water like a miniature sea monster as Vincent kissed him. He reached down to palp Vincent's organ, which throbbed in his hand, ready for action.

Now Vincent disengaged himself from their hot embrace and plunged back into deeper water. He tossed his head in the direction of the waterfall and shouted, 'Race you there.'

Vincent's commanding invitation drew Frank like a magnet. He swam after his friend towards the cascade of water. But what exactly lay behind Vincent's strange behaviour? To excite Frank to boiling point with his kisses, and then to turn tail and swim off . . . It just didn't ring true.

Then, when they neared the waterfall, another surprise awaited Frank. Vincent swam straight for the centre of the foaming sheet of water and abruptly disappeared into it.

Frank trod water and waited for some moments for Vincent to reappear, but he didn't. Where was he? Frank's imagination ran riot. Was Vincent battling an underwater current which dragged him down to the forest of tangled waterweeds that sprouted from the deep pool bed? There was only one way to find out. Bravely Frank struck out. He swam straight for the centre of the cascade, as he had seen Vincent do. Now he passed under the drumming curtain of water, and now he emerged on the other side of it, in a small cave lit only by the sunlight that shafted through the waterfall itself.

'What took you so long?' Frank looked up. There on a broad smooth ledge of rock a little above him lounged Vincent. He lay on his side, and stroked his hard cock lazily like a lascivious satyr.

Frank's penis sprang to attention once more. He hauled his dripping self out of the water and lay down next to Vincent, head to toe. Seeing Vincent caress his own erect prick drew Frank out of his shell, and, before he knew it, he had lowered his head and started to lick the gnarled shaft of Vincent's rod and to kiss the smooth head of it.

'Oh, yes, yes,' murmured Vincent. He removed his own hand from its chafing work, caught one of Frank's hands and laid it on his throbbing organ instead.

Frank needed little encouragement. He began to wank Vincent with firm, regular strokes. Vincent rolled over on to his back and Frank repositioned himself on all fours arched over his lover, still head to tail, but now with his knees either side of Vincent's chest, and his elbows either side of Vincent's hips. Now he bent forward and began to suck Vincent's smooth cock head. He took the whole sticky purple glans, plumlike, into his mouth and ran his tongue lingeringly over Vincent's dimpled cock mouth.

Vincent groaned with pleasure as he caught hold of Frank's cock and started to play with it. He stroked the length of it and caressed Frank's spunk-laden balls as they dangled invitingly above him, like succulent grapes upon a sexual vine. Then he grasped Frank's hips and drew the young lad's pelvis down towards him. He latched his mouth around Frank's cock head, like a young bullock that takes a cow's teat in its mouth and sucks hungrily to draw out the rich and nourishing mother's milk. But this was a hard bull's pizzle rather than a soft udder, and it was nutritious bull's milk – fresh sperm – that rose now within both lovers in a rich creamy white fountain ready to jet.

Frank's whole being tingled as he sucked on his lover's hard cock, and stroked his balls, while under him Vincent's mouth and fingers returned his caresses stroke for stroke.

But then Vincent added something new to the equation. With a spittle-moistened finger he began to massage the tight rosette of Frank's virgin anus as he sucked and caressed the young lad's cock. The sensation proved strange and new, but irresistibly exciting for Frank. His body trembled with wave upon wave of hot desire, and he sucked Vincent's cock harder and faster, and he now also began to move his pelvis so that he thrust his cock repeatedly between Vincent's lips and deep into his throat.

Vincent too began the same rhythmic movements and fucked up into Frank's open and hungry mouth. He also gently insinuated

two spit-anointed fingers through Frank's puckered anal sphincter
and began to wiggle them both around inside the young lad's
arse. Frank shivered as his taut arse muscles relaxed and intense
sexual pleasure thrilled through him.

The surge of desire came full circle. Into Frank's head fluttered
a picture from one of his father's alchemical books – a snake
sucking its own tail. He and Vincent writhed together like twin
sex snakes joined mouth to tail. The waves of sensual pleasure
radiated from cock to mouth and jumped from mouth to cock,
again and again, and, as Vincent's skilled fingers worked their
gentle arse massage, Frank's sensitivity grew. How those tight
bands of delicious erotic spasm racked their naked bodies. Their
two bodies merged into one sexual animal, and the same shared
carnal delight throbbed and coursed through their bodies, locked
together as they were in a heady feast of love.

And then it broke, the crest of the wave. Vincent's cock
stiffened within Frank's mouth, and then reared up and discharged
jet after jet of hot, smoky semen. Frank gulped this warm
nourishing liquid down his throat greedily, and he hungered for
more. How delicious it tasted. And all the while Vincent's gentle
but insistent fingers massaged Frank's arse.

Then – spurred beyond control by the lashings of Vincent's
tongue upon his sensitive cockhead, by the soft suction of
Vincent's rounded lips that gripped his cock shaft, and by the
massage that Vincent gave to his cock root from within his arse –
Frank came.

Frank's arse gripped Vincent's massaging fingers tightly, and the
spunk gushed strongly from his cock mouth. As Vincent pulled
back, the pearly white liquor sprayed his face, his neck, his
shoulders and his chest. Excited, Vincent strained up and lapped
at Frank's cock, fingered his arse, and coaxed another strong
ejaculation out of him, followed by another, and yet another.
Thus Vincent showed his mastery over Frank in the art of sex.

Each time the cocksure young lad ejaculated, his body arched
with pleasure and he gave himself utterly to the knight, who paid
lip service to his cock. Frank offered Vincent all the fresh sperm

his balls had to give. And Vincent quaffed the generous sticky load down each time like a holy communion of manly liquid silver.

With each orgasm, Frank's ejaculate grew less, until finally he orgasmed in Vincent's mouth and no spunk came. But this 'dry coming' thrilled Frank more than all the rest put together. Gradually, though, the fires of lust abated within him, and Vincent withdrew his fingers gently from his arse, and the two lay back next to each other for a while on the rocky ledge behind the fountain, and waited for the pounding of blood in their ears to subside before they swam out from under the curtain of water and returned to the ordinary workaday world.

Once dressed, they breakfasted on a sop of cake dipped in sweet wine. Then Vincent and Frank saddled and mounted their horses and rode onwards. Vincent led the way, as an experienced knight should, and Frank followed – the perfect picture of the dutiful young squire. They said nothing about their bonding in the cave behind the waterfall. There was no need. In that underground, underwater, 'in-between' world they had supped upon each other's living seed, and that holy sexual act drew them close together in a strange sort of wordless complicity.

Frank's mind wandered miles away from Rob at this point. His love for the young woodcutter was, perhaps, only infatuation after all, he reasoned. It had found only one-sided expression and never promised to go anywhere. Whereas with Vincent a different prospect unfolded. At this point Vincent turned back in his saddle and flashed Frank a broad smile which the young lad returned cheerfully. Yes, Vincent had demonstrated his ability and willing-ness to teach Frank a great deal about the mysteries and delights of sex between men, and the young squire's heart swelled within him. He resolved to undertake the exciting journey he was launched on with a wholehearted sense of commitment, and he vowed also to learn as much as he could about himself along the way. The outer quest mirrored the inner quest after all.

As he daydreamed about making love with Vincent in a hundred exciting ways, Frank gradually forgot about Rob and all that the sturdy peasant boy had meant for him over the years –

especially his secret passion for the lad in recent months. A cock in your hand or mouth counts for more than one thrust up a girlfriend's pussy, after all, he said to himself, half sad, half smiling.

After a day's ride, Vincent and Frank came to Castleford – a small hamlet on the banks of Lake Sperma. Even 'hamlet' perhaps was too grand a name for it. A flat-bottomed ferryboat lay moored at the wooden jetty, and only a couple of stone-built thatched cottages stood at the water's edge, with a long low building between them that Frank took to be a stable.

One cottage lay in ruins, utterly deserted; the other looked dilapidated and ramshackle, hardly more than a shack, but the smoke that rose from the chimney told Vincent and Frank that someone lived there. Knight and squire rode over to the doorstep of this second dwelling, dismounted and tethered their horses. Then Vincent strode over and raised a gauntleted fist to rap at the door of the shack. Just at that moment, however, strange noises came from within: moans, panting and curses. Vincent lowered his upraised fist and bent forward to look through a crack in the timbers of the door. A short while later he beckoned to Frank to come and peer through an adjacent knothole, in order to see what was happening within.

Frank's curiosity needed no further encouragement. He applied his eye to the hole in the wooden door frame and squinted through it eagerly.

Once his eyes had focused on the dark interior, he made out two slim naked figures who stood together by the glowing hearth joined in the act of love. At first he took them for two young lads, as they both wore their hair short and displayed slender wiry physiques, but then, as his eyes adapted and became fully accustomed to the inner gloom of the shack, he realised that one was a smooth and graceful young man and the other a boyish lass.

Frank's pupil dilated with lust as he observed the couple's sexual antics within.

The lass stood in the orange glow of the fire, and caressed her clitoris with the slender fingers of one hand. With the other hand she inserted an apothecary's pestle into her moist pussy by degrees, twirling and twisting it around to pleasure herself.

Her young partner stood next to her. He wanked his cock slowly at first and then faster and faster until he ejaculated and jetted his sperm into an apothecary's mortar, which he then put aside.

At first Frank thought that the sexual activity had now come to an abrupt end, but he noticed that the girl continued to thrust the pestle deeper and deeper into her cunt. To magnify her pleasure she now tweaked and fondled her erect nipples. Her small pert breasts sat proud and compact on her chest like two firm apples.

Now the young lad's cock stiffened once more and he anointed the tip of it with some of his previously shed sperm from the mortar. After this he positioned himself behind his masturbating girlfriend and thrust his slender cock between her buttocks. She worked the pestle in and out of her vagina, urgently. As the lad thrust manfully into her, Frank realised that he must be entering her back passage as her front entry was crammed to the limit already.

Frank watched intrigued as the lad's thrusting went on and on. Now he realised the rationale for the young fellow's earlier hand job. As he had already ejaculated once, and fairly recently, he had the stamina to fuck for some time now before reaching a second orgasm. Thus he avoided premature ejaculation and proved more able to satisfy his girl. She now cried out and whimpered as the lad bucked hard inside her. He kept going. Harder, faster and rougher he rode her. Now she laid aside the pestle, which fell to the floor at her feet. She bent her torso forward and reached down, with legs straight, to touch her feet with her hands. And still her young partner pounded away in her arse. He fucked down into her upturned arsehole now, and the penetration was very deep and hard in this posture. He clutched her hips in his hands to pull her arse back on to his cock. He threw his head back and clenched his teeth in a rictus of pleasure as he muttered a string of oaths and obscenities.

Just to look upon such intense sexual passion made Frank's cock pulse hot and stiff in his codpiece. All too soon, in Frank's opinion, the lad let out a great groan, and slumped forward slightly as he shot his jet of spunk in a ferocious second coming into his beloved's arse.

The loving couple stayed locked together for a moment or two, and then the lad drew his cock out of its tight berth, and the lass straightened up.

At this point Vincent rapped loudly on the door and Frank watched as the couple within hurriedly donned their clothes. Then he reluctantly pulled away from his clandestine spyhole and stood upright to wait with an air of innocence next to Vincent before the rickety door, as if they had just arrived there.

The door creaked open after only a short time, and there, framed in the doorway, stood the energetic lover of but a short while before. In the light of day he revealed himself to be a sleepy-looking young man with an angelic round face, pouting lips and a haystack of wiry straw-coloured hair. His slim but shapely legs threatened to burst from the two-sizes-too-small, darned and holed grey woollen leggings he sported. He wore a patched grey linen shirt, open at the front to reveal a smooth nut-brown chest. Frank found the yawning barefoot young man appealing, but he masked his interest for the moment, and waited to see what business they had with the young fellow.

'Ah, Norbert,' cried Vincent, and chucked the young lad affectionately under the chin. 'Do we interrupt you?'

'No, my lord,' he drawled in his country accent, and, as he spoke, the young boyish lass appeared at his shoulder. She was now clothed in a ragged grey woollen dress with a kerchief tied into a loose turban on her head.

She carried the mortar and pestle in her hand, and was grinding the seeds and creamy white fluid inside it into a homogeneous paste.

'Ah, Felice,' smiled Vincent. 'What an unexpected pleasure.'

Felice bobbed a perfunctory curtsy.

'My lord,' she intoned in her low husky voice.

'And what do you concoct there?' asked Vincent, as he pointed to the paste she mixed as they spoke.

''Tis a love charm, my lord. Liquorice, camomile and myrtle bound together in fresh-spilled man seed.'

Vincent turned to Frank. 'Felice is our local cunning woman. That's a way of saying she's a white witch, you know.'

Frank looked wide-eyed at Felice, and she winked impudently at him.

Now Vincent turned once more to Norbert.

'Norbi, my young squire and I need you to ferry us over to the island.'

Norbert's hazel eyes looked at Frank, and with a lazy half-smile he rubbed the bulging packet in the front of his ragged leggings suggestively.

'So, you found a squire then, Sir Vincent?' he said.

'Indeed I did, Norbert, and a fine one, don't you think?'

Frank blushed as he fell once again under the ferry boy's appreciative scrutiny, and his cock grew hard in expectation.

'Yes, sir. A fine one, as you say.'

Then Vincent turned to look at Frank. 'Come, Frank, let's to the boat. Norbert and Felice will put our horses in the stable here and afterwards Norbi will take us over to the island, where the castle of Nonpareil stands. There you will make your new home.'

Obediently, Frank untied the reins of his horse Cinnabar and handed them to Norbert, who winked cheekily at him and then led the nag away at once to the stable. Felice did the same with Vincent's horse Milken.

Frank and Vincent now wandered over to the jetty, and, after Norbert had indulged in a passionate and lengthy farewell kiss with Felice in front of the door of the shack, the ferry boy joined them. Once there, he motioned the other two to get into the narrow boat and to seat themselves. Vincent and Frank faced one another in the middle of the boat – Vincent looked for'ard and Frank aft, and Norbert took up his long punting pole and positioned himself on the raised platform at the rear of the punt, ready to pole them through the shallow water and the reeds and out to the island. He cast one last lingering look back to Felice and waved at her. She waved back and disappeared smartly into the shack, no doubt to get on with preparing her herbal love philtre.

The sun was hot, and as Vincent faced it, he screwed up his eyes. The heat encouraged Norbert to lower his pole for an instant and to remove his shirt, which he knotted nonchalantly around his waist, before he began his poling.

With a few well-aimed pole thrusts, Norbert soon had the boat gliding through the still waters of the lake towards the island at its centre. Frank admired Norbert's sense of balance. He feasted his eyes on the interplay of muscle in Norbert's smooth chest and muscular arms as the ferry boy raised the punting pole aloft, drove it down firmly into the weed and slime at the bottom of the lake, and pushed them onward towards their destination – towards Frank's destiny. Somehow the fact that Frank had seen Norbert engaged in fierce sex with a lithe and nubile young witch but a short while before increased the lad's erotic allure in his eyes.

'The castle of Nonpareil,' said Vincent, as he pointed up ahead.

Frank turned and looked over his shoulder to glimpse his new home.

On a promontory of the island at the head of a V-shaped inlet where two tall red-earth cliffs met, there stood a tall tower of pink marble. It rose into the heights capped by a purple ceramic mosaic cupola. At the base of the tower, at either side of it, squatted two large circular keeps of rose-red brick, each surmounted by a dome of terracotta tiles. Directly below the tower, at water level in the red rock face at the very apex of the sharp inlet, there gaped an ivy-fringed, cave mouth towards which Norbert steered his small boat.

At last the boat entered the coolness of the cave, and Vincent and Frank alighted on to a harbour platform hewn into the rock. Vincent pressed a coin into Norbert's hand and cuffed the lad playfully on the ear, and then the ferry boy began punting back to the mainland. Frank followed Vincent up some stone steps that led up away from the sea cave and into an underground cavern beyond.

The cavern got its light from flaming torches set into the walls by the staircase. All manner of strange stone shapes loomed and flickered out of the darkness as Frank followed in Vincent's footsteps and climbed higher and higher. Human sculptors had given artful finished form to stalactites and stalagmites, once merely rough-hewn products of nature.

As he climbed higher, Frank gazed with excitement at a giant stone eagle which sodomised a handsome youth who crouched on all fours. Then came two young men carved in limestone who crouched and licked up at the huge cock and balls of a proud centaur. Further on, a quartet of cute stone satyrs toyed with each other's massive erection. And a little further on a sculpted quintet of handsome fork-tailed tritons capered in the waves and sucked on each other's cock. After that, Frank encountered the sculpture of a circular chain of six naked stag-antlered young lads each fist-fucking his horned brother.

Finally Frank and Vincent reached an iron-studded gate.

'The door into the castle,' Vincent explained.

He grasped the huge, phallic door knocker and knocked three times. The sound of metal on wood reverberated through the cave. At once a Judas trap opened in the door and the face of a good-looking young lad peered warily through it.

'Oh, it's you, Vincent,' cried the lad as he recognised Frank's companion. 'Welcome!' With that, there was the sound of the drawing back of bolts. Then the heavy door swung inwards, and Frank followed Vincent into the very bowels of the castle.

Frank reeled back in surprise when Vincent approached the young man who had opened the door to them, placed his hand on the lad's codpiece and planted a kiss full on his Cupid's-bow lips. And the young man returned the gesture. He laid his palm on Vincent's bulging packet as his kissed Vincent warmly back. Frank seethed with jealousy. As the two pulled out of their spontaneous clinch, Vincent turned back, smiled, and then caught sight of Frank's Medusa eyes and his stony face of disapproval.

'That's the special greeting of our secret order,' Vincent hastily clarified. 'No need for jealousy. We live like one big happy family here. Frank, meet Shawn.'

Shawn turned to Frank, puckered his lips for another kiss, and reached out to touch the newcomer's crotch tenderly. Frank blushed, gave the young doorkeeper a swift peck on the lips and a brief grope of the groin in return. It all struck him as so strange and new. He clearly had a lot to learn.

'Shawn will show you around the castle while I speak to the master.'

'The master?' Frank queried.

'Yes. Salim du Court. The leader of our order. Shawn will explain. See you later.'

Vincent gave him a goodbye kiss and then, without a backward glance, he strode off down a narrow maze-like corridor on the left. Meanwhile Frank turned to the right and followed Shawn up a stone spiral staircase.

'Vincent has gone to inform Salim that he is back, and that he comes with you as his squire.'

'I see,' said Frank, and then the spiral staircase finished and they emerged into a large baronial hall.

Frank gasped at what he saw there. A large stained-glass window filled one whole wall. It showed a silver fountain that jetted up copiously out of a pink obelisk positioned behind two large pink spheres. In the silver pool below the fountain stood naked men in a variety of postures. They came in all ages, colours, shapes and sizes, and, as Frank interpreted the scene, they were enjoying the experience in different ways.

Frank gazed transfixed, and read the window from left to right. On the left a slender blond youth paddled ankle-deep at the very edge of the pool. A chunky spike-headed lad waded knee-deep and bent to splash his shoulders with water. Next to him, a wiry red-haired fellow stood thigh-deep in the water and cupped his hands to sup up a mouthful of the precious liquid. Just under the fountain – waist-deep and drenched in its spray – a muscular fair-haired young man caressed his naked torso sensually as the rivulets of silver ran down his bronzed flesh. But the thing that most caught Frank's attention was an older man with dark hair that shaded to grey at the temples. He stood to the right of the window, waist-deep in water, and baptised – with silver streams that flowed from a pearly nautilus shell – a young and nearly submerged lad. Only his shoulders and the back of his shaven head rose exposed from the water.

'Beautiful, don't you think?' said Shawn, reverently. It shows the various revelations and the different stages of penetration into the secrets of our order.'

'I see,' said Frank.

He turned to study Shawn more closely.

The young fellow had a narrow face with high cheekbones, beautiful blue eyes with finely arched eyebrows, sensual lips, a mole on his left cheek and a cute cleft chin. He was slim-waisted and broad of shoulder. His fingers tapered, long and thin, to end in well-manicured nails. Frank imagined those fine fingers clasped around his cock, rubbing it rhythmically up and down. At once a powerful erection swelled up inside his codpiece.

Shawn now directed Frank's attention to the high wall that faced the stained-glass window. A most detailed mural graced that surface.

'The ones who sit there are the knights of our order,' he explained.

The wall painting showed six young knights seated, three and three, at either side of an oblong table, while an older man sat at the head of the board. Frank recognised him as the baptiser from the window.

Each of these knights bore his name in red letters on a gold scrip. Frank read the names. Salim du Court was the stern man who presided at the head of the table. To the left of him sat Bastien, Gerard and Dagobert and to the right, Gaston, Jourdain and Vincent. Frank recognised Vincent at once. Smaller figures of young lads stood behind the chairs, and each apparently waited on a knight. Their names appeared in green letters, each on a silver scrip.

'Who are the standing ones?' asked Frank.

'The squires,' replied Shawn.

Suddenly Frank realised that Shawn was in the painting too. He stood respectfully behind the knight Jourdain.

'Why, that's you!' he blurted out, delighted, as he pointed at the painted image.

'Yes, and this is where they will paint you,' responded Shawn.

Frank's gaze followed Shawn's slender index finger and he noticed then that the young squire in the picture who attended Vincent had his head turned away, so that his face was invisible. The name scrip, too, was blank. It was eerie. As if they expected him.

'What do you mean?'

'Each squire belongs to a knight in our order. My knight is Jourdain. He works as the artist here. He made the glass window you see over there and he painted this mural here – to the greater glory of the Tree of Life. I serve as his apprentice. I mix his colours and he allows me to paint the less important bits of his murals. For example, after you sit for him, he will paint your face, but if I'm lucky I might get to paint your cloak, your doublet, maybe even your codpiece.'

Here Shawn's eyes flicked down to size up Frank's bulging packet and Frank's cock swelled proudly under such sweet scrutiny.

He glanced back at the other squires in the painting – Piers, Chance, Tomas, and Kerwen. So many names to remember, so many new things to understand and accept.

'Let me show you to your room now,' said Shawn.

Frank accepted the offer gratefully.

Shawn led the way up a spiral staircase and, as Frank followed, his eyes lingered on his guide's pert rear, in its tight yellow leggings. Determined to make conversation with the cute lad, his mind bubbled with curiosity.

'Are you from Ireland originally?' he asked, as he picked up on a lilting trace of an accent in Shawn's speech.

'Originally,' replied Shawn. 'But that time of my life finished long ago. Now I have been initiated, my existence before the order pales into insignificance. Here I live a fulfilled life. My days and nights have colour and form, and Jourdain is all I could wish for in a knight.'

Shawn grinned. On the one hand Frank found the young lad and what he said very seductive. On the other hand the whole experience disquieted him.

Would he, too, soon begin to forget his life before entering the Order of the Tree of Life? Could he just dismiss his past friendship with Rob as something that 'pales into insignificance'. Frank snorted at such thoughts.

On their way up to Frank's room they met another squire as he came down the spiral staircase. He had the same slim sensual look as Shawn, but a mop of brown hair framed his cute face.

'I'm Shawn's brother, Kerwen,' explained the lad, and he gave Frank the ceremonial kiss and cock fondle of the Order. Frank now began to lose his initial inhibitions and to enjoy this ritual. He kissed Kerwen warmly and caressed his cock lingeringly.

Kerwen's penis strained rock hard against the taut fabric of his codpiece, and Frank thrilled at the thought of making love with the two brothers. His pleasure doubled, therefore, when the young lad decided to turn about and to accompany him and Shawn.

'Here is your room,' announced Shawn, as he opened a door at the top of the turret. 'This is where you will make your bed with your lord, Vincent.'

Frank looked around. The room boasted sumptuous furnishings. In pride of place loomed a large four-poster bed whose pillars were four wood carvings of nude muscular youths who writhed in the ecstasy of masturbation.

A pewter washbowl, a ewer of water and a towel graced a table in one corner of the room, and Frank made for them. He cast off his travel-worn jacket and shirt on a chair as he went over to sluice his head and face with the chill spring water.

As he patted his face dry with the hand towel, he turned to find that Kerwen and Shawn had also taken off their jackets and shirts and lay on the bed side by side. Bare-chested, they watched him mischievously. Frank took in the whiteness of their bodies, and the long silky body hair that graced their arms and chests.

He slowly walked over to the bed. The powerful alchemy of the brothers' erotic complicity drew him. Soon he lay between them, one arm around each. He turned first one way and then the other, and kissed their sensual lips hungrily, feeling their lithe tongues as they probed between his lips.

Frank's sexual excitement mounted when Shawn slid down the bed and began to unlace his leggings. Frank moaned and trembled as the young squire's deft fingers slipped inside his leggings and caressed his cock and balls. Now he thrilled further as Shawn began to kiss and suck at his swollen cock head.

His excitement grew when Kerwen moved up the bed and swiftly unlaced his own codpiece. Once liberated from its cloth prison his glorious cock sprang gracefully to attention. Now Kerwen positioned himself so that his sticky cock head nuzzled at Frank's lips. Frank needed no further encouragement. He took the smooth-domed helmet into his mouth and sucked with gusto.

Frank glanced up at the large mirror set into the canopy of the four-poster bed and observed the two brothers sucking and being sucked off. He gazed excitedly at their three intertwined bodies and felt the power of an intense sexual awakening surge through him. His nostrils filled with the rich musky smell of man sex that oozed from Kerwen's groin; his ears drank in the sensual music of Kerwen's guttural moans, counterpointed by the rhythmic slippery squelching of Kerwen's cock as it thrust in his mouth, and of Shawn's mouth as the lad sucked at his cock.

At last, with a cry, Kerwen shot his hot quicksilver load deep into Frank's mouth, and, a few teetering seconds later, Frank pumped Shawn's throat full of his creamy liquid seed.

Once their lust abated, the lads disengaged, lay back on the bed, and grinned at one another.

After a short while, Frank's sexual appetite sharpened once more, his cock once again sprang erect, and he began to pluck at Shawn's codpiece. Shawn fought off his prying fingers, but this only encouraged Frank to persist.

'Come on, Shawn,' he urged. 'I've already sucked off your brother's cock. Now I want to have some fun with yours. Maybe we could play some more at sucking and being sucked, or maybe you'd prefer a bit of fucking and being fucked.'

'No, Frank, no,' pleaded Shawn, but Frank insisted. When he teased Shawn's leggings down, however, he realised why the young squire didn't want him to go further.

There, encasing the young man's cock, was a finely wrought

metal scallop shell. A steel band and chains snaked about his waist and between his legs to hold it in place. The thing showed beautiful workmanship and was highly polished, but the padlock on it made its purpose plain – it was a personal sexual prison.

'What is this?' Frank asked.

'My cock girdle,' replied Shawn. 'It's a kind of chastity belt – but for men. Only my knight, Jourdain, holds the key to it. In matters of penetrative sex I belong to him now, you see. Ever since my initiation.'

'But why hasn't his cock been caged?' Frank asked as he dug a finger in the direction of Kerwen.

'They have only recently recruited Kerwen to our order. Apart from yourself he counts as our most recent arrival.'

'But when they initiate me and I become a full Brother of the Tree of Life, then I will get my cock girdle and belong to Gaston,' chipped in Kerwen chirpily.

'Gaston?'

'Yes, Gaston Charpentier, my knight.'

'I see,' replied Frank, and he fell abruptly silent. His heart thumped and his mind raced with memories of his handsome fencing teacher. So Gaston lived here as a knight of this order!

'The same will happen to you, of course,' continued Kerwen.

'All squires receive a girdle at their initiation,' added Shawn. 'You will have the honour to wear the lock that fits Vincent's key.'

Frank's blood ran cold at those words. Did he leave Rob for this? To serve as a sexual slave and chattel to one man only. And yet the idea of renouncing his freedom and of giving himself sexually to become part of this strange order had its attractions. If the order had attracted Gaston Charpentier into its folds, could it not welcome Frank du Bois also? Frank considered that power-fully seductive thought with interest.

'We will leave you now,' said Shawn, as he swiftly pulled up his leggings and laced up his codpiece, suddenly serious.

'Dinner is at sunset,' added Kerwen, and he winked at Frank as he buttoned up his shirt.

'A bell will sound,' continued Shawn, while he pulled on his shirt, and avoided Frank's gaze.

'Don't be late,' called out Kerwen as he and his twin brother grabbed their doublets and left hurriedly.

Frank lay back on the bed and rested for a while. No one came to disturb him until dusk, and then, with the clanging of the castle bell, he went down to eat, and to serve his knight.

There were six knights already at the high table when Frank arrived to take his place at Vincent's side. He recognised them from the mural: on the left auburn-haired Bastien, Jourdain with his blond curls, and bald Dagobert with his dark-brown moustache, and to the right, dark-haired Gerard, and blond-maned and bearded Vincent, and there too was his former fencing tutor, Gaston – although Gaston showed no sign of recognising him. A young squire attended each of these knights – again just as in the wall painting.

No sooner had Frank approached and received a kiss on the lips from Vincent than a door at the back of the dais opened and a powerful figure swept in. Salim du Court, the master of the order, certainly commanded respect. With his grizzled beard and iron-grey hair, which lightened to silver at the temples, he cut a compelling figure. And when his eyes – one green and one orange – swept over the assembled knights and squires, Frank trembled at the man's evident authority.

What fascinated Frank also was that du Court had in his retinue a muscular giant who wore a quilted leather jerkin and leather leggings. This young Goliath kept his white-blond hair in a ponytail and, as Frank gleaned from listening to du Court address him, answered to the name of Zarek. Frank took a fancy to Zarek at once, but he served Vincent his soup, his bread, his mead, his meat, his cheese and his fruit, and tried not to dwell on the undeniable good looks of du Court's servant. The situation was far too tangled – what with Gaston's past claims on Frank's affections and Frank's present duty to Vincent. Could he really afford to embark on a new amorous adventure with another man at this moment?

The meal passed uneventfully. The other squires helped Frank. They showed him where to find the soup tureen, the bread basket, the keg of mead, the cheese dish and the fruit bowl. As for the meat, that bit proved easy. A large roast pig and roast goat hung on spits in the vast baronial fireplace and you simply hacked off a slice of meat on to a platter and then took it to your master.

Once the knights had finished their meal, Salim du Court ushered all six of them into the room at the back of the dais. After this, he disappeared into the 'inner sanctum' himself, together with Zarek. Vincent squeezed Frank's hand as he got up to follow.

'See you in your room, later,' he murmured, and left.

Frank stayed with the other squires to have his meal.

As Shawn and Kerwen talked with Piers – a graceful gazelle-eyed lad with straight auburn hair – Frank felt lonely and a little out of sorts. He was not alone for long, however. Tomas, a chunky youth with a crew cut, and Chance, a shy young fellow with a head of tight blue-black curls, soon joined him.

'Lonely?' asked Tomas.

'Yes,' replied Frank. Gaston's lack of attention hurt him. Was it feigned, or did he really not recognise his former charge?

'The rules of the order take a bit of getting used to. We squires always have to serve our knights like that at dinner. Maybe, if we're lucky, they'll come to us later tonight. Then we can serve them in other ways, too.'

Frank looked into Tomas's face. The chunky young lad's hazel eyes twinkled.

'Come and visit me in the kitchens sometime. The knight I serve is Dagobert. He works as the chef here, and I bet I could tempt you to something if you come to see me.'

Tomas reached over and squeezed Frank's thigh.

Frank looked with interest at him. Yes, maybe he would pay a visit to the kitchens sometime soon, and not just to sample Dagobert's culinary creations. He warmed to this thickset cooking apprentice with the laughing eyes.

'Maybe I'll come tomorrow,' said Frank.

Tomas grinned. 'I hope you will, and that, once you've come once, you'll come again and again. If you know what I mean.'

Frank blushed, but nodded. He imagined Tomas's cock, thick and fleshy, and his rump, full and rounded. And then with a sickening feeling he remembered Tomas was an initiated squire. He belonged to Dagobert and only Dagobert had the key to his cock girdle.

Now it was Chance's turn to speak.

'Or maybe you'd like to visit the library. I serve the knight Gerard. He works as the librarian here. Our collection boasts many interesting volumes.'

'Oh, I don't read much,' muttered Frank.

'These contain the most beautiful and revealing illuminations. They show every imaginable position. If you see what I mean.'

Frank did see what Chance meant, especially as the lad's feet played footsie with his own under the table and he pressed his leg invitingly up against Frank's thigh.

For a second or two, Frank fantasised about his cock penetrating Chance's arse in a variety of ways, but then he remembered that the lad belonged to Gerard, and that he wore one of those damned cock girdles, which ruled out penetrative sex.

'Well, will you come soon?' insisted Chance, as he placed an inquisitive hand on Frank's codpiece. 'To the library, I mean.'

'Yes, yes, of course,' murmured Frank.

His heart lightened when the meal was over and he retired to his room alone.

It frustrated him to have all these sexually enticing young men around him when they all wore impregnable cock girdles and in fact each belonged under an initiation oath to his own knight.

Frank stripped naked, and threw his clothes over the back of the chair in his haste. He dived between the cool bedsheets and lay awake. In the dark he stared at the ceiling and waited for Vincent to arrive.

The castle bell tolled the hour, and still Vincent didn't come. Frank heard the sound of laughter and voices in the courtyard below. Some kind of festivity was in progress but no one had invited him. What was more, he didn't share the merrymakers' festive mood. First Gaston had ignored him at supper and now Vincent had forgotten him. It was too much!

After an hour or so, Frank realised with resignation that Vincent definitely wouldn't join him for the night. He punched the pillow and then bit his lip to stop the tears from coming. In the silver moonlight he got out of bed and padded over to the table, where he had left his travelling bag. He rummaged about in that for a bit, and then drew forth what he needed – the acorn-tipped oak wand Rob Oakley had carved for him.

With the wand grasped firmly in his fist he slipped back into bed. There he closed his eyes, and imagined himself back home. He conjured up the image of his beloved childhood friend in his mind's eye. Yes, now he had it. So real he could almost smell the lad's sweaty armpits in his nostrils and touch his stubbly jaw with his fingers. As they wrestled naked in the forest glade, he grappled with Rob on the dew-drenched grass. At first Frank had the upper hand, but now, as they tussled, Rob threw him to the ground and pinioned him there. Frank gazed up at the veins throbbing in Rob's neck, then higher, into his handsome face. His heart raced with desire. His bowels melted to jelly as those large brown eyes stared down hungrily at him. He panted and trembled with excitement as Rob parted his legs and hooked them over his shoulders. All his resistance dissolved. He knew what awaited him – he had longed for it for so many months now. Finally, his secret dreams would be fulfilled. Rob would enter him and they would be joined at the root, bonded for ever, as he had been with no other man.

Alone in bed, Frank moistened the acorn tip of the wand with his spittle and gently eased it into his arse mouth. He imagined it was Rob's firm cock fucking him in the forest glade. He wanked his own cock, and moved the wand up and down within himself. He loved to stretch his anal sphincter and squeeze his cock in this way. His movements became faster, more urgent. Finally, he came again and again and again in spray after spray of hot gobbets of spunk that hit the bedsheets like warm summer rain.

Then he drew the wand slowly out of his arse and laid it on the small table by the bed. Now at last he drifted off to a fitful sleep where he dreamed that Rob and Vincent were fighting together in a knightly tournament with him as their prize.

Four

Early the next morning, a rather drunk Vincent shook Frank awake by the shoulder. Almost at once their lips met in a long and sensual kiss, heavy with the smell and taste of spiced mead. Under this sensual assault, all the sharp criticisms against Vincent that had festered and multiplied in Frank's heart evaporated like wisps of night mist in the rays of the dawning sun.

Frank luxuriated in the eroticism of the moment, his naked body lying below the sheets, Vincent's clothed body sitting next to him on the bed. Frank loved the way Vincent's honeyed tongue probed his mouth, the way Vincent's gauntleted hand caressed and massaged his cock, which pulsed with an undeniable morning erection.

But then a cough from behind Vincent betrayed the fact that they had company. Vincent stood aside to reveal the rather drunken and dishevelled fellow knight who stood two paces to his rear. It was Dagobert the cook, Frank realised, as he took in the fellow's bald head and drooping moustache. Tomas's lord.

'Slept well, have you?' asked Vincent cheerfully.

'Sort of,' replied Frank. 'I counted on your coming to me last night,' he added in an undertone, for Vincent's ears only. The criticisms – so recently forgotten – swarmed back into his brain like angry wasps, ready to sting.

'But this *is* last night for us, Frank. We haven't slept. We drank and roistered all night. Toast after toast. To celebrate your arrival.' He stroked Frank's cheek tenderly. 'I came up as soon as I could. Here, I brought this for you.'

He indicated a beautiful pewter goblet which stood on the table by Frank's bed. At first glance Frank took its shape to be that of an exotic flower with calyx and stem, but he soon realised it was in fact a powerful sexual image. The stem and foot were formed from a slender upended cock that penetrated a pair of lips, and the bowl was a hollow scrotum. Each wrinkle, vein and hair had been lovingly rendered in the cold metal.

'Would you like to drink some? I'm willing to bet that it's the best mead you've ever tasted.'

Frank glanced over at Dagobert, who now sat in the wooden chair in the corner of the room, and gazed avidly at them.

'Don't worry about Dagobert. I count him as a good friend. He's come to see you. I hope you don't mind. I boasted of my beautiful boy all night and he said he'd like to come with me to wake you. Don't turn shy now. I want no mock modesty from you.'

Vincent drew back the sheet that covered Frank's body, and Dagobert's eyes grew wide with interest. The fellow licked his lips, and scrutinised every inch of Frank's naked physique eagerly, hungrily. His gaze lingered between Frank's muscular thighs and pinpointed his erect cock and lust-swollen balls.

'Why, you picked a fine one, and no mistake,' growled Dagobert. 'A nicer piece of boy flesh I never did see, and well endowed too, by Saint Cosmas.

Frank felt excited to be the object of Dagobert's interest. He sat up and took the goblet of mead from Vincent's hand, then knelt on the bed and slowly quaffed it off. It tasted truly delicious. Sweet and nutty, and slightly alcoholic.

Dagobert, for his part, sat spellbound as he gazed at the vision of blond male loveliness, muscular and slim, which knelt in silhouette on the bed in front of him, and obediently drank down its mead. Frank's dark outline had a golden aura to it, thanks to the honeyed rays of the morning sun that shone upon it through the open window. Dagobert felt his stout cock rise in its codpiece like a salmon that strains upriver at spawning time. The sight of this enticing man bait, which dangled so temptingly before his eyes, ensnared him, hook, line and sinker.

Vincent too lusted after Frank as he knelt naked on the bed, and supped the mead from the cup, obedient to his command. When Frank had drunk his fill, he put the goblet back on the table and lay back on the bed. As Vincent gazed at him, he registered, with a twitch of his cock, that a droplet of sticky mead dribbled from the corner of Frank's mouth and trickled down towards his chin. Vincent licked his own thumb, reached forward, and wiped away the glistening track of honeybrew from his beloved squire's face. Bolder now, he continued.

'I came with Dagobert to show him something, Frank. Not just the beauty of your manly form, but also your skill in sexual matters. Especially in matters of mouth sex. No man has ever sucked me off the way you've sucked me, boy. You drew my very spirit self out through my cock by the power of your tongue and lips. And I wanted to share that experience with my fellow knight, Dagobert.'

'Share?' asked Frank suspiciously. 'But don't squire and knight belong to each other in this order of yours? That's what Shawn explained to me last night.'

'Of course,' replied Vincent. 'But sometimes we fellow knights share our squires. Dagobert here and I have often shared his boy, Tomas, in the one bed.'

'And in a variety of ways,' added Dagobert, and he grinned.

'And great sport we all three had of it, I can assure you,' finished Vincent.

'I see,' said Frank. 'So what exactly does Dagobert want to do with us? Will he watch only, or will he take part too?'

'Whichever you prefer, dear lad,' said Dagobert, as he extracted his pulsing cock from his quilted codpiece. 'If you would have me watch the goings on only, why then I shall, with the greatest of pleasure, and Dame Fist shall be my cock's berth for this once.' He took himself in hand, and rubbed his cock up and down with suggestive wanking motions, while drops of viscous lubrication dribbled from its tip.

'So, what say you, Frank?' asked Vincent, as he followed suit and extricated his thick and throbbing pole of man meat from its tailored prison. Its head, too, glistened, slick with excitement. 'I wagered Dagobert that you would be game enough to suck us both off at the same time, but, if you'd like to take us one by one, or Dagobert not at all, then say the word. But hurry, for I fear I may shoot my load in thin air if we don't get at it soon.'

Frank looked down at Vincent's and Dagobert's cocks with interest. The two knights now stood face to face at the foot of the bed. Both looked sideways at him, their cocks reared up in unison, like mirror images, one of the other, and their cock heads touched, and kissed moistly.

The invitation tempted Frank sorely. He may have secretly preferred to keep Vincent to himself, but he had never sucked off two cocks at the same time before, and – ever a lad for novelty and experiment – he yearned to try it now.

'No, Dagobert can stay. I want to suck both your pulsing pricks at the same time,' said Frank, and he positioned himself on all fours on the end of his bed and lowered his head until his mouth closed on those two knightly cock helmets and began to lap at them. He suckled on their manly juices, and soon took both cock heads inside his mouth excitedly.

Dagobert's and Vincent's mouths met in a deep tongue kiss, and they stroked each other's shoulders, and pinched each other's nipples. From time to time they took it in turns to ruffle Frank's blond head and to tweak his ears and nose. Frank took his own cock in hand and began to shag Dame Fist as he sucked and slurped on Vincent's and Dagobert's pricks. It was so very good to have his mouth chock-full of cock meat, for his nostrils to be able to scent the subtle individual aromas that emanated from Vincent's and Dagobert's groins, and for his tongue to savour the distinctive flavours and textures of their pre-come.

Frank sucked away at their cock heads eagerly, diligently, and he felt his own cock rise up hard in his hand, stiff with excitement. He and Vincent and Dagobert were joined together in a close, unholy trinity of sensual interrelation. At last, in a great guttural cry, all three came in quick succession.

First, hot gobbets of Frank's spunk splattered the bedsheet, then Vincent's fountain of seed gushed in Frank's mouth, and, as Frank pulled away slightly to swallow, Dagobert's cock too reared up and spurted strings of liquid pearls all over his face.

Once Frank had washed and wiped himself dry, he dressed and left the bedroom. Dagobert and Vincent now lay together – sleeping the sleep of the exhausted – on the bed. Their arms were wrapped round each other, and their bodies were entwined. Frank felt like an intruder in his own room. He decided to go for a walk in the garden before breakfast.

It was while he walked alone in the garden that the hairs on the back of his neck began to prickle. Someone was watching him, and following him, he was convinced. He quickened his pace. He didn't want to talk to anyone just now. His mind swirled in a welter of confusion about Rob, about Vincent, about the whole idea of joining the Order of the Tree of Life in the first place.

He made towards the 'knot garden', where there was a maze of tall green hedges. There he dived inside the protective green shrub walls. He heard the sound of footsteps on gravel, which still followed him. Swiftly he zigzagged through the hedge-lined spiral paths, ignored the many dead ends that presented themselves, and darted into the very centre of the labyrinth. There he spied the statue of a naked youth, the shadow of whose erect bronze cock pointed to the passing hours on a sundial. Frank sweated and panted as he stood there. He hoped that whoever it was who was following him had given up.

He breathed a sigh of relief at his lucky escape. But this sensation was short-lived, for Zarek, Salim du Court's attendant, now appeared unexpectedly between the green maze walls. He grinned and he had a finger to his lips. He carried a pair of gold Turkish slippers with curled-up toes in one hand, and tiptoed barefoot into the centre of the maze next to Frank. So that was why Frank hadn't heard Zarek enter the maze. But why was he following Frank in the first place?

The tall Polish man approached him. On his lower half he wore baggy, black, Turkish-style trousers and on his top he had only a black felt waistcoat embroidered with gold scimitars. Frank gazed at his strong muscular arms and his hairless but defined chest and abdomen. Zarek caught his gaze.

'You like Zarek's physique?' He lisped slightly as he spoke. Frank noticed then that his eye teeth were filed into points and that his tongue tip was split into two like a snake's forked lingua.

Frank nodded. Zarek put his slippers on the ground. Frank saw with a thrill that the giant Pole had an eagle tattoo on his arm.

'Come!' beckoned Zarek with both arms. 'Come to me!'

Frank gazed with awe at the boy. He stood so tall, so strong. Sexuality oozed from his every pore, streamed from his eyes, his sensual mouth, his pert nipples. Frank's legs weakened at the knees and he felt dizzy. Almost without knowing what he did, he walked over to Zarek. He longed to feel the strong boy's muscular arms around him, to tilt his head up and to kiss him full on the lips.

When Frank was close enough, he ran his hand over the giant's firm pectorals and down his taut belly.

'So beautiful,' he murmured. 'And so strong.'

Zarek shivered with pleasure under his touch.

'Yes, Zarek is strong,' he said and grinned. 'Zarek kills wild boar with his bare hands.'

Frank ran his fingers over the Polish boy's biceps and muscular forearms.

'But Zarek not hurt Frank,' the Pole said seriously. 'Zarek love Frank. Zarek want to fuck Frank's arse. Ever since he saw Frank at supper yesterday.'

Zarek wrapped Frank in his arms. Frank tilted his head up and Zarek bent his head down and they kissed, long and hard. Zarek's attenuated tongue thrust through Frank's lips and teeth again and again. Frank's resistance melted away.

'Zarek want Frank.'

'No, Zarek.'

'Zarek want Frank now.'

'Oh, Zarek, I . . .'

Frank suddenly fell silent and stiffened as the Polish boy bit him softly in the neck, then sucked and chewed with his pointed teeth and licked with his bifurcated tongue.

'Oh, Zarek, please don't, I . . . I can't bear it, it's too beautiful.'

'Now Zarek good and hard.'

The Polish boy grabbed one of Frank's hands and placed it excitedly inside the crotch of his Turkish pants. Frank felt around, turned on by what his fingers touched. Zarek had a huge meaty, uncut cock which now stood rigid. His big heavy balls hung low.

'You like?' Zarek grinned broadly again. He took off his waistcoat and tossed it to the ground next to his Turkish slippers.

'I like,' admitted Frank as he smiled back, 'very much.' He kicked off his blue suede ankle boots.

With a thrill Frank felt the Polish boy's colossal cock rear up with excitement. Zarek now reached down and unbuckled Frank's belt. Frank did the same to Zarek. Both then dropped their leggings to their ankles and stepped out of them.

Zarek now stood gloriously naked before Frank, muscular and tall, and very clearly aroused. Frank had never seen such a massive cock. Willingly he allowed the gentle giant to turn him round, and to push him gently forward until he leaned with his arms outstretched, his hands propped on the rim of the sundial.

Frank felt a delicious thrill of anticipation shudder through his entire body as he heard the young Pole spit. Soon after that he felt a large fingertip, lubricated with sticky mouth juice, penetrate his tight arse insistently. Soon another finger joined that first one, and then a third. As the Polish boy pushed his digits in, worked them around, and stretched Frank's arse mouth to the very limit, Frank rotated his arse and moaned with pleasure.

Now, suddenly, Zarek drew his writhing fingers out of him. Frank felt empty and yearned to be filled again. Excitedly he heard Zarek spit once more. He looked over his shoulder, and saw that his oversized lover had eased back his massive foreskin and was busy anointing his smooth purple cock head with a palmload of spittle, ready to plunge it deep into him.

Frank cried out with the pleasure-pain as the strapping lad

drove his great cock between his buttocks. First only the giant cock tip slipped into him, and butted up against his anal sphincter. Frank's tight arse opened more and more with the constant inward pressure. Then Frank gasped as Zarek's whole flanged cock head entered his arse, and finally his arse muscles relaxed enough to admit the entire length of Zarek's immense cock shaft deep into his soft yielding bowels.

'Oh, that feels so good!' Frank murmured, and he tilted his pelvis back to increase the penetration. Now Zarek placed his strong hands on Frank's hips and began to thrust into him again and again, at first slowly and gently, but then faster, harder and deeper.

Frank's heart raced. This was sexual ecstasy such as he had never known before. All aflame, he reached a hand back to stroke with curious fingers the sticky root of Zarek's huge member as it plunged repeatedly into his arse. It was a great thrill to feel the closeness of Zarek's pubic bush and his own buttocks. He fondled Zarek's sticky cock root as it plunged persistently into him, and his deft fingertips clearly intensified Zarek's pleasure, too. After only a few more inthrusts, the Pole came hard inside him with a forceful and copious ejaculation. Frank cried out with wild desire as Zarek's warm spunk trickled out of his still cock-plugged arse and dribbled down his inner thighs. Frank's cock reared up in sympathy and spat its own generous load of molten man seed all over the sundial.

In the afterglow of sex, when Zarek had finally withdrawn his softening prick from Frank's arse, they sat together, and kissed and cuddled on the grass at the heart of the maze. Suddenly a thought occurred to Frank.

'Zarek,' he asked, 'how come you don't wear Salim's cock girdle?'

Zarek looked confused, and Frank rephrased his question.

'All the other squires have a metal cock cage that only their knight can unlock – to keep them faithful, you know. How come you haven't got one?'

'Ah, but knights and squires are twelve in all, and Salim as the leader of order makes thirteen. I am not Salim's squire,' replied the Pole grinning. 'I am his slave.'

'His slave?' Frank reeled back in horror.

'Yes. Master Salim bought me at the slave market in Constantinople. See. I bear his brand.'

Zarek showed Frank the dark scar on his left buttock where the letters 'SduC' had been seared with red-hot metal into his flesh. Frank shuddered.

'But how? Why?'

'Slavers kidnapped Zarek. Tall blond with lots of muscles and big cock get good price in slave market in east. They about to sell Zarek to sultan as guard for harem, but Salim offer more at auction than Sultan's man – whole heap of gold – so now I belong to him.'

'But that's terrible,' said Frank.

'Not terrible,' replied Zarek, and he grinned. 'Salim very good master and Zarek happy to serve him. Only eunuchs work as harem guards so, if sultan buy Zarek for harem work, he chop off Zarek's balls. Zarek no like.'

He patted his bollocks contentedly, and Frank had to agree that it would have been a great shame if those ripe, spunk-filled plums had ever been pruned from the branch by the castrator's knife.

After a while Zarek stood up and stretched. 'Zarek go now.' He drew on his trousers. 'Many things to do.' He pushed his feet into the Turkish slippers. 'But we meet again.' He pulled on his waistcoat and then, in a moment of tenderness, he knelt down next to Frank, who still sat on the ground, and kissed him on the forehead.

'Zarek love Frank. Nice tight arse good for big dick.'

And, with that, he was gone.

Frank dressed at a leisurely pace and went in to break his fast with the other squires. None of the knights had yet surfaced after the previous evening's revelry.

Over a beaker of small beer and a wooden bowl of curds and honey, Frank talked and joked with the other lads. He gradually began to feel more at ease with them. The fact that he had indulged in sucking sex already with Shawn and Kerwen and with

Tomas's knight Dagobert meant that his inhibitions were fast fading away. He eyed handsome young Piers and chunky Tomas and wondered how long it would be before he slipped between the sheets with one of them. They both attracted him in their different ways.

But it was Chance who made the first move this morning. As Frank got up from the breakfast table, said farewell to the other squires and began to walk from the banqueting hall, the slender purple-clad young librarian sprang up to follow him. He caught up with him at the door.

'Will you come to the library later?' he asked in an undertone. 'Gerard and I have some very . . . stimulating volumes to show you.'

'Of course,' said Frank. 'See you there in an hour.'

Frank returned to his room to freshen up. He could see no sign of Vincent and Dagobert, so he stripped to the waist and splashed his face, neck and torso with cool water. Then he lay down on his bed to rest awhile and to mull over recent events.

Things moved so fast at the castle of Nonpareil that it was hard for his head to keep up with them. Gaston was ignoring him. Vincent cast him off and pulled him on when it suited him like an old glove. Zarek's attentions flattered him, even though – because of the language difficulties between them – they found expression in physical rather than verbal form. But perhaps here lay the secret of Zarek's appeal. A man's cock could not lie – stiff meant interested, and limp signified uninterested. And perhaps the effort he expended as he forced his ideas into a foreign language made Zarek more truthful, and more blunt about what he felt. It was difficult to talk false and fancy in broken English after all.

Frank realised that since he came to Nonpareil he was moving at a rhythm dictated by his heart – or perhaps more truthfully his stiff cock, aching balls and pert arse. It was a dizzying and disconcerting experience. He was now walking along a path of sexual awakening that unfurled fast before him. He reached up to finger the silver chain around his neck, and thought of the horn ring he had taken off that chain and given to Rob Oakley back in the grounds of Woodmere. The path of sexual enlightenment that he now trod led him far away from his beloved Rob, and all the problems that accompanied his unrequited love for the woodcutter, but Frank somehow knew in his bones that their paths would cross again. Somehow he was sure that this journey of erotic and spiritual exploration that he had undertaken was a preparation for a future reunion with Rob, and that what he learned in the Brotherhood of the Tree of Life would stand him in good stead for that eventual coming together when it occurred.

Later that morning, refreshed and full of energy, Frank made his way to the castle library. He went in without knocking and stepped right into the middle of the most erotic scene.

Gerard the librarian sat on a large carved-wood chair. The carvings, Frank noted, showed muscular youths' bodies twined together in different sexual positions. Gerard's codpiece was unlaced and he milked his huge, erect penis into a large silver goblet which was encrusted with amethysts.

In front of Gerard, on the floor, his squire Chance lolled on a boarskin rug. Many finely bound and illuminated volumes lay scattered all around him. He was stark naked except for a studded, mauve, leather dog collar that encircled his neck. With his fine-boned delicate build, it gave him the look of a dun-coloured whippet lying at his master's feet.

Frank noted with pleasure that Chance's cock girdle lay with his clothes at the foot of Gerard's chair. Gerard had clearly freed Chance from all constraints for the purposes of his own voyeuristic pleasure.

'Ah, Frank,' said Gerard, as he looked at him with his dark brown eyes. 'My young squire told me you would come to join us. Come now, strip off and make yourself comfortable on the rug there with Chance. He has some interesting books to show you. Things to make your cock stand on end. I simply want to watch you and Chance as you enjoy yourselves.'

Frank needed little encouragement. He cast off doublet, shirt and leggings and soon lay in the buff next to Chance, while Gerard looked on.

Chance handed him a book called *The Ship of Manly Love*.

'I think you'll enjoy this,' he chuckled.

Frank flipped through the volume. On each page there was a crudely coloured woodcut of a sexual act undertaken by one or more of the sailors on the Ship of Love. On the page that faced each picture was a pithy erotic verse which described the action.

One page showed a handsome young sailor wanking in the crow's-nest with the verse, 'High up in the small crow's-nest, the lookout finds frigging in the rigging best.'

Another spread showed the interior of the captain's cabin. In private the captain, with his cocked hat and nothing else on, taught his well-endowed mate, who wore only a kerchief, the finer points of mutual masturbation. The legend here was, 'The captain shows his well-hung mate the finest way to masturbate.'

On another verso page a gunner rammed his long and turgid tool up the bared arse of a fresh-faced young sailor who lay across the barrel of a cannon. On the recto page the text read, 'The gunner shoves his meaty pole into the raw recruit's tight hole.'

On yet another page, Frank found a picture of a crewmen's orgy below decks. Various sailors in different states of undress fucked, sucked, licked and kissed, caressed and fisted and shot their loads of creamy spunk. The verse here was, 'Here are the able-bodied crew spurting seamen's delight, all in full view.'

As he turned over the leaf, Frank saw a picture of a sailor who wore only a shirt standing at the wheel of the ship. A handsome young naval officer crouched behind him and licked at his naked arse. The words that accompanied this image were, 'The helmsman steers a course due south with the bosun's tongue in his nether mouth.'

And so it went on. The images were vulgar, undoubtedly, the colouring crude, and the poetry unsubtle, but their exuberance and their brash boldness aroused Frank nonetheless. His cock stood fully erect and throbbed.

Frank had so lost himself in the book that he was quite unaware of what Gerard was up to, and directed only the occasional glance at Chance who lay by his side and pored over another erotic text.

After he'd finished with naval gazing, the next volume that Frank grabbed from the pile caught his attention even more closely. Its title was, *The Eternal Triangle: a study in sexual geometry*.

There was a short preface, which Frank skimmed through, that talked of the sublime love that may exist in all its many permutations between two men and a woman – knight, squire and lady. And then the illustrations began.

These were beautifully illuminated miniatures, full of detail. They used tricks of perspective so that they seemed to be in three dimensions, and subtly tinted. They were veritable feasts for the eyes and so real-looking that Frank felt almost that he could enter into each picture and take part in the action. And what action there was! Sexual encounters, yes, but all portrayed with discretion and taste. In a scene in the forest the lord and lady made love naked while the squire looked on from behind a tree. The lord's penis was in fact concealed from view by a cunning and suggestive *cache-sexe* made of acorn and oak leaves that served to titillate and excite Frank's imagination more than the crudely explicit artwork that had appeared in *The Ship of Manly Love*. The caption here was, 'The courtly couple have congress in the woods while the squire looks on.'

In another scene the squire sat on his lord's lap in the minstrels' gallery. The two kissed and the position of the lord's arms as they reached towards the lad's groin suggested they were perhaps indulging in something more than just kisses, though a lute that the squire languidly plucked concealed their codpieces. The unconcerned lady sat embroidering a unicorn on a loom in an inner room. 'The squire plays upon the lord's heartstrings,' read the caption. To Frank this picture caught the idea of snatching a moment of sensuality most keenly.

In a third picture the lord and the squire, stripped for action, made love with the naked lady in a red brocade four-poster bed. Here again, inanimate objects in the foreground obscured and yet suggested sexual action in the background.

The lord penetrated his wife from behind, but the actual point of penetration was obscured by the lord's shield propped against a chair in the foreground, though the lordly coronet that hung from the pommel of the lord's sword intimated what was hidden from view.

While the squire buggered his wife, she simultaneously performed fellatio on the squire, but the view of the squire's penis as it entered her mouth was blocked but symbolised by a red butterfly which landed on a large cucumber in a fruit bowl bearing cucumbers and plums on a bedside table. The lady's breasts were similarly obscured but hinted at by two large ripe pears on the same table. The title of this illumination was 'The lady drinks in the bounty of both lord and squire.'

As he looked at these images of three-way sex between two men and a woman, Frank's mind turned inevitably to Rob and Molly. His bollocks began to ache and his cock began to throb with excitement as he mentally stripped away all artistic conceal-ment and repainted the figures of lord, lady and squire with Rob's, Molly's and his own faces.

Here on the next page was another bed scene: Molly lay legs in the air as Rob's hard pole of man meat pierced her pussy, while Frank penetrated Rob's arse. On the following page there was a standing bedroom pose: Rob thrust his virile rod into Molly's rear while Frank's dick forcefully entered her quim from the front.

'At last. Now you are ready,' came Gerard's voice.

Frank was snatched out of his sexual daydreaming back to the reality of the library in the castle of Nonpareil. He realised that, in his currently highly aroused state, his cock was oozing thick pre-come. Gerard, still in his chair, played with his own cock suggestively, and watched Frank with rapt interest.

'Frank, I believe you are all agog with lust now, my lad. The books have done their work. Now I want you to hold the sexual fancies that brought you to this state firmly in your mind's eye. And now, Chance, my pet, get into position, there's a good lad!'

Chance at once obediently crouched on all fours like a nut-brown dog, his pert arse, slightly tilted in the air like a bitch on heat, pointed directly towards Frank and he whimpered with excitement.

Gerard leaned forward and placed a pot of herbal salve upon the boarskin next to Frank's thigh. Frank knelt and bent down to sniff it with interest. An aroma of mint and bergamot, mixed with almond oil, beargrease and honey filled his nostrils.

'Anoint your stiff key with the salve, Frank my boy. And oil Chance's keyhole well too. And then, once you are both well lubricated, I invite you to unlock the door to paradise!'

Frank did as he was bid, and scooped up a palmful of the sticky gel to rub on to his cock head, down the full length of his throbbing cock shaft, and over his swollen balls. At once a delicious cool sensation spread across his genitals, and made his erection harder and his bollocks contract with pleasure.

He now dipped a finger into the pot and slowly slipped it, coated with unguent, into Chance's tight arse. Chance whined and growled with pleasure and wriggled his haunches as if to work himself back on to Frank's hand. Frank withdrew his finger from Chance's arsehole and dabbled two fingers in the pot. He inserted both of them back between Chance's buttocks once more. Chance's tight arse mouth relaxed a little as Frank's fingers probed and massaged. His wriggles, whines and growls doubled in intensity. Frank now placed three fingers in the pot, and, as they dripped salve, he drove them slowly but insistently into place inside Chance's stretched anus.

'He's ready for you now, Frank, boy. Shove your stout key into place and turn it around forthwith.'

Frank needed no further invitation.

He lined up his pointed cock head with the softly expanding and contracting O of Chance's arse and, like a cobbler's awl entering soft leather, he thrust in. Chance gave a hoarse bark of pleasure at the sudden inrush of hard meat into his back passage. Once deep inside the lad, Frank grabbed Chance's hips for better purchase, and so began the rocking dance of fierce penetrative love between them.

Every time Frank thrust his cock in – deep and hard – Chance rocked back on his knees to parry the blow and to increase the penetration. Soon a delicate rhythm and counter-rhythm was set going between them as if they were one mythical beast that writhed upon itself – driven by its own great power.

By now Frank had his eyes closed and he roared like a lusty dragon with each inthrust. At one moment he imagined himself and Chance as a couple of crew members from the Ship of Manly

Love. At another instant he was the devoted squire who fucked his lord with the geometric precision of an orrery – one of those little models of the planets that spun round, driven with utter regularity by a clockwork mechanism that, once wound up, would never stop.

Chance for his part had his eyes closed also, and moaned, panted and shouted oaths with an urgent desire that built higher and higher. He constantly craved more, and instantly received it as Frank's bone-hard rod pierced him to the quick with implacable insistence.

Now Frank changed rhythm. Remembering Gerard's orders to turn his key in Chance's lock, he began to rotate his penis around inside Chance's arse at the end of every inthrust. It was only a small twist to cap every penetration, like dotting your i's or adding an extra curlicue to your signature, but Chance seemed really to revel in this extra sexual flourish, this teasing erotic finesse on Frank's part.

Gerard watched Frank with great excitement as he tupped Chance so masterfully on the boarskin. He gazed at the two young squires' bodies conjoined in the act of love, and he caressed his own organ in time with Frank and Chance's intricate interplay of sexual forces.

So it was that, at the exact moment when Frank shot his fountain of semen with a cry of triumph into Chance's arse, Chance's cock erupted in a bolt of liquid white lightning that spattered the hide rug with hot seed, and Gerard's cock poured forth a seaspray of white froth that continued and continued until he had finally filled the goblet he held to the very brim.

'Now the sex act is over, the communion of sperm can begin,' intoned Gerard. There was an edge of compelling authority in his voice.

As if bidden, Frank's softening cock at once slithered out of Chance's arse like a glistening snake, and the two naked lads immediately moved over and knelt obediently at Gerard's feet, ready to drink of his holy seed.

'As Lord Baal sent his seed joyfully into the world to make man, so we share our seed now to celebrate our manhood.'

Gerard raised the goblet in the air.

'Lord Baal, bless this seed, shed in an act of unbridled lust by us, your servants. Grant us to grow in your service, to become more perfectly sexual in your likeness. To tread the milky path through the heavens that you trod, and to recruit other young men to our order, so that they may in turn come to know you and love you as we know and love you.'

Greedily they quaffed down the rich and nourishing liquid between the three of them until they had drained the ceremonial cup to its very dregs.

Thus Gerard and Chance formally initiated Frank into the sacred rite of the liquid pearl communion.

Five

———

When he left Gerard and Chance in the library, Frank decided that it was time for him to explore the island a bit. He knew that he would miss lunch in the grand hall, but he opted to skip it. He wasn't at all hungry. Vincent was no doubt asleep in someone else's bedroom in the castle, lying comatose as he recovered from the celebrations of the night before. Frank had no real desire to run into Shawn and Kerwen, Dagobert, Zarek, or Chance and Gerard for a while. To have had so many sexual encounters in such a short space of time made his head whirl. He smiled at the change in himself. He was a long way from his year-long unspoken obsession with Rob Oakley and his half-hearted fumblings with Hal Ashe. The path he trod now, and the journey he had taken, were clearly beneficial for his inner growth. He was pursuing a personal quest towards self-knowledge and self-fulfil-ment. The castle of Nonpareil was certainly teaching him a thing or two about love, about sex and about life.

So, as he took his bearings by the position of the sun, Frank wandered out of the formal castle grounds and walked off around the coast of the island. To the north the isle of Nonpareil rose up in a single, sheer, tall cliff; to the west it descended gently into a reddish sandy beach, lapped by the lake water; to the south it ended in shingle; and to the east it split into a series of rocky inlets. The largest of these contained the landing stage and the cave where Norbert brought all visitors to the island on their arrival.

Frank made first for the south. As he picked his way over the pebbly water's edge, his mind floated in a reverie prompted by Gerard's invocation of the god Baal in the rite of the sperm communion.

This name triggered many associations in Frank's mind. It made him remember various alchemical and mystical-erotic texts which he had pored over as a youth in his father's library at Woodmere.

He had loved gazing at the big-cocked images of Saint Foutin, Saint Guerlichon of Cotentin, Saint Rene of Anjou, Saint Guignole of Landevenic. Or at their pre-Christian forerunners, the heathen god Priapus, or Moloch, the Phoenician god of male bounty. Perhaps Moloch was Frank's favourite sex god when he was younger. Moloch of the bull's head and muscular man's body. Moloch, who accepted sacrifices from male devotees at sunset. Moloch, whose statue in the temple stood on an iron pedestal which contained a fiery furnace within it. Moloch, in whose honour male-only dancing and orgies took place once night had fallen. Moloch, who had a bevy of eunuch priests to serve him. Frank realised that in his heart he had maybe been a servant of Moloch these long years, without realising it.

Just as Gerard evoked Lord Baal to bless his ritual sex acts, promising to recruit new followers to his worship in order to win the god's approval, so Frank felt that Moloch was his godly ideal.

He imagined what it would be like to make love with the divine bull-man. To lie back, to reach up and to caress those smooth and pointed horns above him, to feel the soft moist bull's muzzle nuzzle at his neck, to feel the massive bull's pizzle like an iron rod in a velvet sheath penetrate his arse.

Then he imagined what it would feel like to have his own body invaded and possessed by the powerful taurine spirit as he made love with a new recruit to the order. He shuddered with pleasure and involuntarily ejaculated repeatedly, filling his codpiece with sticky joy.

As he walked on, other thoughts crowded in. Could he really

devote himself to the service of Moloch for the rest of his life?
The idea was certainly tempting, especially the thought of going
out into the world and seeking out handsome young men to be
new recruits. He could see himself using all his wiles to bring
these lads to bed in order to convert them to the service of the
stiff-pricked god and to swell the ranks of the magical order. But
if he were totally honest, and not just using the homoerotic cult
as a pretext for rampant seduction, it would require dedication
and self-negation to abase himself to the will of a god all day and
every day, and Frank was not completely sure that this was what
he wanted.

An hour or so later, after he had finished his tour of the island,
Frank returned to the castle. He was still undecided about promising himself for evermore as a devotee of Moloch.

It was well after lunchtime by now, and he hurried straight to
his room.

He lay down upon the bed to rest, when suddenly the door to
his bedroom slammed violently open. As it swung and creaked on
its hinges, Vincent strode in to the room. He carried a black
leather whip in his hand and his eyes flashed blue fire.

'You young devil!' he snarled, and he cracked the whip at
Frank's feet. 'You have humiliated me before all and sundry.'

'What do you mean?' stammered Frank, as he sprang to his feet
and reddened.

'You failed to turn up at lunch to serve me.' Again the whip
cracked against the flagstones.

'But I . . . I didn't know . . . I thought . . .' Frank's excuses
suddenly rang hollow and died on his lips.

'You owe a duty to me, above all other men. Above even
yourself and your own selfish desires. I rule you as your knight,
and you serve me as my squire. You should obey me without
question. Anything less brings insult and injury to my knightly
patronage. Where did you disappear to, anyway?'

'I . . . I went for a walk along the coast.'

Frank thought it best to omit all the colourful incidents of that
morning – the encounter with Zarek at the heart of the maze, the

visit to the library with Gerard and Chance. He deemed it better to draw a veil over these sexual adventures, especially when he considered the filthy mood that Vincent was currently in.

'You went for a walk along the coast!'

'Yes.'

'For five hours?'

'Look,' Frank rounded on him. 'When I left you this morning you were still sleeping off last night's revelries. I assumed –'

'A squire should never assume anything, Frank. A squire must accept his knight's actions wholeheartedly. Anything else smacks of presumption.'

'But –'

'Don't "but" me. I think you're getting a notch above your true place in the pecking order. You forget your humble station, shall we say? I see you need to be taught a lesson.'

Vincent tapped the whip against the palm of his gloved hand menacingly. Then he reached out with that same hand and grasped Frank's face, pulled it close, and glared at him.

Frank couldn't tell whether Vincent wanted to kiss him on the lips or to spit into his eyes. In the end he did neither.

With his free hand Vincent ran the smooth silver handle of the whip gently down the side of Frank's jaw. Out of the corner of his eye, Frank saw that it was shaped like a large, erect, silver penis.

'Strip!' ordered Vincent.

'What?'

'Take all your clothes off. Now.'

Frank did as Vincent bid him do. Once naked, he turned to face his knight once more.

'Now, my young Frank, what treatment exactly do you deserve?' Vincent asked.

'I –'

'Silence!' ordered Vincent. 'It is not for you to answer back. I take the decisions here. You will simply listen and obey me as a good squire should.'

Frank held his tongue. This was a new, forceful Vincent. A facet of his knightly lover that he hadn't expected or experienced before, but one that he liked. His cock swelled and rose with excitement. It appealed to him to be ordered about, not to have to think for himself, to let Vincent take the decisions. He simply went with the flow of experience like a leaf that floated and eddied on the surface of a lake. And what a lake Vincent was! They could have coined the phrase 'still waters run deep' expressly for him. Frank found it impossible to fathom his thoughts and feelings from outside, but in the end that unreachable quality in him made him all the more attractive. Frank's cock began to pulse rhythmically.

'I believe your truancy over lunch merits a punishment, boy. What do you say?' insisted Vincent.

'I think –' began Frank.

Vincent tapped his squire's bare chest lightly with the looped whip.

'Your job is not to think, boy, your job is to agree.'

Frank's cock reached the zenith of its erection. It now throbbed and bobbed between his legs, and dribbled pre-come tears of happy excitement.

'On the bed, boy!'

'Yes,' replied Frank meekly. He was enjoying every minute of Vincent's playful humiliation. He surrendered willingly to it, eager to see what would come next.

Vincent pushed him forwards and arranged his limbs so that he crouched on all fours in the middle of the bed. There Frank waited, his arse in the air. Vincent teased out the suspense still further when he took the blue silken bedropes from the four curtains of the bed and tied Frank's ankles and wrists to the four bedposts, so that he couldn't escape. Then Vincent ran the cold cock-shaped whip handle down Frank's spine and stroked the cleft of his arse with it. Frank's balls hung full and aching now and his cock oozed with a glistening sheen of love juice, which welled up from his cock mouth and drooled downwards in a continuous fluid cord, to form a sticky pool of pre-come on the bed cover.

'Prepare yourself for your punishment, boy!' growled Vincent, and then the whipping began.

Vincent lashed hard across Frank's back and Frank winced and cried out with the pain, although somewhere that pain contained a pleasurable sense of danger and of humbly offering his body to Vincent for his use and domination. Then after the first blow came a luxurious lull. Waves of warmth radiated out from the weal, so that the next blow, when it came, engendered less pain and more gratification. The third and fourth strokes became intensely delightful and only marginally dolorous. Then Vincent increased his whipping speed, and the rain of whiplashes fell thick and fast.

Frank's body twisted and jerked with pleasure-pain under the onslaught. The whipcracks shot rhythmically through his ears in a beat that matched the quickening drumming of blood in his ears.

As each blow dulled into the next, Frank felt his sense of power over Vincent grow. Just as he needed Vincent to be his lord, so Vincent needed him to be his obedient squire, and Frank had a sense that, in a strange kind of way, Vincent's need was greater.

Frank's pleasure in taking a whipping was the pleasure of inexperienced youth that seeks to experiment with life, to try all sensations out to see if they gratify. If the experience turns out to be cloyingly sweet or utterly revolting you need never repeat it; but, if it brings joy, you can seek it out again willingly and indulge in it again at leisure.

Now Frank's heart sang with joy. He loved the sense of sacrificing himself to Vincent's brute force. The rhythmic pattern of the blows that rained down on him somehow reminded him of Rob chopping wood in the forest glade, and the thought of that similarity excited him all the more.

Now, in between the heavy lashes that Vincent directed to his back, Frank felt a lighter ticklish counterstroke across his buttocks. This brought him to such a peak of moaning and groaning, such a lather of lustful arousal, that, when the rain of whip blows ceased and Vincent's rock-hard cock roughly pierced his arse, it needed only a few deep thrusts on Vincent's part to bring Frank to a sudden intense ejaculation, in which his balls contracted and his sperm shot the length of the bed and spattered the pillow at its head. Almost at once Vincent groaned and his massive organ reared up and poured forth its molten goodness in a warm river of bliss that filled Frank's arse to overflowing.

But, if the build-up to this magical double outpouring of spunk had been gradual, the erotic reverie that filled Frank's mind by the end of it soon shattered abruptly into quicksilver fragments as someone knocked at the door.

'Who is it?' called Vincent hoarsely, and he pulled his still stiff cock swiftly from its soft nest within Frank's bowels.

Frank shuddered and whimpered at the sudden withdrawal of that firm and reassuring column of meat from inside him. He slumped forward on the bed, and his body suddenly smarted dully as all the whip blows he had borne when aroused started to burn and ache. He realised, too, that the silk bedropes cut into his wrists and ankles, but he was too tired and too weak to undo them himself, and he was far too deep in reverie to ask Vincent to loosen his bonds. He pretended to sleep and listened to the door open.

'Dagobert!' came Vincent's voice. 'What are you doing here?'

'I thought I might find you here, Vincent. Salim requires your presence for a meeting of all the knights. Get dressed, man, and follow me. This pretty piece of flesh can wait for later.'

Frank felt Dagobert's rude slap upon his buttock. Then, almost at once, Vincent and Dagobert left the room and closed the door behind them. Their footsteps on the stone flags receded down the corridor and Frank's eyes flicked open. He felt suddenly terribly alone and utterly abandoned. Fragile as he was after this latest violent sexual coupling with Vincent, which Dagobert had so rudely interrupted, his pretence of sleeping turned to reality. As he tossed and turned on the bed – still bound – the waves of exhaustion washed over him and he actually dozed off.

Frank woke some hours later. He lay at an extremely uncomfortable angle, his wrists and ankles still tied to the bed, and his back now definitely smarted. Vincent was nowhere. Frank felt the black resentment rise in him like bile. What did Vincent hope to gain by using him like some plaything, to be picked up and put down at will, without a thought for Frank's feelings? Frank didn't like that idea at all. His madcap scheme of devoting himself to the service of a phallic god came back to haunt him. No, that sort of self-inflicted humiliation was not for him. He had his self-respect and a sense of an identity to preserve and, if possible, propagate.

Games of power, of submission and dominance, were all well and good, but what Frank really craved was the deep love and respect from a man that underlay all else. After Vincent's petty rage about his absence, Frank realised that his knight was becoming increasingly jealous and possessive of him, and he hated that. He wanted implicit trust from his male lovers, and he wanted the personal freedom that came with that trust. He doubted now whether he could ever get those two things with Vincent.

Strange how love and hate make two sides of the same coin, he thought. In their first couple of days together Frank had experienced his love for Vincent as a liberating force. It took him away from the rut he was stuck in at home, and it set him on a voyage of self-discovery, sexual experimentation and spiritual enlightenment. But now, when Vincent abandoned him and then turned vindictive and mistreated him, those feelings of warm affection soon soured into feelings of deep dark hatred. Which were Frank's true sentiments towards Vincent? Confusion reigned in his mind, in his heart, about the matter. Vincent could make Frank run the whole gamut of emotions from love and hope at one end of the scale to hate and despair at the other in a very short time. The future would tell, Frank decided, which of the contradictory feelings towards Vincent that tussled within his consciousness were the most long-lasting. But he felt sincerely that the honeymoon period between them had come to an end, and that it was only a matter of time now before loathing and despair won out over liking and hope.

Someone knocked tentatively on his bedroom door.

'Come in,' groaned Frank huskily. He craned his neck round just as his spiky-haired friend Tomas entered the room.

Tomas took one look at Frank as he lay tied up and naked on the bed, his back crisscrossed with thin stripes of dried blood, and cried out.

'By Saint Cosmas, who did this to you? Was it Vincent?'

'Yes, as a punishment for me because I didn't serve him at lunch. That's how it began at first, at least, though I think he actually enjoyed the experience of beating me for its own sake. Mind you, I quite enjoyed it, too. In the heat of the moment, at any rate. But now I'm not so sure.'

'Here, let me help you.' Tomas's voice softened with concern.

He sat on the bed next to Frank and loosened the silk rope bonds at his wrists and ankles. Then, with the towel and the jug of cool water that he found in the corner of the room, he bathed the welts on Frank's back.

After a while, he patted Frank on the shoulder and said, 'You'll do, now.'

Frank sat up and he and Tomas fell into each other's arms and hugged intensely. Tomas's mouth sought Frank's lips and soon they were kissing passionately.

'My saviour,' murmured Frank as he kissed Tomas over and over again all over his handsome face. His whiplashes smarted less keenly now that his lust was aroused.

At this point Tomas pulled off his jacket and shirt and threw them down on the floor on top of Frank's pile of cast-off clothes. He then pressed close on top of Frank's supine bare body and rubbed his bare chest against Frank's, nipple to nipple.

Frank's cock bounded up stiffly, and Tomas's lips and tongue gradually kissed and licked a glistening path all over his neck, his pectorals, his abdomen, as he worked his way downwards.

Frank shivered with delight as he lay back and felt Tomas's strong mouth close on his cock head. He floated away on waves of hot sensual energy and before he knew it he was ejaculating hard and fast into Tomas's receiving mouth.

Once their lovemaking was at an end, Frank lay on the bed, and Tomas's head lay cushioned in the taut hollow of his abdomen. Suddenly he became aware of a chill breeze that wafted in through the open window. His naked flesh goosepimpled and Tomas sat up, noticed his discomfort and gestured to the pile of their intermingled clothes that lay on the floor.

'I think we'd both better get dressed now.'

'Yes,' replied Frank, meekly. And, after pulling on his shirt and leggings, he turned and looked deep into Tomas's eyes. 'I won't forget this, Tomas. Thank you. For rescuing me and for sucking me off in such a delightful way. I was feeling so low and so bad within myself and you've given me back my feelings of self-worth.'

'Don't mention it,' replied Tomas kindly. 'I know how you feel. When I first became a squire here, Dagobert put me through my sexual paces in a variety of ways – mouth sex, arse sex, threesomes, foursomes, whippings, fist-fucking, pissing. You name it, we tried it. It seemed almost as if he needed to try more and more bizarre things to whet his jaded appetite. I'm his second squire, you see, so he's an experienced practitioner.'

'His second squire?' queried Frank, filled with a sudden curiosity.

'Yes. I'm not sure if the first boy hanged himself or died accidentally while he masturbated with a noose around his neck. The Order of the Tree of Life is a law unto itself, you know. The local sheriff's ordinances count for nothing here, so they never conducted any investigation of the death, and the knights buried the empty shell of his body one night, at midnight, within the castle walls – but without any ceremony.'

'But that's terrible,' murmured Frank.

'Oh, don't take on so,' Tomas reassured him. 'The knights here come and go, as do the squires from time to time. It's like a constantly changing organism: it grows, it casts off dead wood or dead leaves, it flowers, it fruits. You just have to make sure you get what you want out of your time here, that's all.'

To get what I want, thought Frank. And what did that mean exactly? To get his heart's desire would be easy if he knew in his heart of hearts what he truly wanted. He felt hampered by indecision and muddled vision. Did he still hanker for Rob? Or did he long now for Vincent? Or someone else entirely? Like devoting himself to the unquestioning worship of Baal or Moloch, for instance? He turned to Tomas with genuine curiosity. 'And have you got what you want out of the Order of the Tree of Life?' he asked.

'Yes,' replied the lad with confidence. 'I have learned all about herbs and their powers and qualities, which is what I wanted to do when I came here. And I've also come to an arrangement with Dagobert.'

Here Tomas reached into the pocket of his leggings and drew out a small key that dangled on a long silver chain.

'He lets me keep the key to my cock girdle myself, and so I fuck who I choose. The other knights all jealously guard their squires, but not Dagobert. Maybe it's because of the way his first squire died, I don't know. But he gives me my freedom and I value that.'

Freedom, thought Frank, and he looked around at the thick castle walls that surrounded them. Momentarily he glanced out of the window at the lake that encircled the Isle of Nonpareil like a wide natural moat. Was this freedom? To live like a bird without a chain around its leg but to have to hop about in a gilded cage nonetheless.

Tomas placed a hand on Frank's shoulder and interrupted his dark thoughts. 'Let's both finish getting dressed now and you can come with me to the castle kitchens,' he said. 'I'll mix up a herbal plaster for your back.'

Frank's whip cuts now began to smart dully once more, and he jumped at the chance to soothe them with a herbal cure. He threw on the rest of his clothes, and Tomas quickly drew on and buttoned up his shirt and jacket. Then they both left Frank's room and slipped down to the kitchens. Tomas led the way and Frank trotted behind, almost like an obedient pet dog.

Down in the kitchens Frank's eyes and nose detected with pleasure the serried ranks of dried herbs that hung from the ceiling. His ears and nose registered the delicious aromas that floated up out of the pots of herbal brews that bubbled over the fire.

Tomas motioned Frank to a large wooden table that stood in the centre of the room. A bowl of tomatoes and a cucumber sat on one corner of it, ready for salad making, and in another corner a pat of soft, delicious-looking butter lay in a dish.

Tomas, however, clearly had medicinal rather than culinary things on his mind.

'Take your shirt off now and lie face down on the table,' he urged.

Frank did as he was bid, and soon Tomas was smoothing and massaging an aromatic herbal paste across his shoulder blades, and down into the small of his back.

The sensation was of ice that chilled him wherever Tomas laid the paste, and almost at once the lingering smarting of the whiplashes lessened and a welcome calm crept over his skin.

'You can get up now. The cuts don't go very deep. They'll soon fade,' reassured Tomas. 'But best to keep your shirt off for a while until the healing salve dries. You can look around my kitchen in the meanwhile.'

Frank glanced all around with interest. But, when his eyes lighted on a tray on the window ledge, Frank found something that utterly fascinated him. They were small pastries, each moulded in the form of an erect cock and balls.

'What on earth are these?' he asked.

'Oh, those are herb cakes for the Sabbats we hold.'

'Sabbats?'

Tomas scattered flour on the table now, as he prepared to roll out more pastries.

'Yes, the religious ceremonies of the order where we practise sex magic. We hold them once a month at the full moon, and there are four important ones in the year – Samhain, Yule, Beltane and Lammas.'

'But what are these herb cakes for?'

'Well, Dagobert claims they're aphrodisiac, but I seriously doubt that. Would you like to try one in any case?'

'No, thanks.'

Tomas wagged the rolling pin at him admonishingly. 'What's the matter? Are you scared? Frightened your balls might explode or your cock go permanently stiff or something?'

'No, it's . . .' Frank hesitated.

'Go on. Try one. I dare you.'

'All right, I will,' said Frank, and, as good as his word, he picked up one of the pastry cocks and popped it in his mouth. It tasted sweet and good, with maybe a hint of aniseed.

What Frank hadn't told Tomas was that he didn't require an aphrodisiac. The kitchen boy strongly attracted him anyway, and he had no need to resort to artificial aids to passion of any kind. Tomas's kindness and generosity had first woken the spark of interest in Frank, and the oral sex with him had been good. But during Frank's visit to the kitchen – as he lay on the kitchen table, or stood near the heat that radiated from the fire – he had begun to fantasise about indulging in some anal sex with Tomas. So he decided to play along with the idea of the aphrodisiac cock cakes and have some fun.

'Oh, Tomas,' he whispered, as he moved closer to the kitchen table. 'I don't know what's come over me, but suddenly I want you to fuck me, my darling.'

He stood close behind the kitchen lad and circled his arms around Tomas's waist. Then he plunged one hand into the front of the lad's leggings and reached down to stroke his cock. Frank was pleased to note that it pulsated there, and was fully erect already.

'Oh, Tomas. Your cock is so hot and hard for my arse. Don't deny the little fellow his pleasure. Come on. Take me on the table, here and now.'

Tomas needed no more encouragement. Roughly, he pulled Frank's leggings off and pushed him gently but firmly, and now entirely naked again, back on to the floured table. Tomas remained fully clothed.

Frank's arse now hung at the edge of the table, with his legs in the air and his knees hooked over Tomas's jacketed shoulders. He fully expected Tomas to unbutton his codpiece and take out his cock ready for some arse-plugging action, but for the moment Tomas clearly had other thoughts on his mind.

Frank watched with interest as the kitchen apprentice reached over, took hold of the fat cucumber, and dipped its bulbous tip into the soft butter. Frank realised at once what he was up to. He caught Tomas's eye and smiled. Tomas now scooped up some more of the butter on two fingertips and anointed Frank's arse with it. He worked his fingers around to loosen the tightly bunched arse muscles.

Now Tomas's fingers slid out of him and Frank braced himself for penetration by vegetable. When it came it was deliciously strange.

The cucumber felt cool in his insides, and it was long – impossibly long. Even Zarek's enormous member, although it had the same weighty girth, hadn't had that length.

Tomas pushed the vegetable dildo deep into him and then pulled it almost entirely out, before ramming it home once again. Frank groaned hard at each long inthrust and sucked in his breath in a whistle as Tomas slowly drew the cucumber out. He enjoyed this unusual form of deep penetration intensely, and he heightened his own pleasure by scooping up some butter in his hand and rubbing it on his own cock. He masturbated himself with quick rapid strokes to counterpoint the long, low, rhythmic bass notes of the long, green ramrod that slid in and out of his arse like a battering ram at the postern gate of a castle under siege.

In no time at all Frank's body began to flex and twitch orgasmically. Suddenly his back arched, his cock reared up, and he shot his creamy load of spunk into the air like fountain of hot milk. It spattered down again on his taut abdomen, streaked with butter and flour, and from here Tomas lapped it up eagerly like a greedy kitchen cat that laps at a saucer of rich cream.

'Mmm,' murmured Tomas. 'That was sooo good!'

'For me, too,' murmured Frank as the cucumber slid out of his totally relaxed arse. 'I loved it.'

'Now it's your turn to taste my milk,' said Tomas eagerly, and he pulled off his clothes, and got up naked on to the table.

'Frank, go and get that pan that's on the side over by the window and bring it here.'

Frank hopped down from the table and did as he was told. The pan contained a freshly whipped creamy dessert, as Frank discovered when he raised the lid, dipped his fingertip into the yellowy white froth and raised it to his lips.

Once he had brought the pan back to Tomas's side, he awaited further instructions. He noticed that Tomas's thick uncut cock was rising up into a hard erection, and that the foreskin had retracted somewhat and the glans was visible now like a shiny purple chestnut peeping from a split in its pink case.

'Do you like it?' asked Tomas.

'Mmm. It's beautiful,' said Frank as he gazed down at Tomas's bulky prick and balls with hungry longing.

'Not my dick, you idiot, I meant the syllabub. It's my favourite dessert.'

'Oh, I see what you mean.' Frank reddened.

'Frank, I get really excited when people cover my genitals with food and then lick it off. Could you dribble spoonful after spoonful of the syllabub on to my cock?'

'I'd love to.' Carefully Frank spooned the cool and cloudlike dessert all over Tomas's hot and solid cock meat and he poured some spoonfuls over Tomas's massive balls for good measure.

Once Tomas's sexual equipment was wrapped in this frothy outer covering, he motioned to Frank to stop.

'Now lick me clean,' he ordered.

Frank bowed his head and ran his tongue through the delicious tasting froth, lapping it up greedily. It was sweet and sugary and delicately scented with vanilla. As he cleared away the other coating of syllabub, Tomas's genitalia appeared hot and pulsing with lust. Frank delicately licked every last drop of syllabub from Tomas's pubic hair and then he licked Tomas's balls clean, and then the broad shaft and finally the ample head of his penis. Now the sweet flavour of the syllabub gave way to the rich animal taste of Tomas's pre-come.

Frank's salivary glands oozed as he realised he would soon be relishing the flavour of Tomas's fresh and threshing sperm upon his palate.

Tomas writhed and moaned on the table under Frank's oral onslaught, and finally, with a great groan, his massive cock foamed with spunk and Frank drank and drank until he thought he could drink no more.

Suddenly, however, that magic moment of post-ejaculative calm came abruptly to an end for both Frank and Tomas. They heard footsteps and voices on the long staircase that led down from the banqueting hall to the kitchen. From their voices, one dark and serious, the other lighter and more frivolous, they were clearly Salim du Court and Dagobert, and, what was more, they were approaching fast.

'Quick, they mustn't find you here,' whispered Tomas, as he jumped off the table and pulled on his clothes hurriedly. Frank grabbed his clothes in both hands and fled through the back door that led to the kitchen garden. There, screened by the rows of beans, he pulled on his leggings, shirt and doublet. As there was no other way into the castle from that side, except via the kitchen, he decided to walk down to the lake. There he could clean the flour and butter off himself and wash the sweet stickiness from his mouth and chin. There, too, he would also have some time to think over his sexual interaction with Tomas before he had to return to the castle for supper.

Once he had made his way down to the lake's edge, Frank found his way into a little rocky inlet. Here he decided to swim. He couldn't be seen from the castle, and he was sure no one would disturb him here. He wanted to plunge naked into the cool clear lake water and wash away the flour, dried spunk, rancid butter and cloying syllabub that still caked his body. It was the work of a moment for him to pull his doublet and shirt over his head and to yank off his leggings. Freed from his clothing, he hopped from one foot to the other over the spiky pebbles of the beach and at last edged out on to a rocky outcrop. From here he dived in – a beautiful arc of outstretched arms, streaming blond hair, taut muscles of shoulders, torso and buttocks, thighs and calves, and – to finish with – a clean pair of heels.

As he swam and splashed about in the cool depths, Frank revelled in the sensation of his body parting the cleansing lake water. The cool wavelets washed over every contour of his naked flesh so deliciously and intimately. What a subtle lover this lake was! It trickled and tickled between his thighs, lapped at his bollocks, and stroked his limp cock with ripples of feathery lightness. No wonder they told stories of horny old river gods and green-bearded lake spirits, of bell-voiced young merlads who tempted handsome young swimmers down to a watery grave.

Frank shivered as he swam, but his cock stiffened also. Love and death. They weren't so far apart really. Some called the moment of ejaculation 'the little death', after all – a moment when, in the fullness of life, one's soul shot out momentarily from one's body in a spasm of white liquid.

Frank suddenly stopped splashing about in the lake and trod water. He strained to hear something. Could it be? Yes! It was the sound of a young lad's voice, and it was singing sweetly. Had he accidentally conjured up a water spirit? The noise carried across the water, and Frank decided to swim after it.

He swam around a small jutting headland and into the next cove along the coast. The beach here was sandy rather than pebbly, and it was completely deserted except for the naked figure of a young man who stood with his back to Frank as he sang. In addition to his singing, he was drawing something with a long stick in the wet sand at the water's edge.

Frank swam quietly closer. He could now pick out words in the young man's song:

> I am his love and he is mine.
> He has a strong and potent vine.
> Gold moss about its root does twine.
> His ripe grapes give the sweetest wine.
> I am his love and he is mine.

Frank now slowly climbed out of the water and tiptoed towards the young stranger. He wanted to see what it was that he marked in the sand.

Looking over the lad's shoulder, he saw that he had drawn a pentacle – a five-pointed magical star. In the centre of the occult symbol reared a crudely drawn phallus which sat on two large testicles and erupted with a fountain of sperm like a fierce volcano. The letters F and N were intertwined on a cockring drawn halfway up the mountainous organ.

It was then that Frank spotted the ferryboat further along the beach and realised that the young stranger was none other than the ferry boy, Norbert.

He was about to tap the lad on the shoulder and to greet him when he noticed that the slim figure in front of him had dropped the stick and now jerked about as if engaged in a crazy and lively jig. He moaned and groaned and it seemed as if he was suffering some kind of seizure. Tactfully Frank waited for the boy's fit to pass.

It was only when he saw – in the gap between the boy's parted legs – the gobbets of white spunk that rained down upon the letters F and N that he realised Norbert hadn't been racked with convulsions. The cheeky lad had been pleasuring himself – wanking and dripping his freshly spilled sperm on to the drawing in the sand in some kind of solitary magical rite.

'Norbert!' Frank spoke, and the boy spun round. He coloured a little at the sight of Frank.

'Are you surprised to see me here?' asked Frank. He gazed down at Norbert's cock – long and thin and just coming out of an erection now. His own cock stiffened at the sight.

'Surprised, no,' replied Norbert. 'Pleased, yes.'

Frank was thrilled to see that Norbert's gaze fell on his stiffening prick, and that, as the young ferry boy looked down at it, his own prick stopped softening and shrinking and began to harden and stiffen once more.

'What were you doing here?' asked Frank, and he pointed down to the cock within the star traced out on the sand.

'I was conjuring you up in a grey magic rite. I asked Lord Belial to send you to me, and offered him a libation of my sperm to drink to make my spell more potent.'

'Lord Belial.'

'Yes. The Lord of the stiff prick. The Phallic Lord most of the knights in the castle worship.'

'I see,' said Frank. 'And why did you want him to bring me to you, pray?'

'Because I love you, my young lord.'

'You love me?' echoed Frank. 'But I thought you loved Felice.'

'Oh, I do, my lord. Don't get me wrong. I love her as ever a young lusty lad loves his girl. But I run with the fox and I hunt with the dogs, too, sir, if you take my meaning.'

'I think I do, Norbert,' laughed Frank. 'You mean you're as

happy to stuff your cock up a woman's pussy or into her arse, as to suck or fuck your fellow man.'

'You've got it.'

'So although you're together with Felice, and you're sexually very happy with her, from time to time you have erotic escapades with male lovers. Is that so?'

'Indeed it is, sire. And the funny thing is that, ever since I first brought you here, I've dreamed of you at night. And now I want you to love me, my lord, with the same kind of hot passion I feel for you. I want to worship your body with mine. I want to give myself to you as a bodily sacrifice. I want Lord Belial to enter you and to drive you wild with lust for me. I want your cock to become as hard as a sacred dagger, and I want you to choose my arse for your holy sheath. I want to impale myself on your horn. I want to feel the dark god's seed move within me.'

All this talk of sacrifice and dark gods chimed with what Frank had been thinking earlier, and it was undeniably true that, as Norbert stood naked on the sunlit beach with his cock in a throbbing erection, he was an incredibly attractive sexual proposition.

Frank guided Norbert down on to the sand to sit at the very centre of the star he had drawn. Then Frank sat down next to him and the two wrapped their arms around each other and began to kiss sensually.

Their lashing tongues fluttered in and out of each other's mouth, and with sweaty hands each caressed the other's naked body and stroked other's cock. Excited almost beyond endurance now, Frank pushed Norbert gently back on to the sand, reached between his smooth thighs, and tried to prise them apart, the better to thrust his cock under the lad's scrotum and deep into his arse. Norbert, however, sat up. With surprising firmness, he turned the tables by easing Frank's shoulders slowly but surely back on to the sand until Frank lay staring up at the cloudless blue sky.

'You are my god, Frank; you are the altar; you are the living candle; and you are the dark god's instrument of love.'

Frank gave himself up to Norbert's strange words. He watched, almost as if in a trance, as young Norbert straddled his hips, spat into his own hand and anointed Frank's cock head with the sticky mouth juice. He gasped as Norbert sat down on his cock tip and wriggled his hips so that Frank's meaty pole slowly slipped its whole length up into him.

'Oh, Frank. How I love to ride your cock like this!' cried Norbert joyfully, as his anal sphincter finally came to rest hard against Frank's pubic bush.

Frank himself was in heaven. Norbert's back passage gripped so deliciously tight around his hard dick. The sensation of the lad's arse muscles grasping him was truly sublime, and when Norbert started to move up and down rhythmically above him – and to make Frank's cock walk, trot, canter and gallop within his guiding arse – he gave himself up to utter pleasure, bucking up as Norbert sank low and pulling back as Norbert rose high. Truly he felt – as he gazed up light-headedly at Norbert's sinuous body which writhed above him, at the lad's dimpled and smiling face, at his tousled mop of flaxen curls outlined against the blue canopy of the sky – that it was like fucking an angel.

And, with that thought, Frank came copiously inside Norbert's sweet arse. Norbert at once leaned forward and kissed him full on the lips gratefully.

'Thank you, my lord, for gracing my humble body with your divine sperm. Thank you for using me as a vessel for your living seed.'

Then Norbert slowly eased himself up and Frank's detumescing cock slipped out from between his thighs.

Frank glanced at the ferry boy's still swollen organ. He hadn't ejaculated during their coupling and seemed to show little interest in doing so now.

'Can I help you with that?' Frank gestured.

'No, thanks,' said Norbert. 'I've promised my unspilled seed to Lord Belial for seven days and seven nights in return for getting y͘ here today.'

e,' said Frank, and then an idea occurred to him. 'Norbert,
u help me escape?'

'Escape!' The boy's eyes grew wide – though with wonder or fear Frank couldn't say.

'Yes. I want to escape from here. Coming to the castle of Nonpareil was a mistake for me. I realise that now. I don't fit in here. I want to go back home now, but I'll need your help to do it.'

Norbert fell silent and he knelt on the sand and closed his eyes. He seemed to be communing with himself.

When he opened his eyes, he smiled at Frank.

'Yes. Lord Belial says I can help you, and he tells me that you are right to leave. Your place is not here. Bonds of another brotherhood are calling you away. A sticky rope of liquid pearl round your neck is the sign.'

It was Frank's turn to look wide-eyed as he reached his hand up to the pendant that hung on the silver chain round his throat. He remembered the horn ring he had given to Rob Oakley.

After this surprising but welcome sexual encounter with Norbert, whom Frank had imagined as being totally faithful to his girl, Felice, the prospect of being able to return to Woodmere Hall and start up some kind of sexual relationship with Rob seemed suddenly not so unlikely.

Frank's cock reared up in a steel-hard erection as he thought of Rob. Yes, that was where he should go. That was where he truly belonged. Back at Woodmere Hall. Back home with his beloved milk brother. The charm of the castle of Nonpareil and the Order of the Tree of Life was fading fast, and, though it had taught him much about himself, Frank decided that it was not, at the end of the day, a place where he would take up permanent residence.

'Come here tomorrow night, after supper, and I will ferry you away from here,' said Norbert as he kissed Frank on the forehead. Then he turned on his heel and went back to his boat without a backward glance.

Six

———

Frank went back to the castle and waited on Vincent at dinner as his duty required him to do. Vincent seemed to have entirely forgotten his anger and his vicious flagellation of Frank earlier in the day, and he treated his squire pleasantly enough. Frank responded with guarded courtesy. Chance, Shawn and Tomas all turned on their charm and were all three the very models of amiability, and Zarek winked at Frank with a twinkle in his eye at every opportunity, as if to say, 'Tell me the word, and we can make the two-cocked beast again whenever you wish.' Only Kerwen acted a little out of sorts. He dropped a couple of plates and bumped once or twice into other squires as they ran to and fro in front of him. But Frank hardly paid Kerwen any mind, his thoughts too wrapped up with his secret plan to escape.

After dinner Frank retired to his room early. He needed time to think, to plan his flight from Nonpareil, and to pack his things. He laid out a fresh set of clothes on his bed to go in his travelling bag, and was just considering whether the orange hat he had picked out actually went daringly with the green doublet or if it in fact clashed horribly, when someone knocked at the door. Frank hid his travelling bag under his bed and went to find out who wanted to see him.

Kerwen stood at the door. 'Can I come in?' he asked in a low voice. 'I need to talk to someone.'

'Of course,' replied Frank. Although he had no real desire to interrupt his travel preparations and talk to Kerwen at precisely that moment, he felt he mustn't give the game away about his intended escape the next day, so he invited the lad in, and locked the door after him so that they wouldn't be disturbed.

'What's on your mind?' he asked, as Kerwen sat on the broad window seat.

'The initiation ceremony,' said Kerwen. 'I become a Brother of the Order tomorrow evening and it bothers me.'

'Why?' asked Frank.

'I don't know honestly if I want it – to belong to Gaston in that way.'

Frank smiled. 'Listen, Kerwen, I knew Gaston before he joined the order. He taught me to fence, you know. I looked up to him. Anyone and anything impressed me in those days, of course. I suppose I had a sort of young boy's crush on him, really. I trembled when he took my hand in his to show me the correct way to parry and thrust. I almost fainted with delight whenever he stood close behind me, his hot breath on the nape of my neck, as he pushed and pulled at my shoulders and hips, to show me certain tricks of stance and posture. I dreamed that one day I would develop some kind of special relationship with him, that one day I would take the hard column of his cock meat in my fist or mouth, or up my virginal arse, but unfortunately for me it never came to pass. But you have that chance, Kerwen, so take it.'

Kerwen looked into Frank's eyes and flashed him a grateful grin.

'Thanks, Frank. Shawn told me to speak to you about all this, and your words have certainly helped. I imagine you've had similar feelings of doubt and insecurity yourself.'

'Me?' queried Frank, suddenly mystified. What was Kerwen talking about?

'Yes, after all, you'll be initiated tomorrow, too.'

Frank's jaw dropped. The news hit him like the swift onset of a thunderstorm in the midst of a sunny summer's day. All his plans for escape began to tumble down like an old castle tower struck and riven by a powerful lightning bolt. Kerwen looked at him strangely.

'Did I say the wrong thing? Didn't you know about it?'

Frank shook his head and said nothing. His mind raced. The prospect of escape with Norbert – but a short time ago so real a possibility – was shrinking away to an impossibility. He couldn't go to the cove to meet the ferry boy if he had to join the Order of the Tree of Life in the chapel at the exact same time. And, if he tried to escape from the initiation, his fellow squires and knights would immediately note his absence when he failed to turn up to that very public ceremony.

'I don't understand,' went on Kerwen. 'Doesn't Vincent tell you anything?'

'Not much,' muttered Frank, and he rolled his eyes up to heaven. 'He's the strong silent type, you know.' He tried to change the topic. 'What about you and Gaston?'

'Oh, Gaston confides in me a lot.'

'No, I meant how does Gaston perform in bed?'

'Oh, he's a very generous lover,' said Kerwen with a faraway smile, as he lay back on the window seat.

'You mean he gives you more than you can take,' laughed Frank.

'You said it.' Kerwen grinned.

Despite the disappointment engendered by the news he brought, outwardly Frank felt honoured to have Kerwen – the lover of his former friend – there in his room. On the outside he appeared to listen attentively as Kerwen talked so freely and unashamedly of the intimate details and the ups and downs of his and Gaston's love life. Inwardly Frank's plans for escape with Norbert's help needed serious rethinking – and fast. He certainly wouldn't be able to flee to freedom the following day after all, but there would be other occasions, he was sure. Then it came to him suddenly, in a flash, as he sat listening, that it was a pity not to live the present to the full. Kerwen had come to his room at night in private, and, as they were both novices in the order, neither of them as yet wore a cock girdle to restrain his sexuality. The lad was handsome and willing, and this was too tempting an opportunity to miss. So Frank thrust his escape plans to the back of his mind, and crossed eagerly over to the window seat.

He lay down next to Kerwen and the two began to kiss and caress each other. Their mouths met again and again in a sweet duel of tongues. Frank loved the way Kerwen stroked his cock through the thick fabric of his codpiece, and he responded in kind. Now Kerwen roughly unbuttoned Frank's doublet. He actually tore a couple of buttons off and ripped the shoulder seam in his haste. Frank undid Kerwen's doublet with greater care. Now they cast their doublets on the floor and Kerwen began to tug at the buttons of Frank's shirt. Frank raced to unbutton Kerwen's shirt, and soon shirts joined discarded jackets in a crumpled heap on the floor.

Now both lay bare-chested, and myriad new opportunities for sensual stimulation opened up before them. Frank nibbled at Kerwen's nipples and pinched and tweaked them playfully with his fingers until they stood out firm and proud from Kerwen's chest, with its mat of silky brown hair. Kerwen let him do what he would, and in return he massaged Frank's shoulders and moaned and writhed with pleasure under him.

'Oh, that feels good, sooo good!' he groaned.

Frank now took the initiative and unlaced Kerwen's leggings. Kerwen helped him to pull them down round his ankles and then Frank tore off his own leggings and the two lay back now, blissfully naked, side by side once more, on the window seat. Frank snuggled behind Kerwen, and his pre-come-coated cock tip butted up against Kerwen's arse. With a few deft swipes of his sticky-headed organ against the tight rosette of Kerwen's anal sphincter, Frank's manpole gradually sank into Kerwen's arse, like a red-hot poker plunging into the very heart of a raging furnace. Now Kerwen's tight arse mouth gripped Frank's thick and gnarled cock shaft. Frank reached around and caressed Kerwen's prick, which throbbed at the front, even as Frank's own cock pierced Kerwen at the back.

As Frank worked his slippery piston in and out of Kerwen's

arse, and simultaneously ran his hand up and down the length of Kerwen's slick and slippery rod, it seemed that the magic alchemy of sex had somehow fused his cock and Kerwen's together to become one extremely long dick-stick that entered Kerwen's rump, ran him right through, and stuck out in front through the base of his belly like a glistening skewer of hard flesh.

Kerwen now moaned with lust at the rhythm Frank set as his cock pierced the lad to the core again and again. It was not long before Frank's organ exploded in a rush of foamy tremulous sperm that bathed Kerwen's bowels. Shortly afterwards, Kerwen's own organ quivered and shot its heavy load of warm and silky liquid all over Frank's hand.

As the white-hot fire of sexual excitement dulled to a pulsing red, neither lad wanted to break the bond of sexual complicity between them. In the end Frank drifted off to sleep on the eve of his induction into the order with his cock still deep in Kerwen's tight hole.

When they awoke at dawn the next morning, Frank and Kerwen repeated the delightful sexual coupling of the night before, with the difference that now Frank acted as the bodily receptacle and Kerwen became the giver of seed.

Frank lay face up on the window seat, and Kerwen raised his arse up and placed a cushion under the small of his back to support him. Then the lad knelt between Frank's spread thighs and thrust his hard cock straight into place deep inside Frank's yielding innards. Then, with that throbbing living arse plug still in place, Kerwen curved his long sinuous torso over and bent his head down to kiss the tip of Frank's organ. What a sublime feeling it was to have the hard pole of Kerwen's man meat moving inside the tight O of his arse and to feel the soft O of Kerwen's mouth as it kissed and sucked at the stiff rod of his dick. Frank's throbbing dick felt like a thick bone from which the lad would soon extract all the nutritious inner jelly. He loved this exquisite double sexual sensation and groaned as Kerwen's cock and mouth continued to work simultaneously in him and on him.

Then Kerwen came inside him in a rush of hot liquid, and, as

Kerwen's mouth released its hold and he drew his head back, Frank's own cock shot its molten silver load up so high that gobbets of it spattered the raftered ceiling.

They slept fitfully until breakfast time, and then the two of them dressed and went down to breakfast as normal. Perhaps, thought Frank, I may be able to slip away after breakfast.

After breakfast, however, it became clear that neither Frank nor Kerwen would get a reprieve from the Ordeal of Initiation that was fast approaching.

As Kerwen and Frank strolled together to the door of the banqueting hall, Gaston appeared in the doorway accompanied by Jourdain. Neither spoke a word. Both wore long black robes and each bore in his hand a tall black staff topped with a silver phallus. They flanked the two neophyte lads, and led them with silent solemnity to a small tiring room. This lay to the side of the chapel, and measured in depth, height and breadth no more than the dimensions of a monk's modest cell. Someone had closed the blinds in the room and coolness and darkness reigned there, and sweet herbs perfumed the air within.

Two simple beds stood at either side of the room, and, at a sign from Gaston, Frank went to sit on one, and Kerwen went to sit on the other.

Jourdain then ordered them to remove all their clothing and jewellery. Kerwen stripped off dutifully, and Frank followed suit.

While no one paid him any attention he took off the locket and chain from around his neck and stuffed them into a crack in the stone wall, and then propped the pillow from his bed in front of it, to obscure it.

Jourdain brought a large wicker basket into the room and first Kerwen, then Frank, placed all their clothes and jewellery into it. Afterwards Jourdain bustled away with the basket.

'That lot all goes into the furnace,' explained Gaston. 'When you join the Brotherhood of the Tree of Life, you leave behind your old self altogether. You let go of everything from your past and you start anew. You become a naked child that the high priest baptises into the white communion of Belial.'

Was it Frank's imagination, or did Gaston address these words directly to him, as an explanation of why he had held himself so aloof, and had made no reference to their previous acquaintance?

When Jourdain returned from disposing of their clothes and effects, he and Gaston opened a rivet-studded chest and took out eight iron chains attached to velvet-lined manacles. They snapped these manacles around Frank's and Kerwen's wrists and ankles, and then chained the lads to their respective beds.

'What's this for?' blurted out Frank.

'These chains represent the bonds that bind you to the Order of the Tree of Life. Once you enter the order you must never walk away from it, nor should you lift a hand against it. And in all your deeds, sayings and thoughts you should act for the good of the order and its beliefs at all times. And you should propagate and disseminate the creed of Belial to all men, and work to bring as many as you can in time to the pearl communion.'

Now Jourdain sharpened two razors on a strop of leather attached to the wall, and Gaston took two thick hogshair brushes and mixed up two bowls full of sweet-smelling soapy lather.

Frank lay on his bed and watched this activity with interest. He wondered what would happen next. He swallowed hard when Jourdain went over to sit on a stool next to Kerwen's bed, and Gaston came over and seated himself on a stool at his bedside.

Without a word Gaston began to dab soapy foam all over Frank's cheeks, jaw, chin and neck. It was cool, aromatic and refreshing. Frank closed his eyes.

The ripples of pleasure coursed through his body, as he felt Gaston's experienced hand wield the razor over his face and throat. He trusted Gaston not to slip and cut him, but to give him a really smooth shave. With small feathery movements, Gaston trimmed the stubble around Frank's upper lip, under his lower lip and across his chin. Frank felt his face tingle when Gaston at last put down the razor in the bowl and passed a towel over his features to dry him off.

He made as if to get up.

'It's not over yet,' murmured Gaston. 'Lie still and relax.'

Frank did as he was bid and let his body go limp once more on the bed.

Now Gaston raised Frank's arms in the air and dabbed lather into his armpits. The cooling soft soap soon gave way to the sharp razor's edge, which delicately, and without a single false cut, stripped away all Frank's axillary hair. Again the rough towel followed the razor and the cool air kissed those deep hollows under Frank's arms, which now shone resplendent, denuded of all shaggy covering.

Now the lather brush went to work around Frank's cock and on his scrotum. Immediately after the stippling of the bush, Gaston gently lifted up Frank's flaccid member and carefully shaved off the pubic thatch around it. One slip of the razor here could have had disastrous consequences, but again Frank closed his eyes and let the sharp blade do its purifying work. He trusted Gaston completely. Now Gaston grasped first one and then the other of Frank's testicles in one hand and delicately razored off the wiry hairs on his balls pouch. When Gaston patted him dry, Frank gasped as the cool air kissed his clean-shaven genitals. Hair usually got in the way of the breeze, Frank realised, and clogged and dulled the sensitivity of that delicate genital skin. Without that hirsute barrier, Frank felt fresh and new.

Now Gaston picked up a pair of iron scissors and started to shear off the hair on Frank's head. Once he had clipped off nearly all of Frank's golden locks, he put the scissors down, picked up the lather pot once more and ran the foam-thick brush over the dome of Frank's skull. Then the razor followed, and finally came the towel to finish him off. Once Gaston had finished, he patted Frank's glabrous scalp.

'We take off even the hair on your head, to make you like a new-born child, for that is the role you play as you enter the order, innocent and childlike. You know little or nothing of the strange new world you enter, with all its rules and regulations, which you must obey – with a joyful heart – to the letter.'

Once Gaston had shaved off the hairs on Frank's arms and legs, Frank lay on the bed. He felt totally and utterly naked, his skin glowed more alive and vibrant than it had in a long time. The shaving renewed and stimulated him. As Gaston and Jourdain put away the lather bowls and razors, Frank's cock stiffened and throbbed, and his balls swelled and ached with the thrill of being in this fresh new hairless body.

His excitement grew still further when Gaston stripped off his shirt and again came and sat by his bedside. This time Gaston bore with him a bowl of sweet smelling oil into which he dabbled his fingers. Slowly Gaston dribbled the fragrant oil over Frank's chest, his belly, his thighs. The sensation was exquisite and Frank moaned and writhed sensually under the oily flow.

'This is sandalwood essence in almond oil, Frank. The sandalwood symbolises the exclusive and utter masculinity of our order. No man who has ever had vaginal congress with a woman may become a member. And if we ever discover that any initiated member of the cult debases his cock and uses it to pierce a woman's pussy and fill her womb with seed, we will expel that ingrate from the Brotherhood.'

Frank thought momentarily of Molly, Rob's sensual girlfriend, but, with a swift effort of will, he banished the thought from his mind.

'I see,' murmured Frank. 'And the almond oil? What does that mean?'

'That represents the sweetness and goodness that should exist between squire and knight in the order. It stands for the nourishing brother-love bond.'

Unbidden, the image of Rob Oakley's handsome smiling face and naked manly frame flashed before Frank's inner eye, but he dismissed it hurriedly, although a melancholy regret filled his heart in its absence.

Now Gaston laid his hot hands on Frank's shoulders and began a slow and deep massage that started up in the muscles of his neck, flowed over his pectorals and his taut muscular abdomen, and branched off into his arms and legs. Then Gaston rolled Frank face down on the bed and massaged away the tensions in his back and rump. And even as Gaston was Frank's attentive masseur, so Jourdain massaged Kerwen in the same way.

When the massage ended, Frank lay face up on the bed. He felt totally and blissfully relaxed, calm and carefree.

'The massage shows the way your lord should have control

over every fibre of your body, once you enter the order. His wish should be your pleasure, and, if that is so, your pleasure will be his wish. By the way, this doesn't just mean your lord Vincent, Frank: it means your overlord, Salim, too, and the high lord Belial, also.'

Frank floated on a sea of heady pleasure. He gazed indulgently as Gaston and Jourdain drew off their leggings and both came to stand at head and foot of his bed. They were naked except for intricately wrought silver rings that twined around the root of their cocks and balls.

Gaston offered Frank a sweet herbal draught from a silver goblet. Was it this drink, or the heady herbal scent that filled the room, or Frank's state of utter relaxation that turned him light-headed and woozy.

As if in a dream, Frank realised that Gaston had attached the chains about his wrists and ankles to four hooks which dangled from the ceiling. Now Jourdain used a pulley arrangement attached to the wall, to winch him up, so that he hung with his arms and legs in the air and his arse some inches above the bed. Gaston now knelt on the bed and thrust his cock, rock-hard from the restraining ring he wore, deep into Frank's yielding arse. Frank cried out loudly at the first breach, but soon he began to luxuriate in the repeated penetration. He writhed sensually in his manacles and groaned with pleasure at each powerful inthrust of Gaston's hard cock length within his tight arse. His chains rattled faster and faster and then slower once more as Gaston fucked him with a rapid crescendo of cock thrusts followed by a number of slow teasing strokes. Jourdain heightened Frank's pleasure when he buried his head in Frank's groin, latched his mouth around the lad's cock head, and licked and sucked it with all the gusto of a cock expert – and lots of hungry slurping noises.

As Gaston fucked him masterfully, and Jourdain sucked at him like a gourmet delicacy, Frank breathed the herbal aromas, and drifted on an ocean of sexual pleasure. The waves of that erotic sea buffeted him, and made his body tremble, dance and jerk about with pleasure.

When at last the sperm flooded from his cock mouth and

Jourdain quaffed it down, Frank felt his balls, his cock and indeed his whole trembling body send forth its life energy and vital fluids in a searing wave of delight. Then Gaston's cock discharged within him, and Frank relished the sensation as his bowels soaked up all Gaston's precious sex fluids. After a while Gaston withdrew his manpole and Jourdain disengaged his mouth. They both moved away, over to Kerwen's bed, and left Frank to drift off into a deep, dreamless sleep.

Frank awoke with a start to find himself in the chapel. Fumes of heady incense coiled in the air, and he was naked except for a black leather codpiece. His arms and legs stretched out wide either side of him like a starfish, and he couldn't at first work out why he couldn't move them.

As he twisted and craned his head down and to one side, he managed to find the answer to the enigma. He hung in a leather harness from the vaulted roof. Manacles held his wrists and ankles close, and the chains that stretched from them pinioned him to the outer corners of the room. The flagged floor lay some three feet below his dangling toes.

To judge by the incense that burned at the back of the black-draped altar, and by the male voices chanting in pentatonic harmony which wafted up to him from the direction of the tiring room behind the altar, he must already be in the middle of his initiation ceremony.

How could I have slept through the intervening hours? thought Frank, and then he wondered if the herbal draught and the massage and the three-way sex that he had experienced with Gaston and Jourdain earlier, during the shaving ceremony, had been designed to dull the senses, and to ensure that he slept the hours that led up to his initiation, free of all worry and care.

As he looked across the room, he saw that Kerwen, the hair on his head and body closely shaven, hung similarly chained and harnessed from the ceiling. The fact that he had an accomplice, a raw recruit who was about to suffer the initiation with him tonight, acted as a comfort to Frank. He was not alone, so long as Kerwen underwent the same ordeals.

Kerwen was also looking around wide-eyed like a nervous fawn, and the two lads' gazes met and they grinned at one another.

The chanting below reached a crescendo.

On the left of the altar stood a large sculpted silver mountain, as high as a man. It looked like an ornamented case wrought to contain some treasure, but what exactly Frank couldn't fathom.

In the middle of the altar, with steps that led up to it, he spotted a huge gold throne, covered with a tapestry. This richly embroidered ceremonial cloth depicted twelve disembodied phalluses that nestled in a bird's nest with a phallus-tailed rooster, the cockatrice, watching over them attentively.

But what attracted Frank's attention most at that moment was what stood on the right of the altar. There loomed a huge tree, sculpted in black iron. In its boughs hung blossoms of nacre. It was some kind of reliquary – a case for a holy relic – but once more Frank couldn't make out exactly what it contained.

Now, suddenly, the chanting stopped, and all fell silent except for the slight chink and tinkle of Frank's and Kerwen's chains, the crackle of the red-glowing charcoal in the altar braziers and the crepitation of the herbal incense fires that burned in iron sconces on the walls, and threw a flickering greenish-yellow light all around.

Frank gasped at what happened now below him. A group of ten black-robed figures, barefoot and with cowls over their faces, filed in silence out of the tiring room in two lines of five adepts. These were the members of the order.

Behind the two lines processed a majestic figure, shod in silver sandals, and dressed in a black robe with a long silver cloak that trailed behind him. He wore a silver mask of great masculine beauty. Frank recognised it at once as a sort of idealised portrait of Salim du Court, the leader of the order. This figure bore upon his head a curiously wrought silver helmet with horns upon either side of it. At first glance these seemed to Frank to be faithful representations of the horns of a bull, but, as he stared at them, he realised with a sweet thrill that they were in fact two silver phalluses, one on either side, that reached up to the heavens.

What would happen next? Frank squirmed in his harness like a curious cat, and waited to see.

The figure of Salim genuflected now before the altar, and the other ten adepts knelt in two rows behind him.

Now Salim reached forward, opened the black tree up, and revealed to all the treasure it contained. There stood a lovingly crafted sculpture of a god – Belial, supposed Frank – painted in realistic polychrome tints. The supermasculine figure had rippling musculature, and a huge erect penis, and massive balls dangled between his legs. His laughing open mouth also revealed a stiff penis-tongue, and his ten fingers and toes each terminated in a miniature penis head. A tangle of oak leaves and oak apples formed his gilded hair. He had acorns on his chest instead of nipples, and golden oak leaves instead of pubic hair. There was something in the figure that made Frank think momentarily of Rob, and his cock stirred and swelled as a result.

'Bow down before the god of our masculinity, the lord of our order,' commanded Salim, and the two lines of five cowled figures prostrated themselves, as they worshipped Belial.

'We dedicate ourselves to you body, mind and soul, Lord Belial,' intoned Salim. 'You command our cocks to rise and to fall. You command our sperm to flow or to congeal. You command our bollocks to swell and to contract by your unquestionable command over our ever-lustful thought.'

Frank felt his cock grow harder.

'We are gathered here tonight to welcome two new members to our order. Two fresh-faced young novices whose tight arses are eager to be pierced by your massive punishing prick, O Lord.'

Frank watched excitedly as Salim now drew forth from under the sombre altar cloth a metal-studded chest that he opened to reveal a precious load of a dozen ebony rods tipped with silver phalluses. The master gave one rod to each of the cowled figures to hold. Then he turned once more to the statue of Belial and bowed to it.

'Stiffen your proud cock, O Lord Belial. Let the divine love oil flow in abundance from its holy tip,' chanted Salim.

Now he placed two metal bowls of sweet-smelling herbal oil

upon the two charcoal braziers – to right and left of the altar, one below Kerwen and the other below Frank.

Salim chanted spells and incantations over each of the fires in turn, and threw crystallised powders into the flames, so that the flames burned bright green and pungent, and smelled of forests, grass and apples.

'Let the newcomers be as naked children reborn in your likeness, O Lord,' intoned Salim.

It was the symbol for the novices to bare themselves in their harnesses. Frank's cock now dripped a thick ooze of love juice down its whole length and his balls ached. He imagined that Kerwen felt just as he did, a little apprehensive, but aroused and fully ready for the elaborate sexual ordeal to come.

Now the order separated into two files of five brothers. One file encircled Frank's fire, and the other went to Kerwen's brazier.

Frank's cock and balls now throbbed with a potent sexual charge. He craved release. He devoutly wished to be initiated into the Order of the Tree of Life, to become a servant upon earth of the god Belial, to do his bidding at all times and to let the dark lord's energy enter him and possess him during the Sabbat celebrations.

Frank's prayers got their answer sooner than he thought. With one accord the cowled figures below him dipped the silver tips of their long wands into the warmed bowl of oil sitting on the brazier and, with a cry of joy, they thrust the wands upwards one by one, and pierced Frank's arse with their silver cock heads that dripped with warm and sweet-smelling oil.

Encouraged by Kerwen's lustful cries under a similar assault, Frank gave himself over to this new and unexpected pleasure. He writhed and groaned in his chains and still the slow and ritualised assault upon his anus continued. His arse muscles relaxed as the herbal oils penetrated into the delicate tissues of his sphincter. They deadened the pain receptors and enhanced the pleasure of the onslaught.

Now he felt two silver-tipped poles enter him simultaneously, and now three. The fit was tight, but the feeling was exquisitely good. When the fourth pole was added, Frank felt stretched beyond all known limits and he cried out at first with the pain, but soon the pain dulled into a pleasurable feeling of tautness and fulfilment. When the fifth stave was eased into place, Frank had to stifle his groans. He bore the momentary agony, which seemed about to tear him in two, and again, as his reward, the dolorous dark sensations soon dissolved into a sense of joy, golden calm and wellbeing. Then his five attendants withdrew the rods one by one from him, and lowered him to the ground. Frank glanced across to where the other five figures unstrapped Kerwen from his harness. The lad looked shaken and glistened with sweat, but the two initiates exchanged a fleeting smile of complicity as each black-clad band of five led their charge a separate way to face the next stage of the ordeal.

Four pairs of strong hands grasped Frank's shoulders, his upper arms, his elbows and his wrists. Four cowled monklike figures stood to his left and right. One figure in a black habit stood in front of him. At first Frank wondered who this fifth monk might be, singled out so individually, but the figure's height and general build gave him away as Vincent, even though he wore monkish robes and spoke not a word.

Now the figure in front of him bowed low, and then, with a sudden gesture, he threw off the coarse and heavy ecclesiastical robes he wore and stood naked, starkly revealed as Vincent. But this was a Vincent unlike the day-to-day knight that Frank had learned to serve.

This Vincent was a wild beast that gyrated to the rhythm of the chanting and the drumming that went on around him. His fine well-muscled body ran with sweat. He was naked but for one or two ritual ornaments. On his face he wore a silver mask in the form of a unicorn's horned muzzle that hid his nose, cheeks and brow, but revealed his blue eyes and his fine broad mouth and chin. On his upper arms he wore curiously twisted silver torques that hugged the swell of his biceps. Around the root of his cock and balls he wore another silver torque, decorated with two unicorn heads. This constricted the blood flow to his sexual organs and gave him a truly rock-hard erection. Frank gazed down at it with longing, but his arms were caught in vicelike grips and he couldn't reach out his fingers to touch and caress. Also, after his ordeal by hanging and anal penetration by poles, he still felt weak and shaky on his feet, and didn't have the strength to stoop his head to kiss or lick the hard rod of Vincent's man meat.

This figure of Vincent, which was more savage unicorn than man, danced sensually before Frank and led him and his four anonymous black-garbed companions to an altar at one side of the chapel.

Frank gasped with unforeseen pleasure when he looked down at the carved altar top. A beautiful muscular male angel lay there in bas-relief.

The angel's face was broad, open and handsome. With its shaggy locks it reminded Frank very much of Rob. Its face radiated sexuality. The torso, too – with firm pectorals, erect nipples and taut stomach muscles – echoed Rob's athletic frame, and the thick-thewed thighs and well-defined calves also reminded Frank of the sturdy legs of his woodcutting lover. The sculpted wings that sprouted on this angel's shoulders, however, marked this fellow as different from any human lover, and the fact that the figure sported no cock and no balls, but had only a carved hole at the intersection of belly, thighs and groin, gave it a strangely sexless air, although every ripple of its stone musculature oozed utter masculine beauty.

With gestures and gently persuasive hands, Vincent and his four brother monks urged Frank to lie face down on the altar stone, and inserted his stiff cock into the tight orifice between the angel's legs.

Now Vincent ducked down out of view and Frank felt the tip of his cock suddenly surrounded by moist warmth. So that was it! The altar was hollow and Vincent crouched in there and was about to suck him off.

But that was not all. Once Vincent crouched within Frank's altar, the other four monks threw off their robes and stood naked at the head, at the foot, and at either side of the hollow stone table.

Each wore a silver animal totem mask, and a twisted silver torque on his upper arms and around his cock. All panted and gyrated with ritualised lust and sexual expectation. Frank twisted his head around curiously to see who they were.

Dagobert stood at the foot of the altar in a tusked boar's-head mask. Gerard stood at the head of the altar in a spiral horned ram's mask. To his left stood Shawn in a horned goat's mask, and to the right Tomas in an antlered stag's mask.

As he lay back face down on the altar, Vincent sucked at his cock head from below. Gerard now moved forward and placed the tip of his hard pole of man meat temptingly close to Frank's lips. He arched his head up and allowed Gerard to ram the whole hard length of his throbbing manpole deep into his throat. Now Shawn and Tomas moved in close, so that their stiff and pulsing cockrods brushed against Frank's knuckles. With two swift wrist movements he caught each lad's throbbing pole in either hand, made a tight fist around them, and began to wank them up and down in time with the pace set by Gerard's cock as it rhythmically speared his mouth, and by Vincent's mouth as it sucked hungrily at the sticky teat of his own cock.

Then Dagobert's cock nosed for admittance between Frank's buttocks. He gyrated his hips a little and felt the full length of that stiff rod sink into place within his arse. How satisfying it was to have his hands full, his mouth full, and his arse full of hot rigid cock meat and to feel his own cock, buried in the stone angel's groin hole, pierce Vincent's mouth inside the altar. The pulsing dance of orgiastic male love, of which he was the centre and physical intersection, gathered pace, and pretty soon his cock and balls ached and he craved release. And then it came, Shawn's and Tomas's cocks exploded in twin white fountains of liquid lust, and bathed his hands with their warm sticky milk. Almost immediately, Gerard's cock head twitched and sprayed his mouth and throat with copious draughts of rich salty man seed, which he gulped down gratefully. A split second later, Dagobert paused in his thrusting and his cock flexed inside Frank's tight arse, and sprayed his innards with jet after jet of warm and creamy love juice. As the culmination of this ejaculatory chain, Frank's cock reared up, poker-straight, his balls contracted powerfully and the liquid seed spurted up his urethra and surged out of his cock mouth like flames of subtle silver fire. It felt as if the fiery jet of sperm that now pumped from him had been kindled and fed by the four sperm streams that came before it: the two streams that bathed his hands, the one that washed his mouth and the other that soaked his guts with sacred man seed. Frank's ejaculation rode upon the peak of those that came from his attendants, and for that reason his coming reverberated within him as a stronger, more powerful, more truly masculine sensation than Frank had ever known before. With his fellow monks' aid he realised he was on the road to becoming an adept in the art of male love.

There was little respite for Frank, however, for, after the sperm sacrifice on the angel altar, his attendants led him back to the central nave of the chapel. There they met Kerwen, in the middle of his band of attendants. He looked, to Frank's eyes, drained but strangely renewed and fired with a powerful inner masculine energy that blazed from his eyes. Frank and Kerwen now crouched, side by side, naked on the ground, and their ten attendants drew back and doused the herb torches so that the only light in the chapel glimmered from the two charcoal braziers either side of the altar.

At first Frank wondered what would come next. Then he looked up and saw. In the haze of incense fumes that cloaked the high altar, a figure appeared almost in silhouette. Tall and imposing, it was Salim du Court. He cast off his robe and stepped forward. Near-naked he stood now, and proud, as the glow from the red braziers highlighted the contours of his muscular body. He removed his mask, but he still wore the torques on his arms, and the ceremonial silver helmet which bore the two metal phallus horns. He became the horned god in person. Frank looked at Salim's nipples, and shivered with delight when he saw that they were pierced with silver rings. Then, as his gaze sank lower, Frank's cock shuddered with an even stronger thrill to see that du Court's erect cock was a full ten inches in length. What was more, in addition to the twisted cockring that coiled around its base, it bore a line of six or seven silver studs that ran up the underside of it, and added to its strange gnarled beauty.

Frank knew then that he wanted above all else to be this high priest's lover. He yearned for Salim to take him and to make love to him in an utterly bestial way. He wanted to join bodies with this man in a rite of high sex magic, to become the young male consort of the horned god. Penetration by Salim while the god possessed him would be a glorious feeling, he knew.

As if he read Frank's thoughts, Salim approached him, smiled and beckoned. The lad rose to his feet, and followed the master through the heavily perfumed veils of incense that swirled from the herb fires to the altar beyond.

There, on the altar, Frank saw that the statue of Belial was closed up once more in its tree. But there was a new statue where the mountain of silver split in two. This showed a life-sized naked youth who stood with arms outstretched. He was handsome of face and painted perfectly in every detail, almost humanly alive, except that from the base of his belly sprouted ten erect phalluses in a triangle with four cocks as the base line, then three cocks, topped by two more, and with one lone stiff cock that pointed skywards at the apex. Frank found this statue strangely beautiful.

Salim now climbed up the stairs and twitched the tapestry cover off the wide golden throne that stood in the centre of the altar. He beckoned to Frank to climb up also. Now Frank could see the gorgeous love seat in its full glory.

Its arms and legs showed a writhing mass of naked male figures engaged in an orgy of love. Some fucked, some sucked, some wanked. The joys of male-to-male coupling, masculine group sex and the pleasures of lone self-gratification appeared in equal measure. All positions imaginable featured and some that Frank hadn't even believed possible. But the strangest thing of all was that, though the sculpted bodies of the young lads were perfectly modelled, instead of sculpted heads, each neck ended in the mushroom-cap shape of a domed, one-eyed cock head. It was as if all this writhing morass of sculpted male flesh had one thought and one thought only – cock was its master. And, as Salim gestured to Frank to sit down at one side of this broad throne, he noted that there was a gigantic erect phallus which rose up in the centre of each of its double seats.

Like a sleepwalker, Frank sat down and the well-oiled, gold-leafed cock sank deep into him. His own cock reared up with pleasure and his head swam.

Where was Salim?

Now Frank realised his lord stood before him and that Kerwen was sitting down on the carved cock next to him.

Impulsively he reached out and grasped Kerwen's hand for comfort, and Kerwen instinctively returned the gesture and turned and planted a hungry, open-mouthed kiss full on his lips.

Now Salim beckoned and Frank stood up, the carved cock slipped out of him and his arse felt empty, hollowed out, but not for long. Gently Salim manoeuvred him around till he stood, leaning forward, hands on knees. His arse, fully relaxed now, was ready to be breached. Salim stood behind him, and chanted magic incantations. Then, with a masterful thrust of his huge studded cock deep between Frank's waiting buttocks, the master filled his disciple savagely to the hilt, and made him cry out with pleasure-pain. Was this or was this not the sexual reward he had so devoutly yearned for but a short while ago? As the mighty ribbed pole thrust again and again into his innards Frank writhed and moaned. His head turned and swam dizzily, and finally he fainted clean away.

Seven

Frank woke the following day back in his room, lying in bed. The sunlight streamed in through the window. It was already late in the morning. He stirred under the bedsheet and felt his muscles ache. His cock and balls felt inexplicably cramped, and his arse was still raw from the pounding it had received during his initiation ceremony. He thought back to Salim du Court's silver-studded cock as it thrust away inside him, and quivered and moaned with remembered bliss.

'Are you awake, then?' came Vincent's voice from the far side of the room.

Frank propped himself up on his elbows and looked over to where Vincent sat on the window seat. He wore only a brocade robe open at the front, and Frank loved gazing at the muscles of his lover's firm chest and abdomen, the fuzz of his pubic hair, his beautiful sleeping cock and dangling balls.

'I had such a dream,' said Frank, as he vaguely remembered an erotic fantasy of fucking Rob in the arse while he fucked Molly.

'You *are* such a dream,' said Vincent, and he came over and sat on the side of the bed, and gazed down at him.

Vincent's fingers stroked Frank's cheek and chin. Frank loved that.

'And what's best of all,' continued Vincent, 'is that now you're mine, all mine.'

He reached under the cover and patted Frank's cock girdle with his beringed hand. There was a dull metal clanking. Frank realised now why his loins felt so tightly caged about. He remembered now that, without Vincent's key in his lock, he wouldn't be able to indulge in any cock play of any kind, whether solitary or in company.

As if he read Frank's mind, Vincent reached up to a silver key that hung on a long chain around his neck. Frank could see that Vincent's cock now stiffened, strained and throbbed skywards. This vision made his own member swell with anticipated pleasure.

Eagerly Vincent thrust his key into the lock on Frank's cock girdle and with a little 'ping' the tumbrels turned and the cock girdle sprang open. Frank wriggled upwards and Vincent drew the metal belt out from under his young squire's arse, and placed it out of the way on the chest of drawers next to the bed.

'You won't . . . you know . . . try to . . .'

Vincent raised a quizzical eyebrow.

'Fuck your arse?' he queried with mock seriousness.

'Yeah,' said Frank in a low voice. 'You see, I don't know if I could, after . . . you know . . . Salim yesterday. He's so huge – and those studs. Talk about raw.'

Vincent's stern face broke into a sunny smile, and he bent forward and kissed Frank tenderly and with lingering sensuality on the lips.

'Oh, my sweet Frank,' he said. 'Of course I won't do anything you don't want me to. By the way, I thought you behaved superbly last night. Really the best initiation ceremony I've seen yet.'

'Really?' Frank blushed a little but he was pleased to get Vincent's praise and approval. 'In what way?'

'In every way,' went on Vincent, and he stroked Frank's cock absent-mindedly.

'You looked so bloody sexy, and then, when Lord du Court took you and penetrated you from behind, you fainted away for a while and when you came to you seemed to be filled with the spirit of Belial. Your lovemaking was wild and animalistic, you bucked and reared, and pushed back on to Lord du Court's cock to make the penetration deeper. And I admired the way you pinched your nipples, caressed your balls and wanked your cock in such a sensual way in order to heighten your pleasure in the act, and to help relax your arse muscles so that Lord du Court's organ could gain a better purchase and bite deeper into your guts. I was proud of you, my lad. But no wonder you feel a bit the worse for wear today.'

Frank said nothing. He remembered nothing of what Vincent talked about. Had he really pushed back as du Court fucked him, and played with himself in such an erotic way? His memory of events the night before finished with fainting away. Perhaps the god Belial had truly possessed him at that moment, or maybe it had something to do with the herbal draught that Gerard and Jourdain had administered to him before the ceremony. Perhaps that wiped away from his mind all his memories of the end of the ceremony.

Frank had no time to think more on these perplexing things. He couldn't help noticing that under the constant chafing of Vincent's experienced fingers his penis now stood almost fully erect.

'Mmm, that feels so good, my lord and knight,' moaned Frank, and Vincent redoubled his efforts. Now he wrapped his whole hand in a tight fist around Frank's throbbing fleshpole, and began to wank him with rhythmic up-and-down movements.

Frank's body jerked about on the bed and he moaned and writhed in ecstasy. It was as if Vincent were a troubadour who played expertly upon a lute, and Frank's body itself was the finely tuned instrument on which he played.

Vincent, with a few well-directed caresses, knew how to make Frank's whole body vibrate and sing with pleasure, and to Frank it felt glorious.

He knew he would come soon, and in some ways he wanted to reward his skilful lover by ejaculating man's white milk all over his hands, all over his chest, all over his face and neck. In other ways he wanted to hold on to his bollockload of sperm, to refrain from shooting his load just yet, and to teeter on the brink of the pleasurable explosion for just a little longer, and a little longer yet, and yet still more.

Oh, it felt so good to be riding upon these waves of pleasure, like a naked boy upon the back of a dolphin that dived in and out of the foamy crests of the breakers, while all the while the masterful sea god sent wavelets to play seductively with his genitals.

Now Vincent bent low and began to suck and lap at Frank's cock. The pleasure was delightful, delicious, delectable, and now Frank felt the sperm spasm rising in him. His scrotum tightened, his balls contracted and with a whoop of joy he could hold back no longer and willingly, gratefully, he sent rush after rush of his hot creamy man's milk coursing up the length of his pulsing cock. Fiercely it sprayed the back of Vincent's throat and filled his mouth with silvery goodness.

Instead of gulping down that precious load, Vincent, with great delicacy, raised his full mouth up to Frank's and kissed him tenderly. He thrust his tongue between Frank's lips, and, as the squire let his jaw drop to accommodate this lingual penetration, Vincent poured the warm liquid seed he held in oral safekeeping into Frank's open mouth.

It was a strange but glorious sensation to feel the warm seed that his cock had so recently sprayed out now trickle back into his own mouth in this fashion, and Frank luxuriated in Vincent's sensitive sensuality. He appreciated Vincent for indulging in such restrained yet inspired lovemaking the day after the stresses and strains of his initiation ceremony.

Afterwards Vincent lay down next to Frank, and the exhausted young squire drifted off into sleep again.

He woke to hear a knocking on the door. As he looked around he realised that Vincent had gone and he was alone in the room. The sunlight streaming through the window showed that the day was well advanced. He realised that Vincent had locked him into his cock girdle once more before leaving.

'Come in,' called Frank, weakly.

The door creaked open and into the room came Bastien and Piers. They carried a large leather bag full of pots of unguents and leather pouches of herbs. This they placed by Frank's bed.

'How are you today?' asked Bastien.

'We have come with herbal balms and healing salves to nurse you,' added Piers. 'Where does it hurt?'

Frank rolled over on to his front and pointed gingerly at his rump, where the chain at the back of his cock girdle passed between his buttocks. 'Here,' he grunted.

Piers gently eased the chain to one side, and Bastien rolled up his sleeves before examining his patient.

'Yes,' he said after spreading Frank's buttocks wide and peering at the tight rosette of Frank's anal sphincter. 'There's a bit of bruising there, but that's only to be expected. You took quite a pounding last night. The god Belial was in Lord du Court and you responded well. But no matter. I have a salve here that will soon put you as right as rain.'

Frank saw Bastien dip his delicate tapered fingertips into a pot of salve that Piers held out to him. The next moment he felt those fingers working their way gently into the cleft between his buttocks, anointing his puckered arse mouth with a chilled and soothing cream. It was amazing, the effect was immediate. Where up until now his flesh had itched, throbbed and felt feverish, now an icy freshness spread out, radiating from his arse, and his skin felt calm, still and cool.

'Oh, that feels so good,' murmured Frank.

'You must repeat the treatment every few hours this first day after,' continued Bastien. 'Your flesh is young and will soon heal with the help of the herbs.'

'Thank you,' said Frank.

'Don't mention it,' replied Piers, as Bastien put the medicines away in the bag. 'You were superb at the initiation ceremony, by the way. I was only sorry that I wasn't one of your attendants.'

'Were you?' asked Frank, intrigued.

'Yes. I've wished to know you carnally,' went on Piers. 'But always something intervened and prevented me from making my feelings known to you.'

Frank's cock sprang up inside his cock girdle at this revelation.

'I'm sorry to have to disappoint you once again, then,' said Frank ruefully. 'But with this in front –' he patted the protective metal cock guard – 'and being out of commission behind, I don't know what satisfaction I could give you today.'

'We get pleasure out of being watched as we couple,' said Bastien, grinning. He slapped Piers on the rump. 'Isn't that right?'

Piers grinned back. 'Indeed it is, my lord knight,' he replied, and he began to pull off his tunic.

'My erection is always that much stronger for knowing that we have an audience,' Bastien went on, drawing off his leggings.

'And I always find the moment of anal penetration more exquisitely exciting knowing that I am being viewed in the act of taking my knight's cock into me,' laughed Piers, taking off his leggings and standing naked now, except for his cock girdle.

'Would you like us to demonstrate?' asked Bastien, discarding his tunic and standing naked next to his squire.

'Indeed I would,' said Frank. 'It would be a fitting entertainment, a welcome diversion with which to pass the time. For, although I am myself out of commission, my eyes would be right glad of some erotic titillation to while away an idle hour.'

At these words Bastien took the key off the chain round his neck and released Piers from his cock girdle.

The two fell to kissing and stroking each other's naked body, standing in the centre of the room, and Frank sat on his bed and watched, rapt with the beauty of the sexual encounter. It was like observing a living sculpture, he mused.

At a certain point, without saying a word, Piers turned his back on Bastien. He stood facing Frank now. Bastien stood close behind his young squire and, anointing his cock helmet with spittle, he pressed his hard and throbbing organ between Piers's buttocks and began, with gentle pelvic thrustings, to ram it up against Piers's tight anal sphincter, each time making a deeper and deeper inroad.

From the front Frank could see Piers staring at him provocatively. He noted Bastien's hands grasping the young lad's hips, pulling him back on to each of his insistent forward cock thrusts.

With each deeper penetration, Piers's eyes closed momentarily. His face contorted with pleasure, his lips spread wide in a grimace of hard joy, and he let out a low moan of ecstasy.

Frank found it fascinating, and very arousing, to watch the couple making love before him. He delighted in the little idiosyncratic details of their coupling. From time to time Piers turned his head to the side and Bastien leaned around and kissed him full on the lips and their tongues lashed and writhed together like two pink serpents.

From time to time Bastien's fingers closed on Piers's nipples and he pinched and twirled them around, much to the young squire's obvious pleasure. At other times Bastien's hands caressed the pubic hair at the base of Piers's muscular belly, fondled the young lad's balls or stroked his cock.

Every time that Bastien thrust his cock deep into Pier's crupper, the young lad's own penis gave a jerk upwards, and it was now throbbing and fairly drooling with lubricating juices.

Frank could resist the temptation no longer. Even as Bastien continued arse-fucking Piers, Frank climbed gingerly out of bed and moved towards the writhing intertwined couple. When he was close enough, he knelt on a low stool and took Piers's cock into his mouth, lapping and sucking at his sticky organ as if it were the most delicious of sugared sweetmeats.

It was not long before Piers groaned and shot his load of silvery seed into Frank's receptive mouth, and on the heel of Piers's orgasm came a shout from Bastien as he ejaculated long and hard into his squire's soft and clinging innards.

After Piers and Bastien had pulled apart, they got dressed, led Frank back to his bed, and, after administering a sleeping draught, they left him to sleep some more and to regain his strength.

That afternoon Frank woke again. He walked over to sit on the window seat, and study what was happening in the world outside his room.

He saw Salim du Court walking and talking in the knot garden with Vincent. What were they talking about? he mused.

He spotted Tomas scurrying out of the kitchen to pick some

herbs from the herb garden before hurrying back. Was he making more herb cakes for the next Sabbat? Frank wondered.

He spied Chance and Jourdain leaving the library with books under their arms. Perhaps they were taking erotic reading matter to their rooms to study at their leisure.

Beyond the retaining castle walls Frank saw Norbert, sitting on a rock next to the path that led down to the harbour. Was the young ferry lad waiting for him? he wondered. He dimly recalled the plans of escape that he had made with Norbert, hoping to leave Nonpareil and return to take up where he had left off with Rob Oakley, the village woodcutter.

Frank sighed. All that seemed so long ago and far away. Since his initiation ceremony and the ceremonial donning of his cock girdle, it seemed as if a thick curtain had been drawn across the doorway that separated life within the castle and life without. Escape seemed already well nigh an impossibility to him. It would be much easier now for him to stay within the order, rather than to try to leave it and return home. His new home was within the order now, anyway. He had a knight, Vincent, whom it was his duty to serve, and a master of the order, Salim, whom he was bound to obey.

Frank watched Norbert tire of waiting, pull himself to his feet and plod the path down to the harbour with his head hanging forward in a dispirited fashion. Yes, all in all, Frank figured, it was better to stay here at Nonpareil with Vincent than to entertain any more sentimental dreams of having some kind of sexual relationship with Rob.

Shortly after, Salim du Court and Vincent entered Frank's room. Frank blushed to see the man with whom he had coupled in such an animalistic manner during his initiation ceremony, but Salim seemed to feel no shame in the matter. It was almost as if he were a completely different man from the horned master of the order who had presided over Frank's initiation ceremony the night before, but, if the tales of his possession by the god Belial were to be believed, this was in effect the case.

'We have allowed you to rest before the ceremony of exchanging of rings,' said Salim in his deep bass voice. 'But now we are come for that rite. Are you ready?'

'Yes, my lord,' murmured Frank, giving the ritual response he had so carefully memorised.

'Prepare yourself, then.'

Frank stood facing Vincent, and after the knight had removed his squire's chastity belt the two unlaced each other's codpiece and drew out each other's cock.

Salim held a hand over their stiffening members. Two ornate silver cockrings were lying on a velvet cloth spread on a table that stood close by.

'Now you must swear cock-brotherhood.'

Vincent took one of the rings and threaded Frank's cock and balls through it, so that it sat snugly at the root of his genitalia.

'I, Vincent, take thee, Frank, to be my page.'

Frank took the other ring and placed it around Vincent's sexual equipment in the same way.

'I, Frank, take thee, Vincent, to be my knight.'

'Do you promise to be faithful either to other, and to uphold the rules of the Order of the Tree of Life as far as you are able?' intoned Salim.

'We do,' chimed Frank and Vincent in unison.

'Then I pronounce you knight and squire.'

Frank and Vincent kissed tenderly, their tongues fluttering in and out of each other's mouth.

'And now I claim my right as overlord,' continued Salim. 'The first fuck of this sweet ringed lad is mine.'

Vincent left Frank's cock girdle unlocked on the table by the bed, bowed solemnly and left the room.

Alone with Salim, Frank found himself staring into his eyes. How fascinating they were – one green, one orange.

Salim pulled off his shoes, his doublet, his shirt and his leggings and stood naked before Frank.

Frank felt his body tremble with excitement as his eyes took in Salim's huge studded organ, his pierced nipples, his hairy chest and abdomen. How would the master make love to him today? he wondered.

The answer to this question defied all expectations. Where Frank expected to be taken roughly, Salim was tenderness itself; where Frank imagined himself in the passive receiving role, he found himself the active giver.

'Oh, my young stallion,' murmured Salim gently, as he drew off Frank's clothes and stroked and kissed his naked flesh. 'I hope you forgive me for last night, for the powerful way I invaded your body in the act of love. The god Belial was in me, and I could do nothing to mitigate his lust.'

'I forgive you, my lord,' murmured Frank, lying back and looking up at the commanding master of the order.

'But now, today, I am myself, and I want to experience your lovemaking in a different way, my sweet young colt.' Salim gazed fondly down at Frank.

'Anything, anything you desire, my lord. If it is in my power to grant you, you shall have it, I swear.'

'I wish to straddle your young body like so, Frank.' Salim matched his actions to his words, kneeling with his hairy thighs either side of Frank's narrow hips.

'I wish to impale myself on your youthful horn of flesh like so.' Salim lowered his hairy arse down on to the tip of Frank's erect cock, and then, gyrating his hips and relaxing his arse muscles, he eased the whole length of Frank's smooth hard member into him.

'And now I wish to ride you to orgasm, my dear boy. I pray you, make my ride a rough one. Buck up into me with mighty thrusts, my fresh young steed. I long to feel the bite and purchase of your rod within me.'

So Salim rode Frank, and Frank thrust up into him. Salim masterfully put his hot young mount through his paces. First Salim's rising and falling in the saddle was like a slow leisurely walk, and Frank matched that rhythm easily. Then Salim quickened his pace to a trot and Frank's cockthrusts were short and shallow and rapid in succession, rising up to meet Salim's welcoming arse. Then Salim began to canter and Frank responded by giving deeper, longer thrusts with his cockrod. And finally Salim galloped and Frank thrust up into him hard and deep and fast. Their breath came heavy and they were both bathed in rivulets of sweat by now. Frank felt himself soaring upwards towards an ecstatic orgasm, like a handsome angel about to take wing. Then the white stars exploded in his mind and he spread his silvery white swan's wings and he flew, crying out with joy as his cock gushed beneficently again and again, massaged and milked by the pulsing ring of muscles in Salim's arse. Salim's organ, too, now reared up and poured forth a veritable river of white and creamy goodness. It spattered in Frank's hair, it bathed his face, his neck, his shoulders and chest. Frank lay with eyes closed, luxuriating in this warm and nourishing shower of living seed. He could almost feel Salim's sperm threshing to penetrate every pore of his skin. It was such a great sensation. He gave himself up to it and floated on a sea of pleasure.

At last Salim had to go. He hopped off the bed in a sprightly manner, donned his clothes in a trice, kissed Frank warmly on the lips and left.

Frank wiped himself clean with a towel and then dutifully strapped his cock girdle back on. Although the lovemaking with Salim had been exciting and an enriching experience, from now on he knew that he belonged first and foremost to Vincent. He was determined to be faithful to his knight and to live according to the rules of the order he had entered.

Eight

Shortly after Frank's induction, Salim du Court and Zarek, accompanied by Bastien and Piers, left the castle of Nonpareil to go riding the land beyond the lake for some days. No one seemed to know exactly why they did this. Some said it was to survey the lands belonging to Nonpareil. Truth to tell, no one really seemed to care about the reason – either one way or the other.

During du Court's absence life at the castle went on much as before, though there was an almost imperceptible sense of a relaxation of the strict rules of the order among those knights and squires who remained.

Frank's convalescence after the ordeal of induction was over. And, although he was still slightly weak on his legs, he paid a special trip to the tiring room next to the chapel and retrieved the silver locket that contained his father's portrait from the chink in the wall where he had stuffed it on the day of his initiation. However much he might feel committed to his new life in the order, he was determined not to lose some of the special links that he had with his past, with his family. He hid the locket in the secret drawer of a jewel box by his bedside. He might be laying aside his past for the moment, and living intensely in the present, but he refused to take the drastic option of giving up his youth and pretending that it had never happened, or of forgetting his family and his forebears entirely. These things might come back into his life at some point, he felt sure, if the time was ripe.

As he lived for the pleasure of each day, this period at Nonpareil passed as if in a dream for Frank. He felt at one with Vincent, and more truly at ease with himself than he had felt theretofore. He served Vincent his food at lunch and dinner, he did chores around the kitchen with Tomas, he studied in the library with Chance, he made love with Vincent at night and he slept with him until day.

All thoughts of escaping from the castle of Nonpareil and of returning home to be with Rob Oakley the woodcutter had simply evaporated from Frank's mind. He lived for the present, joyful in his sexuality, and made no plans for change.

One afternoon, Vincent took Frank out to have a picnic in one of the meadows beyond the castle walls. After they had picked at their food, they lay close together in each other's arms and kissed each other with intense fervour.

After a while Vincent released Frank from his cock girdle and the two got ready to make love under the dappled shade of an oak tree.

They were too impassioned to remove all their clothes, contenting themselves in their haste with just ripping off their leggings.

Excited, Frank lay looking up at the oak-leaf canopy above him. Vincent knelt between his young squire's thighs, raised the lad's bare legs in the air, and placed his own velvet-clad shoulders under Frank's knees.

Frank gazed up into Vincent's eyes as he felt Vincent's cock head nosing and nuzzling at his arse mouth. With a few well-aimed thrusts, Vincent entered him, and the penetration in this position was excitingly deep. Frank cried out gutturally with pleasure each time Vincent's hard pole gained more ground within him.

'Oh, Vincent,' he murmured. 'Lord of my desire, and commander of my sexual pleasure, how I adore you.'

Vincent stopped his mouth with a passionate, lingering kiss, and began to thrust doubly into Frank with tongue in mouth and cock in arse. Frank absolutely revelled in this double assault. He relaxed his arse muscles and stretched his mouth wide, opening himself and offering himself to Vincent, his lord and conqueror in love.

Vincent now redoubled his efforts, as faster went his cock in and out of Frank's yielding arsehole. Its blunt head massaged Frank's prostate gland in the process so that the lad felt himself tremble with mounting pleasure at every cockthrust. Faster fluttered Vincent's tongue in and out of Frank's pliant mouth. Frank's cock now oozed pre-come and his mouth dribbled freely with Vincent's and his intermingled spittle. He was the vessel of Vincent's love and Vincent was soon going to fill him to the very brim with powerful white liquor.

When Vincent's ejaculation finally came in a gush of wet warmth, which pumped his bowels to the full, Frank felt truly and utterly fulfilled. The two stayed locked together in their coital pose for a while, Frank's legs in the air, his knees hooked over Vincent's shoulder and Vincent's cock still plugging his arse. They kissed and bit each other's lips by turns and every so often pulled back and gazed lustfully into each other's eyes. Vincent's cock, which had for a brief moment softened and decreased in size, now hardened and expanded with lust again. Still with his cock shaft deep in Frank, he lifted the lad up manfully so that his back was pressed firmly against the tree trunk. Once Frank was in this new position, Vincent began to fuck his arse vigorously while standing. Frank enjoyed this new posture greatly. He loved the novelty of sexual experimentation, and Vincent knew just how to please him and tease him, pausing in his thrusting, and playfully wanking Frank's cock to orgasm before he once more plunged up into him with renewed energy, bringing himself to a forceful ejaculation in double-quick time.

Three times they fucked that afternoon without once completely stopping their passionate kisses and caresses. At one point Vincent twined meadow flowers round the root of Frank's cock, and Frank did the same for Vincent, binding the base of his lover's tool with a close-fitting coronet of 'love-in-idleness'. Thus crowned, they fell to kissing and nibbling at each other's mouth, nipples and cock, until they were so aroused that they had to fuck once more. Their third coupling saw Frank lying face down on the grass, his pert arse ready for Vincent to breach with his rigid rod.

That peach of an arse had by now been well pierced by the insatiable worm of penetrative sex, and was totally relaxed by that time. The tendons of Frank's tongue also ached from being so often sucked into Vincent's hungry mouth. Oh, but it was so good to feel the man he loved, the man he was bonded to, kneeling astride his hips. Frank revelled in Vincent's kisses and the playful bites he inflicted on the nape of his neck. He shivered with pleasure as Vincent's hands stroked his shoulders, his flanks, and reached under his armpits to cup and caress his pectorals. Now Vincent had edged back and his skilful hands parted Frank's buttocks and the hard head of his cock soon nosed deep into Frank's back passage.

How gorgeous, thought Frank, to be covered and taken sexually in this way by his man. To lie there completely passive and to be dominated in a manly and masterful fashion by the hard fleshy rod of his lord, which pounded relentlessly deep into his backside.

Again, Vincent's stiff organ paused in mid-thrust, and he cried out throatily, 'Take this!' and sprayed Frank's innards forcefully with spurt after spurt of his soothing liquid essence.

Day after day passed in this way, in lazy lovemaking and close companionship.

During this time Vincent encouraged Frank to experiment and to try novel positions and titillating accessories to ring the changes on their insatiable, ravenous desire for lovemaking.

One day Vincent got Frank to don a fine brocade dress, women's slippers and a high horned hat with a veil. Thus attired, Frank played at being a proud and standoffish lady, busy with her embroidery, while Vincent tried to seduce her. This escapade of course ended with the lady hitching up her skirts and bracing herself against the wall while her suitor fucked her pert rump with insatiable energy.

Another time Frank stripped naked and wore only a headdress of stag's antlers tied to his head and a white deer's scut strapped above his backside. Acting the part of a frisky young buck, he was pursued about the bedroom by Vincent, dressed in hunter's gear, until finally, weary with the chase, the stag lay face down on the bed, at which point the hunter tore off his leggings and plunged his arse-eager tool between Frank's buttocks and fucked him royally.

One night, sated with possessing Frank himself, Vincent asked his squire merely to make love with a number of the other young squires who had been released that night from their obligations, and from their restraining cock girdles, by their lords.

The venue for this orgy was in one of the underground caverns that lay directly below the castle cellars.

On the appointed night, Vincent led Frank to the cavern entrance.

'In you go now. All is arranged. Strip to the buff when you reach the cavern itself, and await the others who are to join you, as I have said.'

'But aren't you coming?' asked Frank earnestly. 'At least to watch, if not to take part.'

'No, Frank. My pleasure will simply be in imagining you coupling with other young squires tonight, at my command.'

With a farewell kiss on the lips to speed him on his way, Frank was off down the narrow stone corridor without a backward glance.

At last he reached the inner grotto. A pale glistening phosphorescence lit its walls, and its arched roof rested upon thick pillars made of striated crystalline stalactites and stalagmites that had dripped down and inched up over the centuries until they kissed and melded in the middle.

Suspended from the ceiling was a splendid and ornate candelabra with a marine theme. Iron lobsters and seahorses were the caryatids that supported the turquoise wax tapers. Here and there around this centrepiece, hanging from silver threads let into the ceiling, or set directly into the walls, were countless cunningly bevelled and faceted crystals and smoothly rounded lenses that shimmered with subtly iridescent rainbow hues and tinkled in the gentle breeze that blew down the long dark tunnel that led from the cave entrance.

In the centre of this natural cavern, a huge bed stood, with a coverlet as blue as the sea, and sheets a creamy white like sea foam, draped across it. The many cushions that lay scattered across it took the form of scallops, conches, nautilus shells, crabs, starfish and other denizens of the deep.

Frank cast off his clothes eagerly and slipped between the sheets as he waited to see who would reach the grotto next.

Chance was the first to arrive. He grinned pleasantly when he saw that Frank was already there, and he cast off his clothes with alacrity. How Frank loved to gaze at Chance's youthful nut-brown body, taking in the almost imperceptible swell of his belly, and the suggestion of slightly rounded breasts that, together with his long-lashed brown eyes and his full lips, gave him a titillating hint of femininity which Frank found irresistible, especially when coupled with the hairy fuzz on his legs, and the pendulous cock and balls that dangled between his thighs.

Chance dived into bed next to Frank, and, as they wrapped their eager arms closely around each other's waist, their two mouths sought each other, hungrily, greedily. They engaged in deep tongue kissing and cock caressing, which began gently and languidly but soon became fiercer and more urgent. As a result they missed the arrival of the next squire to enter the cave – Shawn.

Shawn silently removed his clothes and stood at the foot of the bed, arms folded and cock erect, and cleared his throat. Frank and Chance at once pulled apart and gazed at him, their eyes momentarily out of focus, dilated as they were with passion.

Frank drank in Shawn's angelic good looks as the young lad tipped his head on one side, raised a quizzical eyebrow, and tut-tutted in mock disapproval.

In three-quarter profile, Shawn's pale-skinned lanky body, with its fuzz of blond pubic hair at belly base, was decidedly appealing,

Frank decided. And the stiff and throbbing state of his slender penis belied his apparently uninterested and condescending pose.

Chance glanced mischievously across at Frank, and without a word passing between the two of them, they grabbed Shawn from either side and hauled him into bed between them.

Chance knelt at the head of the bed and offered Shawn the tip of his cock to lick and suck. The offer was not refused. Frank for his part gently eased Shawn's knees wide apart and knelt between the lad's spread thighs. Bending low he sucked on Shawn's cock, licked his balls and fingered the ruched rosette of his arse in quick succession.

Their cocksucking fun and games came to a temporary halt once Tomas arrived. His cheeky ruddy face and short-cropped mop of dark brown hair were the first thing Frank saw when Tomas tapped him on the shoulder, and forced him to let Shawn's cock drop from his mouth, and to wheel round, surprised.

'Oh, it's you!' said Frank.

'Yes, it's me!' replied Tomas in friendly tones. He pulled off his tunic and drew off his leggings. Frank gazed with interest at his chunky torso, his firmly rounded rump, and his sturdy fore-arms, biceps, thighs and calves.

Tomas clambered on to the bed and the four squires now rearranged themselves into a new sexual configuration. Tomas crouched on all fours on the bed, as he sucked at the lust-moist heads of Shawn's and Chance's cocks, the hard shafts of which Shawn held clasped together in his fist. Shawn and Chance for their part snogged hungrily, and drew out purple lovebites on each other's neck in almost vampire fashion, so great was the desire of each to leave his mark and thus impress the other.

Frank watched all this loveplay eagerly. He caressed his cock until he was fully aroused, and he licked at Tomas's arse, moisten-ing it with his spittle and stretching it a little with his massaging fingers. After some time at this, he could bear the sexual tension no longer. Kneeling up, he shuffled forward, positioned his cock at the crack in Tomas's arse, and plunged his stiff organ repeatedly and insistently into the tight cleft between Tomas's buttocks until he gradually gained admittance and his shaft slid completely home.

Thus the four squires made love. Frank penetrated Tomas's arse, and Tomas in turn urgently sucked off Chance and Shawn.

In mid-cockthrust Frank suddenly noticed, or thought he noticed, in one of the lenses set into the cave wall, a magnified blue eye that blinked at him. He thought he recognised it as Vincent's steely gaze. So his master was there after all, gazing intently at every move he made.

At that Frank stared around the cave in wonder and saw other eyes – dark brown, grey and hazel – visible through other lenses dotted around the cavern wall. It seemed that the four squires were in a cunningly disguised observation chamber, and that on all sides these magnified eyes were observing them in the throes of their impassioned sexual antics.

Far from making him feel shy, once Frank knew that Vincent and others were there watching his every move, he threw himself into sexual acts with even more gusto than before, making Tomas writhe and moan with pleasure and suck more strongly in turn upon Shawn's and Chance's drooling tools. The very idea of people studying him in the intimate act of love excited Frank enormously, stiffened his erection to the utmost, and made his spunk-swollen balls ache for gushing release.

At last Frank gave a cry of extreme pleasure.

His back arched, his buttocks clenched and his balls contracted strongly in a spasm of utter delight as he shot his liquid load straight up Tomas's arse. How he pumped that silver flood deep into Tomas's yielding innards!

It was not long after this that Shawn and Chance, hastened to orgasm by Frank's noisy and demonstrative ejaculation, could hold back no longer. Their cocks, too, erupted jet after jet of copiously shed white spume. They filled Tomas's guzzling mouth with generous draughts of their intermingled man's milk – warm, salty and creamy on the tongue.

Yes, indeed, those days shortly after Frank's induction were splendid ones, full of sexual experimentation. And it wasn't always true that Vincent knew exactly what Frank was doing, or with whom he was doing it, either.

Jourdain, for example, was one of the knights whom Frank had fancied for some time. He was lanky, broad-shouldered, slim-waisted and blessed with a deep voice that made Frank's bollocks contract with pleasurable yearning whenever he heard it. One day, when Vincent was off hunting on the mainland, and Frank had opted to stay on the island, he met Jourdain by chance in one of the wine cellars, where he'd gone to decant wine from the cask into the flagons that graced the dining table at lunchtime.

Jourdain was already down in the cellar, waiting for him. When he saw Frank, he drew the lad aside into an alcove.

'Quickly,' he urged. 'We haven't much time before Vincent returns from bagging a brace of hare or a partridge.'

He fumbled with the waistband of Frank's leggings as he spoke. Frank was taken aback and a little confused.

'Jourdain,' he said, 'you forget – my cock girdle. You can't!'

With a knowing smile, Jourdain produced a set of strangely irregular keys like silver fishbones from the leather pouch that hung from his side.

'Oh, yes, I can,' he chuckled.

'Skeleton keys!' murmured Frank, amazed.

'Precisely, and sooner or later one of them is sure to fit. . .'

Jourdain fumbled with Frank's cock girdle, trying one key after another in the lock, until finally the metal cock cage clicked open and Frank stepped out temporarily from his enforced chastity.

Jourdain led him over to a wooden table where the decanters stood.

'Frank, my dear boy, I've long lusted after you. Have you never realised till now?'

Frank's cock sprang to attention at this open admission of another man's desire for him, and a man who was as eminently attractive as Jourdain, too.

Gently, Jourdain peeled off Frank's clothes and manoeuvred him until he was bent over at the waist and lying across the table, his chest and cheek pressed against the smooth wooden table top, his arms outstretched to left and right, and his legs parted wide.

As Frank lay in this position, Jourdain unbuttoned his codpiece and, as he stood behind Frank, he began to push the lust-moist head of his cock between Frank's buttocks. With his fingers he worked the drooling tip up and down Frank's arse crack and rubbed it against Frank's tight anal sphincter.

Frank trembled with hot desire and silently willed Jourdain to thrust his long member deep into him. As if he could read Frank's mind, this was exactly what Jourdain proceeded to do.

Frank cried out with pleasurable pain as Jourdain's cock thrust into him again and again. He wriggled his arse, and jigged it back and forward to counter every inthrust, savouring the sensation of such a glorious specimen of manhood invading and possessing his whole body.

Jourdain, too, cried out a deep groan with every spearing jab his superbly stiff tool made between Frank's madly flexing buttocks.

The sound of Frank's and Jourdain's intermingled groans, blended with the squelching of Jourdain's love-juice-slick cock as it rammed repeatedly into Frank's relaxed arsehole, was magnified by the arched roof of the cellar, so that Frank's ears rang with the rhythmic sound of their shared passion.

At last Jourdain paused mid-thrust.

'Take that, sweet tempter!' he cried out with resonant urgency as his cock loosed a veritable wave of fresh sperm into the cup of Frank's arse like newly broached sparkling wine – a thick spume of rich goodness that came from nowhere and flowed of a sudden so freely. Frank's cock, too, reared and spurted its fine seedmilk in such a copious flood over the table that it covered the top and began to drip from the edges on to the flagged floor on all sides, like a strangely liquid, pearly white, lace table cover.

Many indeed were the moments of exquisite sexual pleasure that Frank experienced during the early days after his induction into the Order of the Tree of Life. Frank found that the routine of the cult – the erotically charged encounters with other members, squires and knights – was highly addictive and highly seductive, too. He forgot, or at any rate seemed to forget, all about his innocent former love for Rob Oakley and threw himself into tasting forbidden pleasures of the flesh with great gusto.

It was as if a rustling rope of shimmering and shining ivy

tendrils was creeping up and strangling a fine upright oak tree. Frank had soon joined the sexual pavane of masculine couplings and recouplings at the castle of Nonpareil, and it seemed to him at that time that the music in his ears – the sighs, the gasps, the moans of his lovers – would never stop. While there was music, his body moved with it – his cock rose up rigid and flopped down flaccidly, his bollocks swelled and contracted with the flux of his sperm, his arse clenched and was teased open by others' probing tongues, fingers and cocks.

During this time his whole being was driven by the tidal waves of interest, desire, arousal and ecstatic erotic self-realisation, followed by short-lived bouts of postcoital melancholy. These brief moments of gloom were soon chased away by the pursuit of yet another orgasm with yet another partner in yet another hitherto unexplored nook or cranny of the castle.

Perhaps the most beautiful of these sexual experiments that Frank indulged in so freely at this time was the night when Gaston and Kerwen came to sup with him and Vincent one night.

The evening started conventionally enough. Kerwen had brought his lute with him, and he plucked out a romantic tune, while he and Frank between them sang a haunting lyric of the deep love between a knight and his sworn brother.

Then Kerwen changed the mood by launching into a ribald song about a shepherd with an insatiable dick who loved to roger whoever or whatever passed him by as he pretended to be asleep in a hayfield.

By this time, Vincent was sitting close by Kerwen on the four-poster bed, stroking his inner thigh with a reverent hand, and kissing his ear, his cheek and neck as he continued playing and singing.

Gaston came over and sat next to Frank on the window seat. He put his arm round Frank's shoulder and Frank felt the same thrill and desire as he felt all those years before when Gaston had been his fencing master.

He reached between Gaston's thighs and patted his bulging codpiece.

'Of all the swords you taught me to wield when you were my

teacher, there was one you never let me lay either eye or hand on.'

Gaston turned to him, a surprisingly tender look on his face.

'Much to my regret, believe me, Frank,' he murmured earnestly.

'Well,' continued Frank, playfully beginning to unlace Gaston's leggings, 'we can always remedy past omissions now.'

'Certainly,' replied Gaston, and he threw off his jerkin and shirt, eager to begin a bout of lovemaking with his former pupil.

'Wait,' whispered Frank, pointing to the four-poster bed where Vincent now had his head buried in Kerwen's crotch, and Kerwen was arched back, his eyes closed in bliss, running his fingers again and again through Vincent's blond mane of hair as the music of rhythmic slurping counterpointed by Kerwen's moans filled the air.

'Let's not disturb them,' said Frank. 'Anyway, I want us to be private, to consummate a passion I had for you long before I knew of Vincent, Nonpareil, Salim and the Order of the Tree of Life.'

They drew the cherry-coloured thick damask bedcurtains around the bed and now Vincent and Kerwen were cut off totally from what was passing in the rest of the chamber. Frank and Gaston returned to the window seat and embarked on a passionate coupling which was all the more intense for having been proscribed and prohibited years before.

'Take hold of my cock as if it were the pommel of a sword!' commanded Gaston, and Frank obeyed.

'Now, run your fingers up and down it, as if greasing a rod!' Once more Frank complied.

'Oh, Frank, you don't know how good that feels, how I've longed for this moment.'

Frank guided Gaston's hand to touch his own throbbing cock.

'Now you do the same to me, Gaston,' he half pleaded, half commanded.

What an utter thrill it was to feel Gaston's firm grasp around his manhood, working him up and down, unceasingly.

'Oh, Gaston, yes! Yes!' Frank urged, and knelt up, so that his and Gaston's cocks were close. From time to time they even touched throbbingly.

He wanked Gaston's huge stiff member rhythmically, and Gaston returned the caress on his own organ, stroke for stroke.

'Oh, Gaston,' said Frank, 'I never realised you cared for me. I never imagined we'd end up making love like this. You've been so cold and distant to me since I came to Nonpareil.'

'Oh, my darling boy,' murmured Gaston, and he kissed Frank lingeringly on the lips. 'That was because I still wanted you, still after all these years.'

'But couldn't you express those feelings before now? Couldn't you have let me know, put me out of my agony of suspense?'

Gaston gazed deep into Frank's eyes. Leaning his mouth close to Frank's ear, he lowered his voice to a whisper. 'I wasn't sure of your feelings Frank. You seemed so happy at first with Vincent, and the rules of the order prohibit –'

'Oh, bother the rules of the order!' hissed Frank angrily, and then he kissed Gaston tenderly on the lips, and began to stroke his cock some more, squeezing it with firmness in his fist with each downward movement.

'Let's forget the past, Gaston,' he urged. 'Let's forget the future, too. Time often robs us of the here and now in our worries about the there and then, and the what-might-be. Agreed?'

'Yes, my dear boy. Agreed. How wise you've grown with the years,' smiled Gaston, his eyes shining bright with love.

Then he began to caress Frank's cock again in earnest, and for the moment their conversation gave way to more basic communication – that of body on body accompanied by animalistic groans, sighs, grunts and growls.

Gaston lay back on the window seat and let Frank kiss him on his nose, on his cheeks, on his lips, his nipples, his cock, his balls and his arse.

'My own dear Frank,' Gaston murmured as he looked up fondly at his former pupil, 'how often I gazed at you in your practice shirt and breeches when I was your fencing tutor. How often I longed to rip your clothes from your lithe young body and to explore every crevice, every secret orifice of you with my tongue, with my fingers, with my cock.'

'Believe me, my body burned with hot passion for you, Gaston,' smiled Frank indulgently, and he ran his hands gently over the muscles in his lover's chest and taut abdomen. 'Remember how I couldn't get the hang of rapier and dagger fighting, and I'd get you to stand close behind me, and to hold my arms so that I could get the moves.'

'Yes, I remember. You were very slow to catch on. I couldn't understand why.'

'But, Gaston, it was for the pleasure of feeling your chest at my back, of sensing your hard codpiece digging into the cleft between my buttocks, of having your arms, strong and muscular, encircling my waist.'

'Oh, my dear Frank,' sighed Gaston, 'if only you knew how that close proximity to your sweaty body drove me wild with desire. My cock fairly hammered to be released, to be allowed to plunge between your downy cheeks. But I held back for fear of arousing your grandmother's ire, and for fear of shocking you, my dear boy. I couldn't bear the thought of losing you entirely, and so I preferred to maintain our sensual and erotically charged friendship, rather than stake all on trying to fuck you and being rejected.'

'But that didn't fool my grandmother. She had you dismissed in any case,' replied Frank sadly, and he twirled a lock of Gaston's pubic hair around his fingers.

'Ah, yes, but now fate has seen fit to bring us back together again, Frank. And now there will be no holding back, believe me. Let us see how well you remember your sword and dagger training. Stand over there, take up your weapons in your imagination. Good. Now face away from me, and I'll come behind you and guide you as never before.'

It was now dark outside the leaded window, and, by the light of a couple of candelabra, Frank stood and gazed at his naked reflection refracted into so many diamonds of flesh in the window glass before him.

He felt Gaston's breath fall heavy on the back of his neck, and at the same time he sensed Gaston's sticky cock head nuzzling up against his arse mouth. Frank spat into his palm. Reaching back, he anointed Gaston's cock head with the warm spittle. Then Gaston put his hands on Frank's hips and drove his rod slowly into place.

'Oh, Gaston, how I love this, and how I love you,' moaned Frank hoarsely, as he felt himself filled to the brink with Gaston's thick and hard pole of meat.

'Me too,' murmured Gaston, and working his cock around in gyres inside his lover's arse.

He reached past Frank's hips and caressed his stiff cock, his swollen balls and his erect nipples. Then, placing his hands on Frank's hips once more, he fucked him fiercely, savagely, and gave no quarter in his assault. Frank cried out again and again in repeated moans and groans of excitement and raw pleasure. These were moans that gradually increased in intensity and volume until finally Gaston shot his hot fountain of love deep into Frank's soft bowels and Frank's cock erupted in sympathy in a spray of terrific force that spattered the floor.

'Now do you feel the force of my love for you?' murmured Gaston, still panting in the afterglow of sex.

'Oh, yes, I feel it most keenly,' murmured Frank, himself somewhat short of breath. Then he pulled Gaston's head forward and arched his own head back so that his mouth was next to Gaston's ear. Into it, he whispered conspiratorially, 'But what have we done?'

'What do you mean?' whispered Gaston back urgently.

'Well, now we've made love like this, and I know what I know, how can I possibly go back to being Vincent's dutiful squire.'

'But you must,' urged Gaston in low tones. 'The rules of the order –' he began.

'Oh, fuck the order!' snapped Frank, once more enraged at the petty rules and regulations that he felt increasingly were hemming him in.

At that moment the curtains of the four-poster were drawn back and Kerwen emerged into the room, his hair rumpled and a satisfied look on his face, like the cat that had definitely got the cream.

Kerwen and Gaston, hastily dressed, conferred together in low voices, and left for their room soon after. Frank, for his part, crawled into the four-poster bed and lay there for a while, feeling shaken and lonely beside Vincent, who lay there snoring and senseless after his passionate love bout with Kerwen. Finally Frank's mind stilled, and he too drifted off into sleep.

Nine

From the moment of his physical consummation of love with Gaston, something changed inside Frank. He began to find the structures of the Order of the Tree of Life irksome. What had before been a novelty now soon palled into drudgery and routine.

Outwardly no one noticed a difference perhaps. Frank was still the same comely youth. He still dutifully obeyed his knight Vincent, served him unobtrusively at table during breakfast, lunch and dinner, and served him at night by being compliant and willing in bed.

But in his heart something had hardened. He no longer felt the same thrill at Vincent's touch, the same ecstasy when he indulged in sexual acts with him. Now he longed always to be with Gaston, and, even when they did manage to snatch some time and even sexual intimacy together, it was all somehow marred by the knowledge that Frank, under the rules of the order, was Vincent's personal chattel, and that Gaston had chosen Kerwen as his squire. This division, seemingly graven in tablets of stone, weighed on Frank heavily, so that he found that even the sweet stolen kisses and the fierce coupling that he and Gaston sought at every opportunity turned sour and lost potency by the implacable rules that officially separated them so cruelly.

Gaston, who was of a more happy-go-lucky disposition, appreciated the present moment for what it was and devoted himself to it utterly. Not so Frank. He heard the tick-tock of the castle clock, saw the candles flicker down in their sconces at night, and felt keenly that time was passing him by in the castle of Nonpareil. Here he stayed, destined to live out his days with Vincent, and he was far from happy at the prospect. He felt increasingly drawn to Gaston, and, when Gaston couldn't tryst with him, Frank went for long solitary walks on the island in order to escape from the comings and goings in the castle, and to wander alone with his thoughts.

And his thoughts, when he could tear them away from mulling on Gaston, were on the rules and regulations of the Order of the Tree of Life. These were fine when one never questioned them and simply went along with them. But, now that Frank found himself at cross-purposes with them, they chafed him with their itemised and seemingly petty restrictions on his freedom. They were like a heavy iron ball and chain that ate into the ankle of a prisoner in a dungeon, except that this hampered and cramped feeling that Frank experienced ate not into any physical part of him but into his very soul, his inner being. He felt, in short, that the Order of the Tree of Life was slowly strangling him and stifling his individuality. Either he bowed and acquiesced to its strictures and became an unquestioning devotee once more, or he would have to break the bonds of the order and run free. But where could he run to? And could he persuade Gaston to make the break with him? Gaston was after all a knight of the order of some years' standing, and he seemed relatively happy with the way of things in the castle. It was as if he had lost his will to an individualistic life and was content to be a faithful and obedient part of the organism that existed at Nonpareil under the leadership of Salim du Court.

The next Sabbat came fast upon them now, and Salim had arrived back in residence with his trusty slave Zarek at his side. Frank was pleased to see Zarek. He also found that the tall young Pole sought him out on a number of occasions for a quiet word. Somehow it fell out that they were never alone together and never had the chance to repeat the intense lovemaking that they had indulged in when they met by the sundial in the maze that time early in his sojourn at Nonpareil.

On the night of the Sabbat, Frank got ready in his black cowled robe, his studded leather codpiece, his silver cockring, his silver cock-headed staff and his silver facemask.

He entered the chapel just before midnight along with the other members of the order, all robed in black and silver, as he was.

At midnight the chapel bell was tolled by Zarek, and Salim du Court, also cloaked in black, came and sat on a carved ebony throne on the candlelit dais in front of the black-velvet-draped altar.

On the final stroke of twelve Salim stood up and threw off his cloak. He was wearing a gold mask in the form of an eagle, gold sandals laced to the knee and a gold torque cockring around his massive pulsing organ. He sat down on the edge of his throne once more, his legs splayed wide.

'Approach, my sperm-brood!' he commanded.

One by one the knights and squires of the Order of the Tree of Life lined up and shuffled forward to kneel between Salim's legs and to place a reverential kiss upon the tip of his cock head and a kiss upon each of his huge pendulous testicles. Du Court leaned back in his throne, and thrust his cock and balls forward towards his devotees' pursed lips. He seemed positively to revel in this worship of him as Lord Belial.

Once all had bent to kiss the rod and fruit, the sperm-brood of knights and squires all drew back and arranged themselves into a standing semicircle.

Zarek entered. He wore a black leather executioner's mask on his face, and an iron-studded black belt around his waist. The difference in his clothing reminded Frank that he was not du Court's squire, only his bought slave, and therefore not a free man. Gazing at the muscular beauty of Zarek's form, Frank felt his cock begin to stiffen.

Zarek placed a large ornately moulded silver bowl on a black iron tripod in front of du Court's throne. He bowed and then withdrew to the shadows.

Du Court stood up. His gold-ringed cock pulsed rhythmically. It looked as if unseen hands stroked it, as if invisible succubi were masturbating the leader of the order, but Frank knew that it was no magic, that du Court could stimulate his own sex organs by the power of erotic mental visualisation achieved through years of Tantric meditation.

Du Court moved towards the bowl, which stood at about crotch height. As he stood with his cock poised above the sacred receptacle, he closed his eyes, raised his arms up to the heavens, tilted his face upwards and invoked Lord Belial to enter him.

At once, his cock erupted into a rich fountain of sperm, which sputtered down into the silver basin for several minutes without ceasing.

When at last the final drop of his liquid seed fell like a pearl from his cock mouth, he opened his eyes and spoke to the assembled throng in the voice of Belial.

'Couple as you will, my sweet sperm brothers, but save all your holy oil for me tonight, I command you!'

Many were the orgasms that they all achieved that night, but always, as ordered by Salim, they meticulously retained the spunk that flowed from each and every sex act and poured it into the silver bowl before the high altar.

As for Frank, he decided to go with the flow of love, and lose himself in an orgy of sensual forgetting that night. So it was that, when Vincent went off with Kerwen up to the chapel belfry to indulge in a foursome there with Tomas and Chance, Frank slipped away down to the chapel crypt with Zarek.

When they reached the depths of the crypt, with its low arched ceiling, Zarek approached Frank and, with passionate energy, began to kiss his lips, his cheeks, his neck, his bare shoulders and his nipples.

Frank felt himself melt under the Polish giant's onslaught, and he put up no resistance when Zarek snapped a manacle round each of his wrists, and he found himself chained to the ceiling.

A small stove stood in the corner of the cellar, and as Frank watched, Zarek loaded it up with fresh wood, and placed branches of wet silver birch leaves nearby. They gave off a delicious aromatic perfume as the temperature in the cellar slowly rose.

The sweat began to pour down Frank's forehead, chest and back in rivulets.

Now Zarek knelt behind Frank, and the young squire was delighted to feel the Pole's muscular fingers prise his buttocks apart and his long pointed tongue begin to lap at his tight anus.

Could anything be so delicious as this sweet and intimate tonguing? thought Frank, as he writhed with ecstasy in his chains. All his thoughts of rebellion against the Order of the Tree of Life swiftly evaporated in the heat of the moment. Even his disenchantment with Vincent and his yearning for Gaston paled into insignificance beside the joyful fleshly pleasure he experienced with every masterly tongue thrust from Zarek.

What was his yearning for Gaston, anyway, but a yearning for times past, for lost opportunities, for the sweet innocence of his youth? He might as well long for Rob Oakley, the woodcutter's son, and he had long ago resigned himself to forgetting that dream. And yet there was something about Zarek that stirred in Frank a remembrance of Rob, now he came to think of it.

The Polish boy now stopped darting his tongue between Frank's buttocks, and began gently to probe at Frank's arse mouth with his fingertips instead. First one, then two, and now three fingers slid gently in and out of Frank's tight nether orifice, making the lad cry out gutturally with the sheer pleasure of the experience.

The heat in the cellar now was intense, and clouds of steam were billowing from the stove, where Zarek now and again poured a ladle of water from a wooden stoup on to the top of it.

Now Zarek took up one of the birch twigs and began to beat Frank's naked body all over with the sweet-smelling leaves. At first he dealt Frank only light pattering strokes, but soon they became harder and more vicious slashes, leaving red weals where they had kissed Frank's bare flesh. The blood rushed through Frank's veins speedily, and his heart pumped faster with excitement at this unexpected stimulation.

GUY EDENBRIDGE

Now, truth to tell, Frank felt his whole body sing with desire, a desire for self-sacrifice, a desire to be taken roughly from behind by the slave boy, a desire to feel Zarek's hot fresh-spilled Polish jism gush copiously again and again within him. All these feelings surfaced within him, summoned by the slashes of the sweet-smelling birch twigs in Zarek's hand.

He thought that Zarek felt the same way for him, too. He reasoned that the careful preparations – the manacles, the stove, the birch twigs – were all evidence of Zarek's desire to possess him. How wrong he was.

Just as Frank wondered when Zarek would finally make love to him, who should appear through the clouds of steam but Salim du Court.

'Have you prepared the lad for me?' du Court asked curtly.

'Yes, master. He is trembling on the cusp of desire,' replied Zarek dutifully.

Frank felt a momentary panic at this unexpected turn of events, but then du Court's magnetic eyes were staring into his.

'Do not be afraid, Frank. You are now my chosen vessel.'

Soothed by the master's velvet tones, Frank relaxed as Salim stood behind him and plunged his studded cock deep into his arse.

'Master, you do me a great honour by fucking me tonight,' rasped out Frank, as his felt du Court move insistently within him.

Du Court redoubled the intensity of his anal assault, and growled with each inthrust. Frank felt overwhelmed by the man's power, helpless and fragile against such indomitable strength and sexual energy, and yet, despite his initial surprise that Zarek had merely prepared him for du Court, there was such a sweet joy in surrendering to the master, that Frank's pleasure and excitement soon mounted once more. If only, came the thought in the back of his mind, Salim were ten years younger, then his joy would be complete.

As Frank now gave his arse wholeheartedly to du Court, Zarek wielded the birch branch and whipped him on the chest and belly to heighten his awareness and his sexual pleasure. Then the diligent Pole went behind the conjoined pair and used the spray of aromatic twigs to flagellate du Court on the shoulders, the broad back, and the flexing arse. Suddenly Frank felt du Court's cock rear up inside him and he waited for the gush of sperm that he knew should come in his bowels, but nothing happened. Then he realised du Court was chanting under his breath. Frank knew at once that the master was deliberately controlling his orgasm, and that he used Tantric meditation to halt the rush of sperm and in fact to send that host of white tadpoles swimming back up their tubes, in order to increase the force and intensity of his ejaculation when it finally came. He could even drink up sperm through his cock mouth by flexing his abdominal muscles.

Frank, on the other hand, was still a novice in Tantric sex, and when he felt the rush of spunk shoot from his balls he knew at once that his bucking cock was going to shoot its load, and he realised with a pang of regret that it would spill and waste his precious seed, breaking du Court's commandment to conserve it for Lord Belial that evening.

Zarek, however, spared him that transgression, for just as Frank's cock mouth gushed with a blaze of hot white milk, Zarek held out a silver chalice decorated with big-cocked satyrs, and deftly caught every last drop of Frank's liquid bounty in it, to save it from going to waste.

Soon after Frank had reached ecstasy, du Court withdrew from him, and Zarek undid his fetters.

'You did well, Frank,' said du Court, and he patted him affectionately on the rump.

'Thank you, master,' replied Frank, still in a daze.

'Take him away now and bring me Chance,' murmured du Court to Zarek quietly, almost out of Frank's hearing.

The Polish boy led Frank away back to the chapel. He carried with him the goblet of Frank's sperm to pour into the silver cup before the great altar as a libation of liquid lust in honour of the god Belial.

Frank ejaculated thrice more that Sabbat. Once Chance's mouth brought him to orgasm, once he came when Piers wanked him off, and he finally shot his load when Zarek fucked his arse.

Always, at the moment of ejaculation, he or his sexual partner held out a silver goblet to catch the silvery rain that spewed from his cock mouth, and they later decanted the collected seed into the silver bowl before the altar. As he looked around at the ferocious couplings of that Sabbat orgy, Frank saw that all his companions in the order were husbanding and collecting their sperm just as Salim had ordered.

At the end of the Sabbat celebrations, the silver bowl brimmed with sperm and Salim beckoned to Zarek. He attached three iron chains that dangled in a pulley arrangement from the ceiling to three eyelets in the vessel's rim. As he went over to a crank on the wall, Zarek turned it round and round until – with a whir of cogs and of ratchets – the silver spunk bowl slowly winched up to the roof. Frank now saw that a fine silver chain depended from the base of the spunk bowl and hung down to shoulder height.

Salim took up his position and stood under the 'spunkoon'. He threw off his robe to reveal himself naked and in all his glory. He was a fine specimen of an older man – with grey hair on his head and chin and chest, and lines of experience on his face, perhaps, but with not an ounce of excess fat anywhere on his firm frame.

Frank gazed at Salim in fascination. 'If only he were ten years younger,' Frank thought, 'I'd be happy to be his bedmate.'

Now Salim reached up, and pulled at the fine silver spunkoon chain. Frank was amazed to see that, by a clever mechanism, an outer skin of the spunk bowl twisted around an inner skin and numerous perforations in the bowl's sides and base came into view. It turned in a trice from a solid silver receptacle into an ornate colander from which the spunk now streamed downwards.

Salim showered luxuriatingly in the pearly streams of man seed that rained down upon his naked flesh. When the sticky viscous spunk streams had played themselves out, he raised his voice and commanded in tones that could not be disobeyed.

'Come now, members of my spunk-brood, and lick me clean!'

All present knelt and obeyed. Some lay on their bellies and licked at his toes, heels and ankles; some knelt and tongued his calves, shins, knees; some crouched and lapped at his thighs, rump, genitals and belly; and some stood with their tongues flickering over his arms, shoulders, chest, back, neck and face. For some minutes Salim became the central focus of a writhing mass of naked male bodies. Then Salim cried out.

'Enough!'

And all stood back from him.

Frank, who had felt increasingly lighter- and lighter-headed as the orgy progressed, stared at the old master of the order, hardly able to believe his eyes.

There stood Salim du Court almost as before. Whether it was the rejuvenating effect of the spunk on his bodily tissues, or whether he had fed his soul on the adoration of his acolytes as they licked every inch of his naked body clean, or whether he was simply pulling off some magical trick, he looked changed. He seemed to have lost ten or twenty years, and to be a younger man altogether. His face had lost its hard, lined look and the grey hair on his head and body was now a stunning glossy jet black.

Frank felt unable to credit his senses, and, weak after losing so much spunk during the Sabbat orgy, his head swam. He teetered and swayed unstably on his feet for a moment or two, and then he slumped to the chapel floor in a dead faint.

Ten

The next morning Vincent opened the bedroom curtains and shook Frank awake brusquely.

'How dare you disgrace me by fainting at the Sabbat?' he snarled.

'I'm sorry,' replied Frank, amazed by the harsh morning light that shone in through the window and made him blink. 'I couldn't help it. It was Salim. Didn't you see? He seemed to grow younger as he showered in our spunk. It was as if he absorbed our sperm through the pores of his body, and it gave him youth and strength.'

'And what of that?' came Salim's dark voice from the bedroom doorway.

'Master, I'm sorry . . . I . . .,' muttered Vincent in cowed fashion. 'Please forgive him, master. He didn't know . . .'

'Enough,' growled Salim, as he stepped forward. He wore a splendid quilted velvet robe and Turkish slippers. 'Vincent, you may go now.'

Vincent withdrew hurriedly, and left Frank alone with the mysterious master of the order. Frank expected the worst, but was surprised and relieved when Salim came to sit on the edge of his bed and gazed down at him with a look of concern.

'Are you all right?' asked Salim, a note of genuine anxiety in his voice.

'Yes, I am,' answered Frank. 'But there's so much I don't understand.'

Salim placed a calming hand on Frank's shoulder. 'Peace,' he said. 'Be at peace and calm yourself. I see your mind is troubled.'

'But Salim, master, I know what I saw at the end of the Sabbat. I saw it with my own eyes, and yet I am hard-pressed to explain it.'

'You saw it with your own eyes, eh?' echoed Salim, playfully, and his stare was so penetrating that Frank had to look away after a while. 'Such a perfect grey they are, to be sure,' continued Salim, and he raised up Frank's face so that their gazes intermeshed once more.

But Frank was not to be fobbed off with flattery.

'Master, I think you owe me an explanation,' he insisted.

'I?' responded Salim, incredulous. 'I owe nobody anything. You came here of your own free will, at the invitation of Vincent. You joined our order not out of compulsion, but of your own volition. How dare you speak of any obligation that I may have to you?'

Frank looked nettled, and Salim at once softened slightly.

'However, out of the goodness of my heart, and because of the claims that youth and beauty may always make on age and power, I will accede to your request for an explanation.'

He got up from the bed at this point, drew some herbs from the pouch on his belt, and threw them into the bedroom fire, which at once blazed up green, smoky and sweet-smelling.

'So, you want explanations,' continued Salim, as he returned to the bed where Frank lay. 'Very well, let me give them to you. You say that you must believe what your eyes see, but I say this is not always so. Observe.'

Salim stepped out of his slippers and let the robe slip from his shoulders and fall to the ground. He stood there gloriously naked. A splendid specimen of an older man. Muscular arms and legs, defined chest and abdomen. Not a spare inch of flesh around the waist. A grizzled mat of hair on his chest and a greying thatch of pubic hair around his cock-root. Frank was spellbound.

The smoke from the fire curled around Salim's commanding

151

figure like morning mist. It gave the master a magical other-
worldly quality that Frank found compelling. He let Salim's words
drip into his ear like sweet dark honey, and they reverberated and
echoed in his head.

'Very often,' said Salim, 'we see what we want to see. You saw
me become a younger man at the Sabbat because that is what you
wished to see. Is it not so?'

Frank nodded as he remembered how he had wished Salim
were ten years younger. 'Yes, master, you are right,' he replied.

'You can make my body become younger in your eyes simply
by the power of your desire,' Salim continued, and Frank stared,
mesmerised, as the grey hairs on Salim's head, chin, trunk, arms
and legs began to darken to black, and then to dissolve in places
and leave him smoother-bodied than before. The creased age lines
that scored Salim's face deeply seemed to fade and thin to nothing.
Even his voice lightened, as if the years had dropped away. And
his very skin tone became that of a younger man.

'Do you now see me as you desire me?' asked Salim. The
herbal mist curled around his magnificent young body suggestively, as if even the elements of fire and air were in love with
him and eager to caress his naked frame.

'I do, my lord,' breathed Frank reverently. He felt his cock stir
and rise at the root as he gazed at the younger Salim, still imbued
with the same majesty and power as always, but twenty years
younger than he usually appeared.

'But we need not stop there,' continued Salim, with great
persuasiveness. 'For you do not only desire men, do you?'

Frank started. How did Salim know this of him?

'You wonder at my knowledge of you, Frank. Is this not so?'

'Yes, my lord. How . . .?'

'I can smell it on you, my boy. I can see it. It oozes from your
every pore. You are not like the others. I could see that from the
start. They respond to their hunger for man's meat, for boy's
flesh. Always they look for a cock and balls to partner their own.
But with you,' he went on wisely, 'there is something else. You
yearn for a male partner, yes, but the lust for a woman also runs
hot in your veins, does it not?'

Frank thought of Molly in the forest glade, and of Norbert's girl, Felice. Both in their different ways had drawn his interest, even aroused him carnally, he could not deny it.

'You seem to see right through me, my lord,' replied Frank. 'Have men no secrets from you?'

'Sometimes, as I have long observed, the most closely guarded secret, the skeleton in the closet that men seek to camouflage and hide away, is the most transparent and apparent part of them. The thing that jumps out – with bones a-rattle and jaws a-chatter – full in the face of any casual onlooker or passer-by.'

The words sank into Frank's ears and he turned them over in his mind, wonderingly. Perhaps this was why a sexual relationship with Rob Oakley still, after all this time, had such a magnetic allure for him. Because Molly was there in the picture, too. It was hard to credit that Salim du Court knew this inner secret of his, when he himself had ignored it up to now. But he had to admit there was truth in du Court's words.

'So, if you lust after a woman, you can see me also in that guise,' went on Salim, seductively.

'In place of my manly square and bearded jaw you see a delicate oval face and pointed chin. Instead of my broad and hairy chest you see two firm ripe breasts. My cock and balls shrink away to a clitoris and labia nestling in my Venus mound. My voice softens and lightens to a luscious contralto, and here I am, the woman you wish me to be. Selina, the sex witch. Your lady and mistress.'

Frank had followed the transformation wide-eyed, as Salim's body underwent the strange metamorphosis to become the gorgeous Selina who stood before him, while the green fire smoke swirled around her.

'Do you desire me thus?' continued Selina, and she gazed at him with her beautiful eyes – one orange, one green. She stroked her full breasts suggestively with one hand, and ran the slender fingers of her other hand up and down her large swollen clitoris, which glistened with lust in a dark pubic thatch dewy with excitement.

Frank's cock sprang up, and it pulsed with animal desire.

'Come to me, Frank,' urged Selina, and she beckoned. 'Come to pleasure your lady and mistress, Selina!'

Without a word, Frank rose from his bed and approached.

'Crouch and lick my clitoris, boy. Worship me there.'

Frank felt unable to disobey, unable to disappoint this powerful and voluptuous woman who stood before him. He leaned forward, ready to kiss and lick her large clitoris lovingly. But then, with a snap of her fingers, Selina's round soft form melted away, and in its place stood Salim, as before, grizzled, mature, but still powerfully seductive.

'Why stop?' Frank blurted out, startled by the sudden rupture of the spell, and the brusque transformation of Selina back into Salim.

'Sex magic, love philtres, seduction by succubus or incubus, all give layers of falsehood and deception to the sex act itself, an act that, according to the philosophy of our order, should be pure and devoid of artifice,' explained Salim. 'In its highest form the sex act should blend body, mind and soul in a mingling of consciousness.'

'I see. So, although we can appear as we are not in our lover's eyes,' chipped in Frank, as he caught on, 'we should never abuse our power and make love by means of illusionist tricks.'

'Precisely. I want you to make love to me as the true Salim, not as the false Selina.'

Frank once again felt his cock stir, but with more intense power and urgency than before. This was his lord and master, Salim du Court, who stood before him in all his naked majesty, and he needed Frank's sexual service. This represented an obligation Frank felt duty-bound but also delighted to honour.

'My lord, let me finish what I was about to do,' he murmured, and he crouched before Salim and took his master's stiff and swollen cock head into his mouth and then deep into his throat. He stroked the huge balls and teased du Court along the delicious road that leads to that earthly paradise – orgasm.

Soon Salim was thrusting his cock hard and fast into Frank's soft, receiving mouth, and rivulets of mingled pre-come and saliva were dripping down Frank's chin.

Finally Salim gave a great growl of pleasure, and his warm seed sprayed Frank's throat again and again as a multiple orgasm racked his whole body. Frank's cock too reared up and spattered its white creamy load on the floor. This was bliss of the highest order.

Later, as Salim and Frank lay together, and caressed each other's nakedness upon the bed, Salim spoke, and what he had to say seemed to justify the time Frank had spent at the castle of Nonpareil. Not only had Frank been destined to go there in order to embark upon the path of sexual awakening and to liberate his true desires. It seemed that he had been sent by providence to learn more about his father, Sir Oliver. And the man with the missing piece of the jigsaw was none other than Salim himself.

'You must know that I yearn for a young apprentice, Frank,' began Salim. 'As I was sexually and magically apprenticed to an older man when I was but a youth, I wish to transmit what I learned from him to another younger man.'

'I am not sure that I am the one, my lord,' began Frank.

'I know that, Frank. Don't think that I don't. Your lust for both men and women marks you out as exceptional. You are a misfit in my order, and in my heart of hearts I doubt that we can keep you here for ever because of it. But I am willing to try you as my apprentice if you are willing to undertake the burden. For the sake of your father.'

'My father?' queried Frank, his face suddenly sharp with interest.

'Yes, your father, Frank,' continued Salim, and he traced his forefinger delicately down Frank's nose and round his mouth.

'But how do you know him?'

'Quite simply because he was my sex mentor when young.'

Frank could hardly believe his ears.

'Your sex mentor?'

'Yes. He taught me all I know about sex magic. Of course, I was too young to understand all that he tried to pass on to me, but then I myself have refined and added various elements to the core of what I learned from him over the years.'

This was it! Now perhaps was Frank's chance to find out about his father and Ursula Oakley. To find out if he and Rob were truly half-brothers as the village gossips at home made out. He tried gently to probe Salim and learn more.

'So you knew my father intimately, then?'

'Indeed. Oliver du Bois and I were bedfellows for many a long month. He was the man who took my anal virginity, you understand. I could deny him nothing. I looked up to him, worshipped him when he came out on a military campaign to the kingdom of Outremer. And he seduced me with his fine looks – much like yours, Fankr – and with his hard cock and his exquisite lovemaking.'

'What proof have I that what you tell me is true and not mere hearsay?' asked Frank.

'You have my solemn word on the matter,' said Salim. 'And that should be enough for you. But there are tangible proofs, too, should you wish to see them, in the form of letters that I still have in my possession, and also in the form of a present which I gave your father that I believe lodges to this day in Woodmere Hall.'

Frank's bollocks tingled as he asked his next question.

'And did you know my mother?'

'No. My time with your father was just before he returned home, and a short while before he went to his marriage bed with the lady Isolde. I never met her.'

Frank licked his lips nervously.

'There are some who say that my mother was not the lady Isolde, and that Ursula Oakley was my dam.'

'Then they lie,' replied Salim. 'As I said before, I received many loving letters from your father, and sent many letters that burned with devotion in return. Your father had no secrets from me and would not lie to me. And he told me that you were Lady Isolde's child. Ursula was your wet nurse, nothing more.'

'But then how do you account for the frequent visits my father made to the woodcutter's cottage some months before my birth if not to tryst with Ursula Oakley and to get her with child?'

'Frank, Frank.' Salim chucked him tenderly under the chin. 'Your father went to the cottage not to plant his cock in Ursula's quim, but to meet with Will Oakley, and to be penetrated by the earthy woodcutter's sturdy tool. Will Oakley was your father's lover, my boy, and out of such a union no child can come. No, you are Lady Ursula's child, take my word for it.'

Frank's heart fairly sang at those words. If he was not Ursula's child, then he was not Rob Oakley's half-brother! And, if he was not Rob's half-brother, then whole new vistas of sexual desires and possibilities opened up before him.

'If you doubt my words, you only have to remember how Will Oakley died.'

'And how was that?' queried Frank. Now perhaps he would truly get to the bottom of those rumours about his father's death.

'Do you not know?' Salim was incredulous. 'It was a feat of great fealty, great love and great devotion on Will Oakley's part. Your father was on a boar hunt, and the beast – a large ferocious male – had been cornered in a thicket. Sir Oliver dismounted from his horse and approached with a spear to finish the savage animal off, but the brute charged out at him, and broke the spear, which entered your father's side, and wounded him fatally. When all who stood present saw what was happening, they were frantic to rescue Sir Oliver, but the boar was cornered and menaced any approach. In the end it was the faithful Will Oakley who rushed forward to drag his dying master – his secret lover – to safety, but the boar chose that moment to rush at him. Sadly it gored him strongly through his jerkin before it thundered off through a gap in the ring of hunters that Will had left, to disappear into the forest.

'So it was that Sir Oliver died in Will Oakley's strong arms. And it happened too that Will Oakley lingered only a short while alive before he followed in his beloved master's footsteps, and trod the lonely darkening path that led down to a silent grave.'

Frank felt the tears course down his cheeks as Salim reached the end of his tale. Du Court's eyes, too, swam with emotion.

'A beautiful and noble end for such a devoted pair of lovers, don't you think?' said Salim.

'Indeed,' breathed Frank sadly, and he thought back to the strange mishmash of reality that Mad Quentin's brain had concocted, the strange half-true things he had blurted out in Woodmere and at Millhaven. Salim's words certainly rang true in his ears, but he wanted to be sure. 'How do you know all this, Salim? You speak as if you were there and had seen all.'

'That is because I *was* there,' replied du Court. 'Your mother was away on a lengthy visit to your grandmother's castle some leagues distant at the time, and your father invited me to the castle to join him for some hunting. I jumped at the chance to join him. And I brought with me a gift for him, too: a fine tapestry from the town of Gobelins.'

'A tapestry?' Frank's heart beat faster.

'Yes. Perhaps you have seen it hung on a wall somewhere in Woodmere Hall. It shows Zeus as an eagle carrying off a delectable young Ganymede, with Hera looking on indulgently. Do you remember ever seeing it there somewhere?'

'Indeed, yes,' said Frank. 'It hangs in the great hall at Woodmere. That tapestry fascinated me from an early age, but I never really understood it. Could you explain exactly what it means?'

'Let me explain rather what it meant to me when I was a young man of twenty-seven or so, visiting your father. I saw myself then as young Ganymede, carried off forcibly by your father, who was like a Zeus for me. It was a plea, I suppose, to be accepted still as your father's lover, although he was by then married to the lady Isolde. That was what the smiling Hera meant in the corner of the tapestry. I wanted Zeus's wife to condone her husband's little indiscretion with his cute young cupbearer.'

Frank nodded. It all made perfect sense. He was inclined now to believe all that Salim told him about his father without question.

'So you took the tapestry with you as a gift when you went to visit Woodmere?'

'Yes. Little did I realise that what Sir Oliver had planned as a pleasant few days of boar hunting, falconry and archery would have such a tragic end.'

'It must have come as a terrible shock.'

'It did, let me assure you. Of course I stayed for Sir Oliver's funeral, a hurried affair, but then I left Woodmere – never to return – before Lady Isolde came back. I was not sure, in the circumstances, of the welcome that she would have afforded me.'

'Quite.'

'So, now that you know of my past links with your father, will you accept my offer of being your mentor. Will you be my young apprentice?'

Frank considered for a moment. What du Court had told him put such a new complexion on everything. His sexual attraction for Rob, which until so recently he had dismissed as futile, now welled up in the pulsing chambers of his heart, in the erectile fibres of his cock. His former feelings of distrust towards Salim du Court were now also strangely metamorphosed into sentiments of the deepest trust. Here was a living link with his father, a way that he could take from Salim what Salim had received from Sir Oliver – the mantle of an adept in sexual magic. Perhaps, once he had mastered the different techniques of erotic sorcery, he could use them to ensnare Rob and win his sexual favours. It was an idea that had a strong appeal for him.

'Yes,' replied Frank, 'I will become your apprentice – for the time being at least.'

'Good,' breathed Salim, relieved. 'I could not hope for more. I am pleased with your decision, Frank. I will inform Vincent at once that he must leave Nonpareil and go in quest of a new squire – for from now on you belong to me.'

The next day, Vincent left with fairly good grace to find a new squire to attend to his bed and board. The relationship between Frank and his former knight had cooled to such an extent that this official rupture of the connection between them presented no real hardship to either.

Frank, for his part, was glad to be rid of a relationship that had proved sterile, seemed to go nowhere for either party, and had actually become harmful and destructive for both. The new role he had as Salim's apprentice was something he welcomed with both arms wide open. Who could tell how long it would last? Mutability was the name of the game, as far as he was concerned. Grab hold of opportunity by the forelock and make him your servant while you can, else he might not present himself to you again. This was Frank's motto during these days. Salim himself was under no illusions.

'Frank,' he said, as they stood on the battlements of Nonpareil and watched Norbert ferry Vincent off to the mainland, 'why do I offer you this apprenticeship when by your very nature I see that you are destined to leave me sooner or later?'

Frank gazed deep into his mentor's eyes and made no reply, forcing Salim to speak again, and answer his own question.

'How like your father you are. Strong and silent. I think that must be the hold you have on me, the root of the destiny that I feel I must fulfil with you. Because of the way your father took me to him and inspired me to cleave to him and his memory, I must take you to me in the same way.'

He bent his head down and kissed Frank tenderly on the lips. The warm breeze winnowed their hair like a third, invisible lover who blessed their union.

That night Salim took Frank to his bedroom, which Frank had not seen before. It had two superb gold-framed mirrors along the walls to left and right of the bed. They bounced their reflections off each other, and showed the bed again and again, smaller and smaller each time, as it receded into infinity.

Salim's bed certainly proved an impressive object. It took the form of a black swan, with a silver brocade canopy hung above it. Salim threw back the sheets and Frank cast off his clothes and slipped into the bed, and Salim removed his cock girdle.

Salim cast off his brocade robe and slipped into bed naked beside him. The two men – older and younger – at once began to kiss hungrily. It was a joy for Frank to have this older, powerful man worship him for his youth and beauty. He felt Salim's experienced hands caress every inch of his body with masterful assurance, like a carpenter that strokes a prized mahogany carving.

Soon Frank lay face up on the bed, his legs in the air, and Salim gently licked at his arse, then tenderly probed it with a moistened finger. After a while Frank felt his mentor's superb cock head slide into place within the tight channel between his rounded buttocks and below his scrotum. Frank gave himself up to the pleasures of sex, and Salim thrust away firmly inside him. But, after only a short while, the door to the bedchamber opened, and Zarek, Salim's slave boy, entered the room. Salim seemed entirely unabashed at this interruption. He merely paused for a moment in his penetration of Frank's arse, while Zarek slipped out of his clothes and hopped on to the bed behind Salim.

Frank watched in the bedside mirrors with fascination as Zarek thrust his cock deep into Salim's arse. He felt Salim's cock rear and swell into an even bigger, harder erection within his own back passage.

'Ah, yes, my faithful Zarek, that feels so good,' groaned Salim. 'To have your fine cock buried deep within me and to feel mine planted in my young apprentice here, this is bliss indeed. I am female and male. The furrow and the plough. The legendary alchemical hermaphrodite. Now, my fine Polish stallion, ride me hard until your manly mercury flows within my bowels.'

Zarek needed little encouragement. He fucked Salim's arse fiercely, and Salim fucked Frank's arse in turn, until the three of them orgasmed in quick succession.

Zarek threw his head back and crowed with erotic triumph, Salim groaned with supreme sexual joy and Frank's cock erupted with a flood of sperm which, because of his upended posture, spurted down deliciously into his own mouth. He drank it down eagerly, curious for every new experience that might come to him now he was Salim's young apprentice.

After they finished, Frank, Salim and Zarek lay side by side together in the same bed. Salim occupied the centre and Frank and Zarek flanked him on either side. They suckled on his erect nipples and caressed his spunk-heavy bollocks for a while as the afterglow of coitus gradually melted away. Then – their bodies intertwined tenderly – the three of them drifted off exhausted into sleep.

That night Frank dreamed of Rob. It was the first dream of his boyhood love that he had experienced for ages, and it was almost as if, now that he knew Rob was no blood relative of his, his inner self was urging him to go home and to try his luck in seducing Rob to be his lover.

Deep in the thrall of sleep, Frank's mind flitted up through the ceiling of Salim's bedchamber and out of the roof of the castle of Nonpareil. He glided high over the lake, above Norbert and Felice's little lakeside cottage, retracing the way he had come with Vincent what seemed like so long ago.

In spirit Frank passed the waterfall, the hollow tree where he and Vincent had slept once in the forest of Sombredell, Millhaven, where he had seen the village lads caper naked in the stream. Finally he was back in his own village, and his dreaming self floated in through the window of the woodcutter's cottage. There before him, on a truckle bed, lay Rob, just as Frank remembered him, blissfully naked, his muscular body sprawled on one side. Depending on which way he looked at his friend, Frank could gaze admiringly at his fine well-muscled chest or his broad back, at his muscular rump or his large cock, stiff and throbbing with excitement.

Probably dreaming of fucking Molly, thought Frank.

Rob's eyes were closed, but his eyelids flickered and there was a smile on his face.

Frank leaned close over him, and with a misty finger he drew up one of Rob's lids and peered inside his dark, dilated pupil.

There in the jellied depths of his friend's eye, he could see the dream Rob was having. He lay on his back in a forest glade. The blue sky hung overhead. Molly, naked, sat astride his hips, with her thighs pressed close against his flanks. Rob's cock thrust deep in her cunt, and her breasts bobbed up and down as the woodcutter's boy fucked up into her.

Frank let Rob's eyelid fall. With a translucent hand he grasped hold of his friend's cock and began to wank him, tenderly, lovingly. Surely there was no harm in this, he reasoned. While his friend dreamed of fucking Molly, Frank would ease his sexual hunger and bring Rob's cock to ejaculation.

Rob now rolled on to his back, and the dream form of Frank took advantage of this, and assumed Molly's posture, straddling the young woodcutter's thighs.

Frank's guided Rob's cock into his astral arse. It so satisfied him after all those years of yearning to feel Rob's hard pole of man flesh slip deep into his spirit self. He and his love were now joined together. He rose and fell, like a jockey in the saddle, and Rob fucked up into his arse and dreamed he was piercing Molly's cunt.

Finally Rob's cock spat out a stream of hot semen, at which point Frank realised with dismay that his flimsy dream bowels could not contain the warm wetness of his friend's seed. It spattered down in milky gobbets on to Rob's firm abdomen, and, with a start, Rob's eyes flicked open and he stared up into the smoky simulacrum of his friend's face.

'Frank?' he cried out into the night.

And although Frank wanted to reply, the words stuck in his throat, and at once he felt a yank at his belly. An invisible umbilical cord drew him swiftly up and out of the cottage window, and he hurtled high through the night sky at breakneck speed, and landed with a jolt back in Salim's bed at the castle of Nonpareil.

Salim lay asleep next to him and Zarek snored on the other side of the bed. Frank looked at the receding mirror images of himself as he sat up wide-eyed in bed. He pondered the real meaning of the dream. After he had turned it all over in his mind again and again – Salim's stories of the boar hunt, his gift of the Ganymede tapestry, the dream in which he had sent his own spirit body to visit Rob – Frank decided that he could never be truly happy in the illusory Order of the Tree of Life. Despite Salim's kindness to him, and the honour of apprenticeship that the master had so recently bestowed upon him, Frank decided that he had to leave Nonpareil soon, and that he would return home to seek his erotic destiny with Rob before the next full moon.

But, before he left, he knew he would have to glean all he could from Salim du Court about the art and techniques of sexual magic, and also about what his father, Sir Oliver du Bois, had been like in his youth.

Eleven

Over the next few weeks Frank learned as much as he could of what Salim could teach him. He learned how to achieve an immediate and powerfully throbbing erection and even a copious ejaculation through the power of thought alone. He learned about 'coitus reservatus', or the retaining and reabsorbing of his ejaculation by the recitation of calming spells. He learned how to rhythmically flex his anal muscles so that, by a process of inverse peristalsis, he could actually sup up liquids – water, ass's milk, sperm – through his gulping anus. He learned also how to use abdominal muscles to reverse the flow of semen from his cock so that his cock mouth could actually drink up sperm instead of spewing it forth.

He learned about the antiseptic powers of urine and the nourishing powers of sperm when used as a skin cream. He learned how to conjure with his voice and about a sex magus's ability to transform his outward appearance by appealing to the desires of the beloved sex-partner.

He learned about the stimulation of the perineal gland, the different sizes of cocks and arses, and the most sublime combination of the one in the other. He learned about all the different sexual positions known to male lovers, the advantages and disadvantages of each, and variations that one could introduce to ring the sexual changes.

During this time, Frank was like a sponge. He soaked up all the sexual knowledge that Salim chose to cast his way. Salim for his part was like a bubbling, generous fountain, so pleased to have found a young apprentice to whom he could impart titbits of erotic lore, that he constantly gushed and spouted new facts that Frank drank in with an insatiable thirst for enlightenment.

Frank continued to wear his cock girdle, but now Salim held the key. Vincent still had not returned from his quest for a new squire, and Frank wondered idly when he would, and what his replacement would be like. Frank had felt that the cock girdle trapped him and coerced him into fidelity when he was with Vincent, but now as Salim gave him a freer rein to come and go as he pleased, and to associate with whomsoever he wished in the castle, Frank hardly noticed the bodily restrictions placed on him.

Frank learned too during this time about the power of herbs to excite love and even extreme sexual licence when mixed up in love philtres. But Salim charged him never to use these herbal stimulants for his own benefit and never to administer herbal concoctions in order to dupe any of his sexual partners.

Frank also learned about the relaxing quality of some of the herbal scents and aromas when a sexual magus cast herbal powders into the fire, or massaged herbal oils into the skin. Salim permitted and even encouraged Frank to perfect both these techniques of enhancing sensuality through herbal magic.

Some months later, when Frank's head felt stuffed full of sexual learning, he was wandering down on the beach one day, when he met Norbert.

'Master Frank!' breathed the young ferry lad, his eyes bright with pleasure at seeing the object of his male desire after so long.

'Norbert!' cried Frank, and the two fairly flew into each other's arms. Frank planted a long passionate kiss on the boy's lips.

'I waited for you to escape with me, Frank, but you never came,' said Norbert at last, reproachfully.

'Yes, I know. I'm sorry. I couldn't come to you that night as we planned because of my induction into the order.'

'But then the months went by, Frank, and I thought you'd forgotten me.'

'Forgotten you? Oh, no, Norbert.' Frank grinned, and he tweaked the young lad's throbbing cock through the crotch of his woollen leggings. 'I could never forget you. But I was stuck with Vincent – a jealous knight who hardly ever let me out of his sight. Because of his possessiveness, I couldn't come to you these past months.'

Frank stretched the truth a little in what he said in order to save face. He didn't want to admit to Norbert how Vincent had initially charmed him. Nor did he wish to describe his other sexual conquests – or sexual conquerors – in the castle, who had delayed his intent to escape, and made his purpose to return home waver.

Norbert looked at him with a puzzled expression on his face. 'And now how come you can get away?'

'Now I have a new master – Salim du Court – who is not jealous and who lets me do as I please, and doesn't ask questions afterwards. This is why I can come down to the beach now.'

'I see. So now you are the squire of the master of Nonpareil.'

'His apprentice, actually.'

'I suppose that means you have given up all idea of escape from the island, then.'

'No, Norbert, far from it: I feel even keener now to escape than before. I feel my home call to me more strongly now, and I cannot delay my return there overmuch. In these days my studies here will be finished, and in the next few days, when the full moon shows her face in the sky, I will signal to you from my window, and you can come and ferry me over the lake to freedom. If you still agree to help me, that is.'

'Of course, my lord. I will tell Felice, too. She will be so pleased.'

Frank's cock bounded in its cock cage at the thought of slender, boyish Felice and Norbert making love in their shack, as he had first seen them.

But the next day Vincent returned, and he brought with him

his new-found page, and Frank was constrained to delay his departure a little longer.

When Frank saw Vincent arrive with his new attendant in the great hall of Nonpareil he was flabbergasted. For Vincent's page was none other than Hal Ashe, Frank's graceful and slender former valet.

Frank found an opportunity to get Hal on his own when the lad went to get Vincent a flagon of beer from the cellars.

'Hal, what a surprise!' he murmured in friendly fashion, as he got a flagon of foam-topped beer from the neighbouring cask for Salim.

'Oh, Master Frank, I hoped I'd find you here.'

Frank heard the note of tension in the young man's voice, and saw the drawn look of worry on his face.

'What is it, Hal? What's the matter? How do you come to be here and not back at home, ministering to my brother Philippe's every whimsical need?'

'Don't speak to me of him, my lord.'

'Why not?'

'He's behaved terribly, scandalously even, ever since the lady Yolanda died.'

'My grandmother is dead?' asked Frank in a hollow voice. He felt a sickening blow to the pit of his stomach at the shock of the news, but afterwards no really deep emotion welled up within him.

'Yes. She's been dead these four months now. Did you not know?'

'No. No one saw fit to tell me.'

'Philippe probably wanted to keep the news for himself.'

Frank's mind raced. If his grandmother was dead, Philippe had now inherited Woodmere Hall, and the chest of his grandmother's treasures along with the rest. With Frank away at Nonpareil, Philippe was now undisputed lord and master of all the du Bois estates. The possibilities for him to abuse his new-found power and position were enormous. No wonder he had been reluctant to write and inform Frank about the new state of affairs back at home.

'Is that why you left? Were things too unbearable at home?'

Hal drew himself proudly up to his full height and spoke through clenched teeth.

'I left, my lord, because your brother was out to kill me. He learned that I had overheard something I should not. He has surrounded himself with cronies and stooges, "yes men" who will never gainsay or check his vilest proposition. So he runs riot, and squanders the du Bois riches on debauched parties, on worthless gewgaws, and on flatteringly tailored fine suits to bedeck himself in. I was so sick of his ways that I made the mistake of hinting at what I knew, and he decided that I had to die for that.'

'I see.' Frank swallowed nervously.

'Sir Vincent came riding up to the castle on the very day I ran from it. I fairly jumped at the chance to come here to Nonpareil, and to become his squire, when he offered it, and so here I am.'

'And what of Rob Oakley, the woodcutter's son, Hal?'

He imagined Philippe would take great pleasure in cruelly teasing and torturing Rob for the simple fact that he had been one of Frank's closest friends and associates.

'Ah, my lord. Things bode ill for him. Philippe threatens to take his young bride-to-be, Molly, to his bed. Rob sends you this token, by the way, and asks to be remembered to you.'

Hal took something out of the leather pouch on his belt and pressed it into Frank's open palm. Frank looked down at it. There sat the horn ring he had given to Rob all those months ago, when the young woodcutter came to bid him farewell on the road to Nonpareil.

Frank remembered his own words: '. . . if you ever need my help, send the ring, and I will return to Woodmere immediately.'

'He needs your help, Master Frank,' said Hal.

'And he shall have it, Hal. He shall have it. But what is it you know about Philippe that nearly cost you your life?'

Hal was about to reply when Vincent appeared.

'Hal, I think you have talked more than enough. It is not fitting for you to stray so far from my side for so long,' he commanded.

Hal obediently bowed his head in silence and trotted away after

168

Vincent, and Frank was left to gaze at the horn ring in his hand, and to ponder on all that he had learned.

His resolution to leave with the waxing moon that very night was strengthened. Whatever secret it was that Hal had tried to use against him, it was clear that the evil in Philippe was growing stronger and had to be nipped in the bud before it flourished and grew to fruition. There was no turning back now.

That night, while Salim met Vincent and the other knights of the order to discuss the welcoming of Hal Ashe to Nonpareil as Vincent's new squire, Frank placed a lighted candelabra in the window of his room, took his silver locket from its hiding place in the box by his bed, fastened it around his neck and then made his way down to the shingled shore. He carried with him a small bundle of his belongings, and a 'dark' lantern, with a tallow candle inside and outer metal casings that could open or close to reveal or conceal the light that flowed from it.

Once down on the beach, Frank began to signal with the lantern. He opened and closed the shutters on it at intervals. This and the candelabra in his window were the signs he and Norbert had agreed to show that he was ready to leave.

After only a short while Frank spotted Norbert's ferryboat as it drew close to shore. Not long after that there was a crunch as the prow of the boat touched the pebbly beach.

Frank hurried over, pushed the boat back out into the water, and hopped in. Norbert greeted him with a lingering kiss and then they sat side by side, placed the oars in the rowlocks, and rowed for the freedom of the mainland shore.

When they arrived at Norbert's cottage, Felice was there to greet them.

'Your horse is saddled and ready, Frank,' she said.

'Thank you, thank you, both,' said Frank, warmly, and he swept both Norbert and Felice into a tight embrace.

'Will you stay awhile and have supper with us before you go on your way?' asked Norbert, his eyes shining.

'No, I cannot,' replied Frank. 'Who knows when Salim will discover that I am missing? I want to be well on my way by then.

But listen, I must pay you – or give you something at least – for your help.'

'The payment that we exact from you, Frank du Bois, is that you stay and sup with us,' said Felice playfully. 'Lord du Court will not notice you are gone until midday tomorrow.'

Frank had to admit that this was true. The meetings of the order usually lasted for several hours, after which Salim would go to bed. Not finding Frank there, he would expect him to be asleep in another room in the castle. When he rose later, after breakfast was over, he would miss Frank only when he failed to turn up to serve at the luncheon table.

'Very well, I *will* stay and eat with you,' said Frank. 'But I must be on my way again before morning light.'

Felice served up a simple light supper of curd cheese, home-baked bread, home-cured hams and home-grown salad stuff and fruit. It was plain fare, but Frank had eaten no other supper that night, and to him it tasted utterly delicious.

After supper, Norbert and Felice went with Frank to the stable to saddle up the horse and to see him off, but there, as Felice and then Norbert kissed Frank goodbye full upon the lips, the passions of all three became enflamed.

First Felice slipped out of her simple homespun dress to reveal her lithe and sensual body, which lurked completely naked underneath. Frank and Norbert began to kiss her all over. They suckled at her nipples, inserted their fingers into her pussy and her arse, and caressed her clitoris.

She lay back on a bed of hay, and now Frank and Norbert cast off their clothes so that Norbert stood nut-brown and bare, and Frank stood clad only in his metal cock girdle. Unfortunately he had not had the chance to remove this before leaving the castle.

Frank was amazed by the beauty of Norbert's and Felice's naked bodies. He was so smooth and sinuous, she so wiry and sensual. As they lay together on the hay before him, they kissed and thrust their fluttering tongues in and out of each other's mouth. Frank felt compelled to join them. He knelt at their feet, reached forward with one hand to caress Norbert's stiff and throbbing cockhorn, and wanked it with slow strokes so that the pre-come began to ooze copiously from its smooth tip. With his other hand Frank began to caress Felice's dewy love cleft. He teased its convoluted folds gently with his fingertips, so that Felice's soft pussy lips dribbled with glistening love juice. And slowly the two young lovers writhed and moaned. Encouraged by Frank's skilful massaging hands, they kissed each other fiercely, hungrily. Norbert reached out his hand to cup Felice's breasts and to tweak her nipples playfully. Felice ran her nails down Norbert's back, and scored his skin lightly with superficial white scratches, to intensify his pleasure.

Now Frank not only caressed Norbert's cock with his hand, but bent forward to lick at it and to suck at its fleshy cap. Norbert moaned under the sweet assault and the lubricating juices flowed out freely into Frank's hungry mouth. Frank continued to wank the length of Norbert's sticky organ from tip to root. Now he turned his mouth towards Felice, and nuzzled his face into her sweet-smelling pubic mound. Here his tongue ran with soft, feathery strokes up and down her moist cunt lips, and now he suckled on her large and stiff clitoris.

With Frank's expert help, Norbert and Felice experienced a level of sexual arousal neither had known before, and they loved it.

In a shift of roles and positions, Frank and Felice kissed and licked Norbert's body all over. They took it in turns to pinch his nipples, suck his throbbing cock tip, and insert their probing tongues between his buttocks.

When all three were excited by such antics beyond measure and beyond containment, Frank urged Felice to stand up, her torso angled forward, her legs astride, her arms outstretched, her hands clutching either side of the straw-filled manger, her rump provocatively tilted upwards. Now Norbert stood behind her, his legs astride, his stiff cock pulsingly full of blood, as it throbbed up against Felice's buttocks. He reached round to caress Felice's breasts eagerly.

Now Frank knelt under the aroused couple and looked up hungrily, first at Felice's dripping cunt cleft, and then at Norbert's swollen balls and love-engorged prick. He lapped alternately at

Felice's gaping hole and Norbert's hard rod. Then, at last, he brought the two together with his urging hands. How blissful the moment was when Norbert's flanged cock head bit into Felice's love cave and his urgent thrusting began. Slowly but surely, Norbert's cockpole slipped inch by inch into Felice's lust-swollen vagina, and all the time Frank arched his neck up and licked at the sticky root of Norbert's organ as it disappeared again and again into Felice's tight but welcoming womb tunnel. He caressed Norbert's dangling bollocks with his fingers and ran his tongue again and again over the taut V of pussy skin that was stretched to the limit every time Norbert's cock thrust into it.

It was unfortunately out of the question for Frank to penetrate Norbert with his own cock. The hard steel shell of his cock girdle prevented that.

Then, in a moment of inspiration, Frank reached for the pouch that normally hung at his side. It lay now discarded on the floor at his feet. Out of this bag he took the carved acorn wand that Rob Oakley had made for him all those months before. He felt sure Rob would approve of his using the gift to make payment in full to Norbert for his help in organising his escape. He moistened the tip of the rod with his saliva, and slipped it slowly but surely deep into place in Norbert's arse.

The ferry boy groaned with pleasure as Frank moved the rod around within him, plunging and rotating it. Norbert redoubled his fucking of Felice and she redoubled her moans of delight under him.

Suddenly Frank noticed Norbert begin to tense up and slow a little in his thrusting. He knew in his heart that the lad was about to shoot his creamy spunkload up deeply and forcefully into Felice's pulsing vagina, and he couldn't bear the beauty of the moment, couldn't bear not to be a part of this sacred communion of sperm. Felice would feel the rush of Norbert's liquid seed as it entered her many times in the future, he reasoned, but he, Frank, would be gone and on his way home on the morrow. Felice couldn't deny him this one pleasure, this one favour, he felt sure.

As he tugged gently backwards on Norbert's scrotal sac, Frank encouraged the young lad to withdraw his glistening tool fully out of Felice's cunt throat, and to leave her pussy lips puckering forcefully with rhythmic contractions. Now Frank's lips rounded into an O and he took Norbert's warm and sticky rod of man flesh deep into his mouth gratefully. It smelled delightfully of Felice's cunt juices – an unexpected pleasure. At the same time Frank thrust three fingers into Felice's cunt mouth and began working them around.

No sooner had he done so than Norbert trembled and growled and again and again, in urgent rush after urgent rush, he filled Frank's mouth with precious bollockload after bollockload of hot, salty man's milk, which trickled teasingly down his throat.

'Oh, my lord Frank, I so wanted you to have that,' murmured Norbert. 'My Felice here can drink my seed, and I can bathe her womb or her bowels in it whenever she chooses. But you, my lord. Once you have left us tonight, will we ever see you again? At least this way you will go with the taste of both of us on your tongue.'

Frank drank their mingled love juices down greedily, and he worked his fingers round tantalisingly within Felice's lust-clenched pussy, so that she orgasmed powerfully in counterpoint to the pulsing and spewing cock of her lover, whose orgasms slaked Frank's thirst for fresh-spilled man seed.

Afterwards they separated and Frank thanked Felice and Norbert both for their kindness and for sharing this exquisite last moment of their intimacy with him.

Then, their farewells said, Frank threw his clothes on, picked up his things, saddled his horse, and was about to jump on it, when Felice thrust a soft parcel of cloth into his hands.

'Take this. Only open and use this in an emergency,' she said.

'An emergency?' queried Frank.

'Yes, if Lord du Court is hot on your heels, and you are in danger of his catching you, then open it, and it will help you on your way in your hour of need.'

Tucking the bundle into his saddlebag, Frank gave a cheery wave to Norbert and Felice and rode out of the stable and off into the night.

Twelve

Frank rode through the night, and stopped for nothing. At the first light of dawn, he found himself by the hollow tree in the forest of Sombredell, where he and Vincent had sheltered on their way to Nonpareil.

As Cinnabar, his horse, was quite ridden out and could clearly go no further that day, Frank removed the bridle, saddle, stirrups and saddlebags and, with a smack on the rump, sent him off across a muddy banked stream to caper among a field of wild colts that they had passed in a valley which bordered the forest. Soon all the horses – Cinnabar included – stampeded away and off across the grassy valley, and left Frank alone with his thoughts in the early-morning silence.

He grabbed the saddle, the bridle and the other things and hulked them into the hollow tree. There he stripped to the buff. After that he hared off to the nearby waterfall pool. He intended to indulge in an early-morning swim, before retiring to the tree to sleep a little, and to renew his energies for the onward journey.

It was while he was in the water, however, that he saw the posse of horsemen go riding by. He sank down into the frothy spume by the waterfall's edge until only his eyes and the top of his head peeped out, breaking the surface of the water, and he watched.

As the line of horsemen drew nearer, he saw that it was a search party from Nonpareil, and they were obviously looking for him. At the head rode Salim, and behind him Dagobert, Gerard, Chance and Jourdain. Frank was pleased to see that Vincent, Hal, Gaston and Zarek were not members of the group.

He had a momentary pang of anxiety as the group neared the hollow tree and slowed their pace, but they then rode by it. Vincent had obviously not told them of his usual stopping place.

At this point, Jourdain, who brought up the rear of the line, noticed horse's hoof prints where Frank's horse had but a short while before forded the muddy stream to join the herd of wild horses. Jourdain called out the news of his discovery and the line of knights and squires from Nonpareil turned about and rode to the stream. After a hasty conference, and much examining of mud at the water's edge, the posse forded the stream and galloped off, away down the valley, in pursuit of Frank's liberated steed.

When they had gone, Frank slipped out of the pool and ran to the hollow tree. Now, if ever, he knew it was time for him to open the mysterious bundle from Felice, and to see what it contained. He couldn't for the life of him figure it out, and could scarcely see what exactly *could* save him in his present situation, but it was certainly worth a try. Anything rather than fall prey to the search party and be taken back to Nonpareil in shame.

When he opened the bundle, however, all became clear. It contained a peasant woman's outfit: a full dress, a shawl, a wimple to cover his head, thick woollen stockings for his legs, and a countrywoman's clogs.

He swiftly donned this disguise, rolled his own clothes up in a bundle, which he slung over his back, and began to trudge off along the road that led through the forest of Sombredell to Millhaven.

About midday, he heard the sound of a wagon that was bowling along the cart track behind him.

He looked back as the vehicle drew near and – to his great surprise and pleasure – he saw that the drivers were none other than Dickon Pine and Martin Sycamore, two of the village lads from Millhaven whom he'd seen capering and fucking in the river all those months ago on his journey to Nonpareil.

'Where are you going, then, missus?' Dickon called down to the disguised Frank.

'To Millhaven first, and then on to the du Bois lands,' replied Frank. He pitched his voice up a little and lisped to disguise it.

'Jump up in the back, then, good dame, and let us take you there. For we're bound for Millhaven also.'

Frank did as he was bid.

As they spun along the road to Millhaven, Salim's posse of horsemen rode up fast behind the cart, and when they were parallel, Salim motioned Dickon and Martin to pull over. The Millhaven lads, who saw and respected the evident rank of their interloper, dutifully reined in their horses to a walk and pulled over on to a grass verge. There the horses cropped the herbage while Dickon and Martin sat on the driving box and waited for Salim to address them.

Frank sat hunched up and pretended to doze in the back of the cart, but he shrewdly observed all that passed between Salim and the lads from under half-closed eyelids. He used an adapted form of magical image projection to emanate the aura of an old countrywoman.

'Good day, good lads,' called Salim as he rode up beside the cart.

'Good day, good sir,' replied Dickon.

'Where are you bound, my good fellows?'

'To Millhaven, sir. To the market there.'

'I look for an escaped fugitive. A young man who has fled from my castle. A rich reward awaits the man who returns him to me. You haven't seen such a man in your journey?'

'Indeed not, sir.'

Frank silently thanked Felice for her foresight in providing him with a female disguise. But he feared that he could still be exposed if Salim questioned Dickon and Martin about the old woman in the back of their cart.

'And who do you have in the back that travels with you?' asked Salim, making Frank's worst fears come true. The young

176

lad's blood ran cold and a deathly hush within him made Salim's words reverberate prominently in his skull. 'Your old aunt or grandmother, is it?'

'Old auntie, sir . . .?' began Dickon, a perplexed note creeping into his voice, but at that moment there was a halloo from the field.

'Come quickly, Lord Salim,' came Gerard's voice. 'We found the horse young Frank used for his escape, and it led us to a hollow tree back by the lake where the saddle and bridle are stowed. He can't be far from there.'

Salim turned back to Dickon and Martin.

'Well, I thank you, young men,' he said. 'And salutations to your old aunt, too.'

And the next minute Salim and his entourage had cantered off back up the road to search near the hollow tree. Frank breathed easy, the blood pounding heavily in his veins, but he felt safe once more.

That night Dickon and Martin stopped off at an inn, and, as the innkeeper there had only one free sleeping chamber left, Frank had to room with the two lads.

When the two boys stripped naked to sleep in the same bed together, Frank kept his woman's disguise on, and sat hunched in the rocking chair.

The lads began to tease him.

'Afraid we might get at you in the night, are you, dearie?' goaded Martin.

'Don't you want the cocks of two of Millhaven's best to plug you fore and aft, auntie?' chimed in Dickon.

They came over to where Frank sat and began to pluck at his woman's clothing.

Suddenly, in the midst of this playful assault, Frank's wimple came off in Dickon's hand and the lads saw him at once for what he was – a young man in disguise.

'Interesting,' said Martin as he studied Frank with new eyes. 'Do you dress up like this for your own pleasure, or to excite the young men you meet and make love with?'

'Or are you perhaps,' enquired Dickon, 'the fugitive on the run from that lord we passed on the road?'

Frank saw that the game was up. It made no sense for him to try to dissemble any more, and so he made a clean breast of it. He told them plainly that he was Frank du Bois, and recounted how he'd gone to join Salim's sexual-mystic order, explaining in brief how he had eventually become disillusioned with its repressive strictures and had decided to escape.

'And what proof have we that you are telling the truth this time, and that you really are Frank du Bois?' asked Dickon.

'This,' replied Frank. And he took out the silver locket from around his neck and opened it. 'This is my father,' he said, showing them the miniature portrait. 'Lord Oliver du Bois.'

'Indeed, it is. And I recognise the du Bois crest on the locket, too,' replied Martin.

'I'm still not satisfied,' continued Dickon. 'Granted, you are Frank du Bois, but what proof do we have that you are really trying to escape from Lord du Court's repression? You could just be a renegade lordling who has abused a great hospitality!'

'This is my proof,' replied Frank, and he slipped out of his peasant woman's dress and woollen stockings, and stood there before them, naked, except for the steel cock girdle that bore Salim's crest. This was the metal cage that kept him from sexual unfaithfulness to Salim, unless by his master's will his key should unlock it.

'This is how Salim du Court enforces chastity in his order.'

'Inhuman!' gasped Dickon.

'How ghastly!' added Martin.

Their sympathy was obviously with Frank now. He breathed a sigh of relief.

'Frank, we'll have to take you to the blacksmith in Millhaven when we get there,' continued Dickon. 'He'll soon strike that off for you.'

'And in the meantime . . .' began Martin.

'. . . no penetrative sex,' finished Frank for him.

'That wasn't what I meant to say,' chuckled Martin teasingly. 'Let's show him, shall we, Dickon?'

'Yes,' agreed Dickon.

Dickon lay face down on the bed, and Martin took a pot of sweet-smelling unguent from his haversack. He opened it and smeared some on his index fingertip. Then he began to anoint the inner cheeks and tight rosette of Dickon's arse with it.

'Of course, ordinary penetrative sex would be out of the question for you at the moment,' said Martin as he moved his finger around in the cleft between Dickon's buttocks. 'But Dickon and I practise other kinds of penetration.'

'Yes,' chimed in Dickon, and he gasped as Martin's deft first and second fingers now worked away and gently pierced his anus. 'We've been fuckmates for some years now. At first we got a lot of pleasure by stuffing our cocks up each other's arse.'

'But after a time we got bored with that. It was always the same, always too tame,' went on Martin. He slipped a third probing finger now into Dickon's arse along with the other two. 'We wanted to capture that same feeling of someone taking us up the arse for the first time. That unbelievable tightness. That sensation of a hard manpole stretching the arse mouth to the limit.'

Frank watched, fascinated, as – greased with the unguent – Martin slipped his fourth finger into Dickon's arse.

'We began to experiment with other objects – candles, poles and each other's fingers and fists,' gasped Dickon, as Martin wriggled a thumb into place alongside the four fingers already buried inside his fuckmate's anus.

With Martin's hand now firmly lodged in his arse up to the wrist, Dickon hauled himself up on to hands and knees on the bed, his arse tilted provocatively in the air. Frank's cock stiffened as he watched the two lovers, obviously so closely attuned to each other's body, make love in this way, which was so strange to him, but obviously so familiar to them.

Martin now plunged his bunched fist slowly in and out of Dickon's arse, which gaped now, totally relaxed. Sweat beaded Dickon's brow and he groaned with the intense pleasure of the experience as Martin sank his fist into him up to the forearm, and gave a little twist at the end of each inthrust to heighten the pleasure. Frank could see a silver thread of pre-come drip from both Dickon's circumcised cockhead and from Martin's foreskin-sheathed cock as they went on with their powerful, slow-motion fist fucking. They both clearly revelled in every movement and every moment of the experience.

Frank wanted to become a part of their sexual joining. But how? Suddenly an apt idea jumped into his head. He plucked a riding crop out of his bundle of clothes, and began to beat Martin's rump and Dickon's flanks repeatedly with feathery strokes of it. His rapid, teasing whipping overlaid a high melodic line on top of the regularly rhythmic bass notes of Dickon's and Martin's groans and moans of pleasure, and the delicious squelches as hard fist and forearm pierced soft and succulent arse tissues with a sweet insistent susurration.

After only a short time, Martin's cock tensed and erupted in a flurry of silvery sperm. Frank just had time to latch his mouth to Martin's cock head. Hurriedly he gulped down the fresh-jetting seed like nourishing marrowbone jelly. Then Dickon's cock tensed and reared, and Frank eagerly transferred his lips to its pulsing tip. Now he drained Dickon of copious draughts of deliciously warm and salty new-ejaculated man's milk. At the same time Frank felt his own cock rise up, and in an instant it pumped out hot ejaculate through the steel mesh at the front of his cock girdle.

Frank felt privileged to join Dickon and Martin in their fist-fucking antics. And now they considered him as a friend. A fuckmate. Accordingly, after their lustful thoughts had subsided, he wrapped the woman's apparel he had worn as disguise into a bundle and unpacked his own clothes and drew them on instead. Dickon, Martin and Frank then went down to dine in one of the inn's private dining rooms.

The innkeeper's young son, Yves, attended them at the meal. He was a fine, gangling, dark-eyed young lad with hair cut short apart from a single, long, straight lock that fell down, cutely, over one eye. And Yves waited on them most attentively. After they had consumed a fine roast boar's head, together with roast carrots and parsnips, the three diners called for more wine, and they asked Yves to clear the table and then to join them in a game of cards.

They played a game with a tarot pack whereby, for each hand lost, the losing player had to remove an article of clothing. Frank suspected Dickon and Martin of some sharp roguery with the dealing of the cards for – strangely – they managed to remain fully clothed, while Frank and Yves gradually lost all the things they were wearing to the pile on the table.

Soon Yves wore nothing but his pair of coarse leggings, and Frank was naked except for his steel cock girdle.

Yves eyed it curiously when he first caught a glimpse of it.

'Is that a gift from your lady, to keep you faithful to her?' he asked uncertainly.

Dickon and Martin exchanged knowing glances.

'More or less,' said Frank matter-of-factly. He felt himself strangely drawn to this awkward, ungainly youth before him, and gazed with fascination at the lad's large nose and the proportionately large swollen packet of cock and balls that filled out the fore of his breeches. They said that a man's nose size correlated to his cock size, didn't they? Frank didn't have to wait long before Yves's last scrap of modesty was lost to the game. The young lad's leggings came off, and his long, slender cock and huge pendulous balls were exposed in all their glory.

'What a fine lad you are, Yves,' said Frank with admiration.

'And such a cock on you, too, my boy,' added Martin.

'Like a young stallion or a bullock,' chimed in Dickon.

Yves blushed to the roots of his hair, but he seemed also strangely to revel in this admiration.

'Would you like to have me, sir?' Yves asked Frank with innocent candour.

'Indeed, I would,' replied Frank, 'But, you see . . .' Here he gestured wordlessly to the hampering cock girdle.

'That doesn't matter sir,' replied Yves eagerly, indicating Dickon and Martin. 'These two fine gentlemen have been to this inn many a time and have taught me a bunch of fine tricks to use in bed if need be.' He raised his fist in the air and stroked it with his other hand suggestively.

'Yves, what a good idea. I think we'd like to watch you and Frank in action,' said Dickon.

'Yes, but not in the bed. That would be too boring. Right here, on the table,' added Martin.

'As you wish,' replied Yves. He got up on to the table and lay down lengthways on it, his face upward, his legs in the air, and his arse towards Frank, who stood at the head of the table.

Dickon reached into the pouch at his side and took out a pot of salve, which he handed to Frank.

Frank dipped his fingers one by one into the salve and inserted them one by one into Yves's arse, just as he had seen Martin do to Dickon earlier. Soon he could bunch his hand into a fist and he plunged it slowly but firmly in and out of the lad's now relaxed anal sphincter.

'Oh, yes, master. That feels so good. Your fist is like a great hard cock head entering my soft arse again and again. You stretch me to the very limit, sweet sir.'

Dickon and Martin watched appreciatively. They had both drawn their stiff cocks out of their codpieces, and now stood either side of the long table and wanked faster and faster as Frank's forearm disappeared again and again into Yves's arse up to the wrist. Yves, too, now wanked his stiff cock and stroked his spunk-heavy balls to increase his pleasure to the utmost.

Suddenly, with a triumphant cry that issued from his throat, Yves reached a powerful orgasm. His cock shot a great fountain of spunk that spurted high in the air with such incredible strength that droplets of it spattered against the raftered ceiling. Meanwhile, his arse tightened firmly, and his arse muscles grasped Frank's wrist in rhythmic spasms of joy.

Almost at once Dickon's and Martin's pricks shot their creamy load across the table. It landed in a swirl of mingled sperm on Yves's smooth torso. Frank then proceeded to withdraw his fist delicately from Yves's stretched rectum, and he licked the glistening coating of spunk off the lad's chest and flat belly, lapping at the aroused boy's stiff nipples, and at the pool of pearly man seed that had gathered in his navel.

Thirteen

The next day Frank set off early on the cart to Millhaven with Dickon and Martin. They arrived mid-morning outside the smithy, and Frank got down and thanked his travelling companions warmly for their help, their good company, and not least for their timely instruction in the use of fists. At that point the swarthy young blacksmith's apprentice, Jack, came out of the smithy and joined Martin and Dickon. He was taking a mid-morning break from his duties. The three young lads quickly decided to go off for a dip in the River Werry together, and there Frank arranged to meet Martin and Dickon later. They waved goodbye cheerily, and Frank at once entered the blacksmith's shop.

It was dark inside, except for the glow of the forge. The blacksmith stood in front of the fire and went unhurriedly about his work. He seemed oblivious to Frank's presence.

He was a tall stocky lad, bathed in sweat, and he currently held a red-hot horseshoe over the anvil with tongs, and was battering it into shape with a thick hammer. Having finished, he then dunked the horse iron into a wooden pail at his feet and a hiss of steam rose up as the red-hot metal kissed the cold water held therein.

Only then did the blacksmith down his tools and come over

to speak to Frank. He wiped his hands on a grimy rag as he did so.

'Xavier the blacksmith at your service. What can I do for you?' he asked.

'I am Frank du Bois, and I need you to strike this off me,' said Frank, and he dropped his leggings around his knees, to expose his cock girdle. Its sleek steel contours glinted in the orange light from the forge.

Xavier whistled and then tutted. He fingered the cock girdle to test the metal's thickness and the robustness of its construction.

'Nice workmanship. Pity to spoil it. Lost the key, eh?' he said tersely.

'Yes,' grinned Frank. 'That's why I came to you.'

'Oh, well, soon get this off you,' said Xavier. 'Though it won't be easy to mend once it's off, mind.'

'Oh, I don't care about that. I won't need it any more, you see,' said Frank.

'Oh, I see. Well, that's all right, then,' replied Xavier.

Frank admired the blacksmith more and more as they talked. His cock stiffened as he mentally undressed the stocky lad. In his imagination he caressed the blacksmith's handsome, manly physique with reverent fingers. In his lustful daydreams he planted kiss after kiss upon those full and sensual lips. And all the time those large bullish eyes gazed at him unflinchingly.

Just to stand close and talk with Xavier made Frank tremble with desire. The blacksmith was thick-waisted and heavy of thigh and calf, just as Frank liked a man to be. And, although his full arse and sturdy legs were encased in thick brown leather knee-boots and brown corduroy leggings, his torso was covered only by a brown leather waistcoat much worn with oil and singe marks. This showed off to advantage the rippling muscles of his hirsute chest and belly, and his thick, muscular, hairy arms. Frank drank all this masculine beauty in with furtive but eager eyes.

In the end, Xavier ignored the lock, which was of too devilishly cunning a design for him to open by using any of the ready-made wrought-iron keys that hung on the rows of hooks against the back wall of his smithy. Instead he went over to the forge, and, with a bevy of puffs of wind from the bellows, the fire blazed up red and hot.

Now Xavier motioned to Frank to sit astride the anvil. He thrust a pair of metal tweezers into the heat of the forge until the tips glowed first red, then orange, then yellow and finally white. At last, the stocky blacksmith spat on his hands, and he brought the tweezers out of the blaze. With surprising delicacy of hand movements he teased the hinge of the cock girdle apart. He took great care not to singe Frank's naked haunches. Both Frank and Xavier laughed with nervous relief when finally the cock girdle fell apart in the blacksmith's strong hands, and Frank could step free of the restraining device for ever.

'Now, lad, that's a job well done, and now I think we both deserve a beer for our pains,' chuckled Xavier, as Frank pulled on his leggings and laced his codpiece over his now liberated organ.

As they moved out of the smithy, Xavier took off his waistcoat and sauntered bare-chested over to the horse trough, which stood in the road before his shop. He splashed his head and shoulders with the cold water from the stone trough, and, as his curly black hair dripped over his eyes, he grinned at Frank and took the towel that a willowy slip of a girl, who had just joined them from the house, held out to him. She whispered something into Xavier's ear, and he flashed her a smile of complicity and nodded.

'This is my wife, Judith,' he said, as he presented her to Frank. 'And this fine young friend of mine is Lord Frank du Bois,' he said grandly to Judith. She dropped a little curtsy to him.

'And now for a beer and also the matter of payment,' said Xavier, and he beckoned Frank to follow him into the house. Judith trotted behind them, and cast sidelong glances of interest at Frank, who was a fine sweet-smelling gentleman compared with her swarthy and sweaty tough man of metal, Xavier.

No sooner had they reached the interior of the house than Judith brought them each a flagon of cool beer. They sat at the table in the sitting room and drank. After they had quaffed down the rich brew thirstily, Xavier reached across and swept Frank unexpectedly into a tight wrestling hold. Judith then proceeded to lock the door. After that she approached and stripped Frank of all his clothes.

When he stood stark-bollock-naked, Xavier let him go.

'What do you mean by this?' asked Frank, blustering hotly.

'Just the matter of payment for services rendered,' said Xavier, and he eyed Frank's naked body with the look of a horse dealer who checks over a handsome young colt he wants to buy. 'I don't want any money from you.'

'What do you want, then?' asked Frank, though his suspicions were beginning to grow. Under Xavier's lingering scrutiny, his cock started to swell and rise up into a pulsing erection, and his bollocks began to swell and ache.

'Well,' continued Xavier, and he slowly peeled off his boots, waistcoat and leggings until he, too, stood naked. His cock also throbbed upright. 'It's not so much what I want, but more a question of what my dear lady wife here craves.'

Judith, too, now began to strip off her blouse, skirt and petticoats until she stood naked between the two men.

'And what is that?' asked Frank, running his eyes over Judith's willowy frame, her slim waist, her pert breasts and the triangle of golden pubic fuzz at the base of her belly.

'I want to be fucked by two men at the same time,' began Judith in a soft, low voice, and she caressed her pussy with one hand and tweaked at her nipples with the other.

'I want one to pierce me afore, to fill my pussy with his hard man's meat. And then, while he's still in me, I want to be pierced aft by another fellow's tool. So that my arse is crammed with his prick, too.'

Judith paused, and Xavier continued.

'We both like the look of you, Frank. Judith saw you out of the casement window and suggested to me that we invite you to join us in forming a magic triangle of lust. Not on a regular basis, mind. But just this once. What do you say?'

Frank looked from the muscular and well-endowed Xavier to slim Judith, and back again.

'Such a payment would be an honour and a pleasure for me to

effect,' he replied at last, feeling his belly flutter, his cock stiffen, and his bollocks tighten even more as he spoke.

'Very well, then, Frank, my lad,' said Xavier. 'Do you fancy fore or aft duty?'

Frank was about to say 'fore', when Judith turned to him. She gazed deep into his eyes, touched her forefinger to the centre of his lips, and slowly traced a line down to his chin, down his throat, over his Adam's apple, between his proud pectorals, down his chest, over his muscular abdomen, and across his navel to end up at the base of his cock. This she proceeded to grasp firmly and to wank with gentle wrist movements.

'Oh, my sweet young lord. I want to feel your seed spurt in my arse. Will you oblige me?'

Frank felt his resistance melt, and Xavier chuckled.

'Seems like the missus has made her mind up, eh, Frank? Best just do as she bids you then, lad.'

As Judith's deft fingers continued to work at Frank's cock, the pre-come oozed from the tip of it. Xavier took up his position in front of Judith. His thick fingers twirled and tweaked at her nipples, and turned them stiff and proud with excitement. Occasionally, too, he reached down and ran a fingertip down the moist crack of Judith's pussy, and caressed her lust-engorged clitoris.

Now all three were ready, eager and hungry for intense sexual conjoining. Frank parted Judith's buttocks and thrust a spit-moistened finger into her tight anus, to ready her for his cock. Judith for her part bent forward to suck at Xavier's cock head, to ready him for her pussy.

Now Frank lined up his thick cock at Judith's arse gate and plunged into her. She cried out with the power of his firm thrusts, and her pussy wept with tears of excitement.

At this point Frank reached around and drew the lips of Judith's pussy apart, so that the sweet shell-like inner convolutions of her sex gaped pink and moist in the cool air. Judith pulled Xavier's hips to her, and his cock, its tip positioned at the sticky outer entrance to her cunt, slipped sweetly into place – head, shaft and root inside her.

Xavier began to thrust hard into Judith's cunt, and it was sheer joy for Frank to feel the blacksmith's mighty member as it rubbed against his own through the slender membrane of Judith's arse wall.

In counterpoint to Xavier's stalwart cunt-plugging, Frank thrust repeatedly into Judith's arse, and soon all three were lost in the sheer energy of the tripartite sexual experience.

Judith whimpered and flailed with pleasure at this double assault. So powerful was the penetration from fore and aft that at times she danced on tiptoe and rose and fell into the air, like flotsam that floated on a tempestuous sea.

Xavier growled like a beast as he lunged repeatedly with his iron-hard dick deep into Judith's soft-yielding pussy. His cock felt like a red-hot steel blade that he tempered over and again in a pool of cool water.

And what of Frank? Frank moaned with extreme pleasure as his cock slid slickly in and out of Judith's palpitating arse mouth. He deftly parried the movements of Xavier's mighty cock as he felt them through Judith's elastic arse wall. It was an erotic fencing match where all who took part won and there were no losers.

At last Frank groaned and loosed his pent-up jet of spunk into Judith's bowels. It left his cock like a lightning-fast, white meteor, and it seared in its intensity and trailed a sticky mane of silvery swimming sperm behind the forerunner.

Xavier orgasmed almost at the same instant. He arched his head back and gave an ululating cry of sexual joy as he did so, like a wolf that howls at the pleasure of the kill.

And between them Judith's body quivered and jerked about in spasm after spasm. Her eyelids fluttered wildly, and she groaned and whimpered again and again. She was clearly experiencing an all-consuming multiple orgasm at the very moment of realising her sexual dream to the full in all its glory.

After this payment in kind, Frank got dressed and left Xavier and Judith still naked. They embraced and kissed each other tenderly in the afterglow of sex. Frank had half a mind to stay with them for a little longer. He yearned to take full part in another erotic coupling with them, if it should take place.

However, he had pressing business at home – a meeting with Rob and a reckoning with his evil brother Philippe to attend to – and so he forwent that transient present pleasure.

From the smithy he went straight to the river, where Dickon and Martin had arranged to meet him. There they were, bare-arsed and playing at the water's edge with Jack Hawthorne the blacksmith's boy, when Frank arrived.

'Come on in. The water's lovely!' shouted Dickon, as he splashed about, but Frank shook his head.

'We could have some fun together,' called Martin, and he lay on the bank and caressed his semi-erect cock invitingly, but Frank, though the vision sorely tempted him, and made his uncaged cock leap up in sprightly fashion, resisted the temptation with an iron will.

'I must be on my way,' he called back. 'Can any one of you take me to Woodmere Hall on the du Bois estate?'

'Are you turning down a chance of a fuck with the three of us?' asked Dickon, incredulous.

'Two of you,' said Jack to Dickon laconically. 'I must ride over to my uncle's today. He lives right next to the du Bois lands.'

He scrambled out of the river and called to Frank, as he pulled on his clothes. 'I'll take you where you want to go, sir, and with no delay.'

So it was that Frank ended up riding back to his father's estate on the back of the same weary nag as Jack Hawthorne. It was a highly erotic ride for Frank as he was seated close behind the handsome burly lad, and had his arms around his waist to keep him steady. But, despite the fact that Jack oozed with heavy male sexuality, Frank fought against the desire to make passionate love with him. He was travelling home to Rob now, and that was more important than any quick and furtive fuck along the way with a passer-by, however good-looking.

Jack stopped his horse at the gate to the du Bois estate, and Frank hopped down.

'Best of luck, sir,' called Jack and he rode off without a backward glance.

Frank dismissed the slight feelings of regret that he still harboured at losing the opportunity to fuck such a sweet young lad. He strode purposely through the gateway, but ignored the broad trodden earth path that led through the trees and up to the castle. Instead he veered at once to the right and made off towards the woodcutter's cottage.

Frank heard the sound of chopping wood as he hurried along, and, as he grew nearer, he hoped that it would be Rob that he met.

Rounding a spinney of trees, he suddenly saw the powerful arms, broad shoulders and narrow waist of his old friend. Rob's back was to him, his arms raised in mid-axe-swing, and Frank watched him at work for a while, marvelling at the compelling beauty of his musculature in motion.

Once Rob had chopped down the tree he was working on, Frank darted forward and clapped his old friend on the back.

Rob wheeled round, startled, but then his face split into a broad grin when he saw who it was.

'Master Frank, sir. You came back!'

For reply Frank smiled and held up the horn ring, which Rob had sent via Hal to summon him.

'I knew you'd come, sir, when I sent that ring. A friend is a friend, after all, and a promise is a promise. I knew you wouldn't let me down!'

'How could I?' replied Frank, and then he looked at Rob in earnest. 'Now, tell me all.'

'Well, sir, I don't rightly know how to begin. Hal will have told you about Philippe, no doubt.' Rob spat the name of Frank's brother out with hatred.

'Yes, he did. But what about Molly?'

'Well, sir. She's now working as a servant at the hall, and I'm worried for her safety, sir. Your brother! He's a demon, sir. A very demon since he inherited all. I fear for Molly's honour, sir, and I fear for her life. We're to get married tomorrow, sir, but I fear that your brother wishes to prevent, or at the very least to mar, our wedding with his perverse interference.' Rob was quite worked up by now.

'Don't worry, Rob!' Frank used the magical voice of power on him. 'Don't fear for Molly.'

Rob quietened down, and Frank decided to test his command of the tricks that Salim had taught him.

'You'd like Molly to be here, right now, wouldn't you?' he went on.

'I would that,' said Rob, his eyes slightly glassy.

'You'd like her to be sitting next to you, as I am, wouldn't you?'

'Indeed I would,' replied Rob, his eyes now becoming unfocused. A faint smile played over his lips. He reached down and scratched his groin. Frank could see the bulging erection that swelled beneath his tight leggings.

'You're excited by Molly being here, aren't you, Rob?'

'I am that. My cock's rearing up in my breeches as I look at her.'

'At me, Rob. You're looking at me. And I'm glad to see you, too, Rob,' continued Frank, entering magically into the role of Molly.

'I want to take you, Molly, here and now,' continued Rob, and he unlaced his codpiece and let his superb cock spring free. 'You send me wild with desire as I look at you. I want to drive my manpole hard into your sweet pussy.'

'Lie back, then, Rob, and I'll ride you to ecstasy,' commanded Frank, and Rob lay back on the leafy forest floor, a beatific smile of expectation on his face.

Frank now cast off his leggings, and knelt down bare-arsed astride Rob's hips, but, just as he was about to impale himself upon the sticky tip of Rob's tool, Salim's words of advice, of commandment, came to him: 'You mustn't abuse this power!' He had been so beguiled by getting Rob to fall under his magical influence that he'd got carried away. He wanted Rob to fuck his arse while the lad believed he was fucking Molly's pussy. This was no good at all. It was sheer deception, and no good would come of it. Frank snapped his fingers at once and Rob's unfocused gaze jolted sharply back to see reality.

'What on earth . . . ? Where's Molly?' the woodcutter gasped, and he lay there, and rubbed his hands with his eyes as Frank rose and went over to retrieve his cast-off leggings.

'I'm sorry, Rob, I was about to trick you into making love with me,' said Frank penitently. He waited for Rob to turn angry with him, but the anger never came.

'And why would you want to do that?' asked Rob, and he gazed up at Frank in wonderment.

'Because I love you, Rob, as I've loved no other man. More than a brother. And I wanted so much to feel your hard cock inside me that I was prepared to stoop to trickery to gain my desire. But I stopped myself just in time.'

'Good thing, too,' said Rob sternly, and he raised himself up on his elbows.

Ah, now I'm for it, thought Frank.

'Trying to make me think I was making love with Molly when it was you all along,' said Rob indignantly as he sat up. 'It isn't right.'

'I'm sorry,' blurted out Frank, and he wished the earth would swallow him. 'I knew you'd feel repulsed by the truth. I knew you'd reject me because of my feelings for you.'

'No, Master Frank. You misunderstand me,' went on Rob, and he lay back down on the forest floor once more. 'Look at my cock!'

Frank looked. There was Rob's cock, thick, hard and pulsing with masculine strength. It was such a tempting vision. Frank longed to take it inside his mouth, inside his arse. What was Rob playing at now? Was he tempting him with forbidden fruit he could never taste?

'What do you mean?' asked Frank, confused.

'I mean that I want to fuck you, Master Frank. Not as Molly, but as yourself. I've long dreamed of making love with you. I lusted after you in secret, like. But I always held back, afraid you'd look down on me because of my humble birth.'

'I . . . I don't understand. But you and Molly . . .'

'I love Molly, to be sure. The man part of me does, but the other part of me longs to make love with you, Master Frank.'

Frank could hardly believe his ears.

'So, you actually want both of us?'

'Yes,' grinned Rob. 'I want to have my cake and eat it, so to speak. So, if you've got no objection, why not lie down next to me and let's us two make love now, long and hard, to make up for lost time and lost opportunities.'

Frank took Rob at his word. He lay down next to his milk brother on the leafy forest bed, and the two men moved closer. Each kissed each other's face and caressed his body lovingly.

Frank felt a thrill of pleasure as Rob's hand closed on his stiff cock and began to wank him with slow and sensual strokes. He reached out and grasped Rob's sturdy organ and began to masturbate him until the pre-come oozed from his cock tip. It dripped down his whole cock's length in sticky transparent rivulets, coating Frank's hand with its warm moistness.

Now Rob pressed his cock tip to tip with Frank's organ. And carefully he unrolled his loose foreskin so that it covered Frank's cock head as well as his own. Frank revelled in the sweet feeling of Rob masturbating both their cock heads wrapped up together in the same soft prepuce.

At length, when Frank judged that Rob's excitement was high and that he would soon be ready to penetrate him anally, Frank withdrew his cock head from Rob's warm and enveloping foreskin and pushed his friend gently down on to his back. Once again he positioned himself with his thighs astride the woodcutter's hips, but this time as himself, not as a magical simulacrum of Molly.

The excitement thrilled through Frank's body as Rob lined up the tip of his thick cock against the crack of his arse. Frank wiggled his hips slightly and sat down on top of Rob's massive dick, and he willed that hard pole of man's meat into him. He shivered with pleasure as his long-awaited dream came true. Rob's mighty prick entered the bunched portal of his arse. Frank opened himself to receive the hard and throbbing rod in its entirety. He joyed in the intensity of feeling as Rob's pulsing phallus stretched his anal sphincter to the very limit. This was what he had yearned for over so many months, and now it was happening. He and Rob Oakley were making love.

Frank gazed down lovingly at the handsome lad under him. He felt Rob's cock helmet sink comfortably and gradually into place inside his arse. Now, rising and falling gently in the sexual saddle, he took inch after inch of Rob's veined cock shaft into himself. He marvelled at how utterly right it felt, and what a gorgeous sensation it was to welcome Rob's length of hard man's flesh into him in this way.

Rob for his part gazed up at Frank with such love in his eyes, as he ran his hands gently over Frank's pectorals, and toyed with Frank's cock and balls to increase the young lord's pleasure.

Frank, meanwhile, gazed down at the woodcutter's brawny shoulders, his hairy chest, his muscular abdomen, his slim hips, his rugged thighs, and he felt the best part of the lad buried deep, hot and hard within his own arse. His heart melted with pleasure at the sight and feel of this long-sought penetration, and his cock oozed a flood of glistening pre-come from its swollen tip.

Now Rob began to plunge up into him, and Frank rose and fell like an experienced jockey riding a skittish stallion. He bobbed up and down on the peaks of Rob's thrusts like a small boat that rides the crests and troughs of mighty waves in the midst of a fearsome storm. And it was a veritable tempest of passion for Frank that seemed to seethe and boil in Rob's heart. It found physical expression in the young woodcutter's sexual performance, as he rammed his turgid tool in a powerful, animalistic way deep into his friend's yielding bowels.

All at once, while Frank still rode Rob with a regular rise and fall, making towards his own distant orgasm, Rob's body tensed and he let out a great cry of deep sexual satisfaction. A split second after, Frank felt his bowels washed by the warm flood of Rob's spunk. It was such a delicious sensation, to feel his innards swimming in Rob's silky ejaculate, and he indulged in the sensuality of the moment. He felt flattered at the intense sexual excitement that he had engendered in Rob, an excitement so intense that he had caused the lad to ejaculate so soon. But Frank's own peak of erotic pleasure was far off, and he was disappointed that he had not been able to shoot his own milky load in this act of sexual joining which held so much significance for him.

His momentary worries subsided, however, for Rob seemed keen to ring the changes in their sexual position.

'You've ridden me to orgasm, Frank. And now I want to do the same for you.'

'Do you really, Rob?' The words were like music to his ears.

Now Frank rose up, and Rob's flaccid cock-snake slithered from its nest hole behind Frank's dangling bollocks. Frank felt the lack, the absence, of Rob's hard rod inside him keenly. But the prospect of being able to stuff his own cockpole deep into Rob spurred him on.

Now Frank lay back, and gazed up as his burly friend straddled his thighs. Rob sat down on Frank's hard and throbbing cock head. He threw his head back, let out a deep sigh of satisfaction, and closed his eyes as Frank's rigid cockrod slid deep into him. Frank began to thrust up with short shallow jabs of his cock and Rob bore down on him. His muscular arse soon swallowed up Frank's prick to the hilt.

This is pleasure indeed, thought Frank as he continued to thrust up into his friend's accepting arsehole. Rob's cock had now stiffened into the hard horn of an erection again, and Frank grasped it and wanked it rhythmically as he penetrated Rob again and again.

At last Frank shot his jet of liquid lust like an arrow deep into Rob's warm bowels, and this triggered Rob to come again. His massive cock spattered Frank's face, neck and chest with pearly droplets of his hot seed.

'Oh, Frank. You can't imagine how I've longed for this!' whispered Rob, and he kissed Frank fervently on the mouth, the chin and the throat.

'But what about Molly?' Frank asked nervously.

'Oh, Molly won't mind.' Rob was definite in his rebuttal. 'If we can rescue her from your brother tonight, then I'm going to marry her tomorrow the same as we've planned. Why should she care about what you and I get up to? It's not as if she's losing me to you. She'll just gain another man in her bed through me. And one so handsome and so powerful in love as you are is sure to win her heart. Between us, Frank, we'll satisfy her every sexual craving, believe me.'

With Frank's cock still firmly embedded deep in his arse, Rob ran his fingertips over Frank's cheek. He bent forward, and kissed him lingeringly full on the lips once more. 'I want both you and Molly in my life and in my bed, Frank. You must believe me.'

'I do,' replied Frank fervently. 'I do believe you, Rob.'

After they had finished their lovemaking, Frank and Rob got dressed and hurried off to the du Bois castle to find Molly.

Night was just setting in as they arrived, and through the leaded casement windows they saw Philippe holding court in the great hall with a gaggle of five of his sycophantic cronies in attendance. Their five woollen travelling cloaks hung discarded on a wall rack, and all five were now wearing ceremonial hooded uniforms. They were drinking copious draughts of red wine, and clearly, judging by their ribald singing and the red faces visible under their hoods, had been at it for some time.

The tapestry of Ganymede, which in happier times had hung in that very room so carefree and joyful in mood, now brooded over the fireplace, dark and ominous, as if it were a portent of some vile act of humiliation about to be perpetrated.

Through a broken pane in the window, Rob and Frank could hear Philippe's voice, strident and harsh.

'Bring in the wench now, Carl,' he shouted, and one of his burly hooded friends left the room hurriedly and returned in a trice with Molly on the end of a rope.

Her wrists were bound together, and there was a tight gag tied across her mouth to prevent her crying out. The long rope, by which Carl led her like a dog on a leash, was fastened around her waist.

Once they had reached the centre of the room, Carl tied the free end of Molly's rope to a large iron ring set into the flagged floor. Thus she could pace around and around like a caged wild animal, but she could never entirely get free.

'Well, my dear,' laughed Philippe evilly, 'it seems I have you in my power now. No handsome young woodcutter to save you from your fate, I fear.'

Molly tried to speak, but the gag cut into the sides of her mouth and prevented her from articulating any words. Instead, her eyes flashed defiant fire at Philippe.

'Now, my dear, you are at my mercy,' continued Philippe. He drew closer to Molly, who was at the very limit of her rope. She backed away from him slightly, and he continued to advance upon her.

Suddenly he reached out and grasped with two hands the front of the bodice of her dress, pulling it violently apart. It ripped open and Molly's full breasts tumbled out. Her eyes spoke outrage and she darted forward to knee Philippe in the codpiece, but he skipped back beyond the limit of her rope once more and taunted her from there.

'No, no, no, my dear,' Philippe went on – his voice full of icy suaveness. 'You don't want to make me angry with you, do you, my sweet?'

Philippe turned to Carl, now. 'Put the irons in the fire,' he commanded.

Carl went over to the baronial fireplace. Some branding irons stood propped up against the wall of the inglenook. Carl took them, and laid them down with their brand marks in the seething hot embers of the log fire that crackled and blazed merrily.

'You have such beautiful breasts, my dear girl. But soon they will be beautified still more when they each bear my brand mark seared upon them.'

'Noooooo!' yelled Rob, and he sprang from Frank's side, and dived through the casement into the hall. He shattered diamond panes and snapped the crisscross web of grey leading as he went through the window and landed in a heap on the flagged floor.

Philippe turned and looked curiously at this intruder.

'Carl, the rope, quick!' he snapped, and before Rob had time to stir he found his wrists tightly bound. Carl then tied him by a length of rope to another ring in the floor some six feet from Molly, on the other side of the fireplace.

'Well, well, well,' said Philippe, and he eyed Rob up and down with an evil expression on his face. 'How touching. The young woodcutter comes to save his girl from the branding iron.'

Frank, who had stayed unnoticed outside the window, watched and listened intently, but what could he do against Philippe and his five hooded cronies?

Rob spat full at Philippe. He aimed at his face, though he missed. The gobbet of spittle landed on Philippe's starched lace collar, where the arrogant young lord brushed it off with disdain.

'Rob Oakley. That was an unwise move,' he snarled. Then he turned to Carl and barked, 'Gag him!'

Once the tight band of cloth had stopped Rob's mouth, Philippe drew close once more, though he kept beyond the limit of Rob's tether.

'I was going to content myself with branding Molly on the breast or the rump, but now I see my original intent falls short of the full range of possibilities. I feel that a gang rape would be more in order.'

Philippe's hooded cronies smirked and chuckled evilly at this suggestion, and they eyed Molly hungrily.

'What's more,' went on Philippe, 'now that you have opted to join us tonight, I wish to include you in things, my dear young Rob. What do you say to a spot of anal rape? First I bugger you while Molly looks on, then I bugger her while you look on. That should be amusing, don't you think? Especially on the very eve of your wedding!'

Rob's eyes flashed lightning bolts at Phillipe, and he struggled against his bonds angrily.

'Strip them naked!' barked Philippe, and Carl and another crony ripped off first Molly's dress and then Rob's shirt and leggings.

'What a fine rump,' muttered Philippe, and he slapped and palped Rob's muscular buttocks with his hand, like a rich farmer at a livestock fair examining a stud bull. 'And it will look even finer once it bears the du Bois crest branded upon it.'

Frank stood outside the window and watched. No one within the hall paid him any attention, for no one knew he was there. What Philippe was planning to do with Rob and Molly was evil, wicked. He had to stop it, but how? His mind raced. And then it

198

came to him. He knelt down and scrabbled in the dirt at his feet until his fingers closed on what he needed.

Now he stood up, leaned in through the broken window, and flung a sharp pebble hard at his brother's head. It struck true, and blood flowed from just above Philippe's ear. Philippe turned sharply and fell back, his face distorted first by horror and then by rage when he saw that Frank was there.

'You!' he cried.

'Shame on you, brother,' taunted Frank. 'Reduced to taking men and women sexually by force, are you? Not attractive enough to get them any other way, I suppose.'

Philippe's lip curled.

'And what are you doing here, you bastard? Tired of that monastic order, did you?'

'Indeed,' replied Frank. 'So I decided to come home.'

'Did you, eh? Well, as you can see, things have changed here. Grandmother is dead and I am master of Woodmere Hall now. All men here obey me and serve my will.'

'Not me,' replied Frank.

Philippe goggled angrily at him.

'Then I will bend you to my will,' snarled Philippe. He turned to Carl and two of his other hooded cronies. 'Carl, Jorick, Haakon, after my half-brother and catch him! And the one who does so gets first fuck of the woodcutter and his wench on his return.'

Frank turned on his heel and sprinted off, and Carl, Jorick and Haakon grabbed flaming torches and ran into the night after him.

But Frank had the advantage of them. He had played in the castle grounds as a young lad and he knew all its secrets, all its various nooks and crannies.

First he hared off to the upper terrace. There he grabbed an urn of flowers, and scrambled up on to an empty plinth, where he stood motionless, like a statue. He saw his three pursuers split up and hurry off in different directions. Jorick went on to the lower terrace, and came closer. In the end he stood directly beneath Frank as he looked from right to left – scanning the garden for any sign of Frank. When Frank dropped the flowerpot on his hooded head, Jorick crumpled up unconscious on the path below him.

Frank then ran off in the direction of the gardener's tool store, where Carl had headed. This was in fact an ivy-covered door that led into a windowless cave in the base of solid rock on which the castle stood. When Frank arrived there, he saw the door stood ajar and he could also make out the flickering light of a torch inside the cave. He smartly slammed the door shut and swiftly turned its rusty iron key around to lock it from the outside. Carl could hammer and pound all he liked, the door was thick and its hinges strong, and he would not escape from there in a hurry.

Now there was only Haakon left. Frank had seen him make for the gatehouse and so he followed him there.

When he arrived, he was surprised to find Philippe's hooded thug interrogating Jack, the blacksmith's apprentice, who was backed up against the gatehouse door.

Frank noticed with a smile that the heavy beam of wood that bolted the outer gate against enemy attack in time of siege lay propped against the gatehouse wall on his side of the twosome. He tiptoed towards it.

'So, you brought Frank du Bois here earlier and you just thought you'd pay him a visit, did you?' grilled Haakon.

'Y-yes, sir,' replied Jack uncertainly.

'You're lying, boy!' snarled Haakon. 'You came here to meet him by arrangement.'

Frank waited to hear no more. He hefted the heavy beam of wood from its leaning place and thwacked Haakon on the head with it. Haakon slumped at once to the ground like a dead man.

'It's good to see you, my lord!' said Jack with relief.

'Glad I could be of service to you, Jack, to repay your earlier kindness to me.'

Frank pulled the hood off Haakon's head, wrested the still flaming torch from his hand before it sputtered out on the ground, and beckoned to Jack to follow. As they hurried off across the dark castle grounds, he explained briefly what was happening and what exactly he intended to do about it.

They ran back to the castle by way of the terraces. Jorick was beginning to stir groggily on the ground by now. For good measure Frank hit him once again on the head with the flower urn. Jorick collapsed into a crumpled heap once more.

Now Frank tore the hood off Jorick's head and handed it to Jack, who pulled it on hurriedly. They lit Jorick's torch again from the torch that Frank held, and then returned to the great hall.

A rescue plan was swiftly forming in Frank's head. For it to work, he relied on the fact that the hoods they wore would conceal their faces to some degree, and also that Carl was Philippe's especial favourite. He hoped that Jorick and Haakon, who were about the same build as Jack and himself, had not so keenly attracted the attention of the new Lord du Bois and that they would not merit more than a cursory glance when they came into his presence. He also figured that Philippe's two remaining cronies would be so busy ogling Molly's and Rob's naked bodies that they would not notice the substitution of two of their number by hooded impostors.

In all these surmises Frank proved to be correct. As soon as Frank and Jack rushed into the hall and placed their burning torches into a wall bracket to the side of the huge tapestry of Zeus's rape of Ganymede, Philippe, without a second glance in their direction, barked angrily at them.

'Where's my brother?'

'Don't know, sire,' said Frank, and he hung his head as if shamefaced.

'Reckon Carl might find him, sire,' continued Jack. 'We all went different ways, you see.'

'Very well,' snarled Philippe. 'But my lust is rising within me and I can delay no longer. You two!' he shouted at the other two cronies in the room. 'You hold the wench.'

They ran to do his bidding.

'And you two!' Here he turned back to Frank and Jack. 'Restrain the young woodcutter, here. I want him to see exactly how I bugger his girl.'

Frank and Jack moved close to either side of Rob, and Frank whispered hurriedly in his ear.

'It's all right, Rob. It's me, Frank.'

Rob glanced for a moment at him, a look of relief in his eyes. Then he turned back to see what Philippe was about to do to Molly.

Philippe had unbuckled his codpiece, and one of his cronies knelt before him, and kissed and wanked his master's cock into a hard erection.

When Philippe was fully aroused, he stepped close behind Molly. His cronies pinioned Molly's arms and forced her to incline her upper body forward so that her arse stuck out provocatively close to Philippe's drooling cocktip.

Frank had secretly untied Rob's wrists and waist by now, but he made a sign to the lad to stay calm and to hold back. The odds were against them. Philippe and his two cronies bore swords in their belts. Frank and Jack had a dagger each, but Rob and Molly were unarmed and vulnerable. It would be a very uneven fight if it came to it.

Suddenly, just as Philippe seemed about to grasp Molly's buttocks and fondle her there, while she shuddered with revulsion at the thought of the anal penetration to follow, Frank noticed a crackling, a popping and a fizzling sound that came from behind him, coupled with a smoky smell of burning.

He wheeled round at once to find that one of the torches had slipped to one side in its wall bracket, and that tall flames now licked the tapestry of Ganymede in the eagle's arms and some even shot up to the ceiling.

'Oh, my god!' screamed Philippe, who had also now become aware of the sudden blaze, and was panicking. 'We must stop the fire. It mustn't spread. Quick, fetch pails of water from the castle moat, piss upon it, anything.'

But his words were in vain. The dry old tapestry flared up unstoppably. It was wholly a sheet of flame by now and the fiery orange tongues began to lick at the dry uprights and crossbeams of the wooden scaffolding that shored up the ceiling of the great hall, as they did in so many dilapidated parts of the du Bois castle.

It was clear that the fire was swiftly taking hold of the castle and that all the pails of water or pisspots in the land would not be enough to put out the conflagration.

Acrid smoke filled the great hall now, and the roof beams started to char and some spontaneously burst into flame as the fire spread.

'Escape! We must escape!' yelled Philippe. 'This way.'

He beckoned to his two cronies, who fled hurriedly through the main door, out of the hall, and into the castle grounds after him.

Frank ripped the gag from Rob's mouth, and Jack rapidly untied and ungagged Molly. Frank grabbed two of the long woollen cloaks from the pegs where they hung on the wall and threw one around Rob's shoulders. The other he draped around Molly. She smiled at him gratefully.

'Quick now!'

Jack beckoned to Molly and Rob to follow him through the main door too, but Frank pulled them back.

'Too dangerous!' he shouted over the roar of the blaze. 'Philippe and his cronies would run us through with their swords as we came out. Like ratcatchers who smoke out rats from their hole.'

'But we can't stay here!' shouted Jack back at him. 'We'll be burned alive if we do.'

Suddenly an image from the past – a dark corridor to safety – flashed into Frank's head.

'Follow me!' he yelled, and he made for the far side of the fireplace. The three others ran after him, the fire hot on their heels.

When Frank reached the wall, he touched the carved stone boar's head on the du Bois crest, and a secret door clicked open in the masonry. Frank dived into the dark tunnel beyond and the others followed.

This was the tunnel where Frank and Rob had played as young boys. It led out of the castle, twisted around underground, and emerged in a stone grotto at the end of the castle garden.

When Frank, Jack, Molly and Rob at last came out of the tunnel's far end, they looked back to where the castle stood. Its stones no longer looked grey and still in the moonlight. They were dancing orange walls of flame.

Frank could clearly see Philippe and his two cronies in silhouette as they stood between them and the fire.

Philippe shouted and stamped his foot in impotent rage.

'Oh, my god! My house! My heritage! It's burning to the damn ground!'

Frank crept closer, unseen in the darkness. The fire was spreading apace now. The constant wind that rippled over it fanned it to new heights. The greedy flames neared the chapel. Heavily supported by wooden struts and wooden ties, this was where Yolanda lay buried.

'Oh, my god in heaven! Not the chapel, too,' screamed Philippe, and his voice took on a hysterical edge. 'Is nothing sacred?'

'I must go in before it's too late!' he shouted. 'I must rescue what I can.'

'My lord,' pleaded one of his cronies, 'you would be going to your death. See how the chapel burns.'

Frank watched the snaking orange flames engulf the small church.

'I have no care for my own life. That is of little account,' Philippe sobbed in a paroxysm of grief. 'But all that I count most dear is about to be swallowed by the fire. I must do something. Unhand me, cowards.'

He pulled away from his cronies, who desperately tried to restrain him, and rushed headlong through the chapel door, screaming, 'I am here to save you from the blaze, my treasure!'

A second later there was a loud report of breaking timbers and the roof of the chapel collapsed inwards. Frank fancied that he heard Philippe's voice scream with the pain of hellfire, as if he had been crushed by a falling beam and was now being roasted alive, his leg trapped under rubble, at the very entrance to the underground vault where his grandmother, Lady Yolanda, lay buried.

Fourteen

During the night Philippe's fair-weather cronies left the castle to burn. As there was nothing they could do to stop the blaze, Frank, Rob, Molly and Jack took what they could from the different wings of the great house before the fire reached and consumed them, though nowhere did they find the great chest of gold and jewels that had once graced Lady Yolanda's bedroom while was still alive.

Then, just before sunrise, a fierce storm broke. The rain tumbled down in sheets and did what human firefighters could not – it doused the flames. In the dawn light, Rob and Molly excused themselves from keeping further vigil with Frank. They returned to Rob's cottage in the woods, there to get dressed and make ready for their wedding, which was to be celebrated, as they had planned, later that day.

Frank now had only Jack for company as he explored the smouldering remains of the castle. His first act was to enter the blackened chapel interior solemnly, followed by Jack. There, under a huge beam that smoked pungently, they found Philippe's fire-ravaged corpse. It lay face down on the floor, and its blackened arms reached out, with soot-black fingers charred to bone, pointing like talons towards the carved flagstone under Frank's feet.

'What was he doing here?' asked Jack, curious.

'It's my guess he wished to save our grandmother's remains from the flames. He lies near the entrance to her tomb. Here, under our very feet. You can see her crest.'

'Was he a pious man, then?' asked Jack, curious.

'Pious, no. But devoted to Lady Yolanda, and she to him.'

'A strange tale,' said Jack. 'And one that fairly beggars belief. From what you have told me, and from what I myself saw and heard of Philippe, he was a purely selfish man. There must have been some other reason for him to brave the flames as he did.'

'Be that as it may,' said Frank. 'It is a reason that we shall never know. It goes with my brother to his fiery grave.'

There was a bronchitic cough behind them. Frank spun round. It was old Quentin Holly. Mad as ever, it seemed. Or maybe not quite so mad as Frank had once supposed.

'Welcome home, young master,' the old man said, and he shuffled forward and dropped arthritically to one knee before Frank.

Frank suddenly realised that what Holly said was true. With Philippe dead he, Frank du Bois, was now indeed the official master of the du Bois estate.

'Rise up, Quentin,' said Frank, and Quentin stood up on his bowed legs. 'Now I am in truth master here, you are welcome to return to the castle to live out your days in my service.'

'I thank you, sir,' said Quentin, and he kissed Frank's hand. 'I knew all would turn out well when Lady Yolanda called for Philippe to come to her on her deathbed. This I had from your page, Hal, sir.'

'I don't follow you, Quentin. Why should Philippe being at her bedside when she died make any difference?' asked Frank, bemused.

'It was what she said to him then that was the important thing, sir.'

'And what was that?'

'She told him the truth, sir.'

'And what "truth" do you speak of now?'

'That you and he are not full brothers but half-brothers only.'

206

Frank drew himself up to his full height and rounded on Quentin angrily. 'Enough of your crazed slanders, Quentin. I have it on excellent authority that I am the true son of my father and mother, Sir Oliver, and the Lady Isolde, and anyone who says otherwise is a liar and a scandalmonger.'

'Oh, but sir, your birth was not the issue. It never was. It was the birth of your older half-brother that was in question.'

'Philippe's birth? What do you mean?'

'Did you not know, sir? He was the offspring of a union between the woodcutter, Will Oakley, and the Lady Isolde.'

Frank reeled back with shock. Philippe a half-brother both to himself and to Rob! It seemed impossible. And yet he remembered Hal Ashe's words at Nonpareil. He recalled how there were physical similarities between Philippe and Rob.

'That was when Philippe went a bit mad, sir,' continued Quentin. 'After Lady Yolanda died, he realised that *he* was the bastard, sir, not you. And he knew that he had less right to the family estate than you did, sir. But the world was never meant to find out his secret. That was why Hal Ashe fled in fear of his life.'

No wonder Philippe had reacted so desperately when he realised that Frank – the true du Bois heir – had returned from the castle of Nonpareil and intended to live at home once more.

'That was why he buried the chest of gold and jewels in the family vault with his grandmother. For safekeeping should you ever return, sir.'

Frank's head spun with this fresh information. So the family riches had neither been squandered entirely, nor destroyed in the castle fire. They were here, under his feet, safe and sound in Lady Yolanda's vault. He laughed at the irony of it. Philippe had preserved the jewels at the cost of his life, and now Frank would sell them and spend the proceeds. There was a crazy kind of logic to it. It was a sort of divine retribution.

'What did I tell you, sir?' chipped in Jack. 'I thought there was something fishy about Philippe's sudden devotion to his grandmother's remains. All is plain now. He didn't rush into the burning chapel to save her at all. He wanted to save the family jewels from the blaze.'

'Right,' said Frank. 'So let's see how they are.'

Using Phillipe's fire-blackened sword as a crowbar, they raised the crested flagstone together. Once it stood fully upended, they descended the narrow stone staircase that lay underneath it and went down into the vault. It lay dark, dank and untouched by the fire, and there, by Lady Yolanda's carved coffin, stood the treasure chest, just as Quentin Holly had described it, whole and intact.

Frank was relieved to know, with the discovery of Philippe's hoard, that he now had the wherewithal to rebuild the burned-out shell of Woodmere and refurbish it over time in order to bring it back to its former state of glory.

His heart alight with euphoria brought on by this unexpected treasure trove, Frank asked Jack to help him hulk the chest to the one castle tower that remained unravaged and unspoiled by fire. Once it was there, he locked the tower door, and, for even greater security, he stationed Jack outside the tower as guard. Then he rushed off at once to the village church, where Rob and Molly were getting married, for, as Rob's closest friend, Frank was destined to be best man at the ceremony.

The marriage ceremony passed smoothly; the groom looked handsome and the bride radiant, and there was a roast-boar-and-mead wedding breakfast at the Boar's Head Inn afterwards.

The wedding speeches there flowed freely, as did the mead, and, after the roast boar, waiters served a sweet syllabub to all. Finally Rob and Molly cut up the marchpane cake and divided the pieces between the guests. And at last all went back to their homes.

For the time being, until his castle could be rebuilt, Rob and Molly invited Frank to lodge with them. And that wedding night, as the custom was, Frank, as the lord of the manor, was to have first fuck of the new bride. And in this instance, as Frank was his long-lost milk brother, Rob wanted to observe this custom to the letter.

No sooner had they retired to the bedchamber than Molly stripped off her wedding finery. Inspired, Frank tore off his leggings to reveal a cock that pulsed with hard virility. Rob looked on fondly as, top to tail, Frank began to lick at Molly's quim, and Molly began to stroke and suck at Frank's hard manhood. It was not long before the two of them teetered on the very brink of sexual release solely as a result of their heated foreplay.

Now Molly lay back on the bed and raised her legs high in the air, and Frank positioned himself to service her. His sticky cock tip pointed straight at her lust-engorged pussy mouth. With a few well-aimed thrusts he slid his whole length into her, reached his mouth down to suckle at her full breasts, and caressed her clitoris from time to time with his deftly exploring fingers.

As he plunged again and again into Molly's slick cunt, Frank knew now that he would never be able to return to the Order of the Tree of Life. Vaginal sexual congress with a woman was strictly forbidden to all cult members. But, as Molly's vaginal fluids moistened the length of his hard tool, Frank felt no regrets about closing the door that led back to the castle of Nonpareil. Instead vistas of a delightful future together with Rob and Molly opened up to him.

Suddenly Frank realised that Rob had joined them on the bed. Even as his own cock plunged deep into Molly, Frank felt excruciating pleasure as Rob parted his buttocks and began to thrust his thick cock into place deep inside him. Frank's cup of joy fairly overflowed at this double assault on his senses. To fuck and be fucked deliciously at the same time. Could his bliss be more complete?

His flexing arse danced on the slippery pole of Rob's hard man meat. He could hardly bear the sweet suction, this intimate intrusion. Rob was the pestle, he the mortar, and the grinding was heart-achingly intense, and below him, Frank's own pintle ground away in Molly's sweet cup.

At last they came, simultaneously. All three breasted wave after wave of foaming pleasure as Rob spent his silver load into Frank and Frank transmuted Rob's jism into his own and charged Molly generously with the same, plus interest.

In the warm afterglow of lovemaking, all three bodies separated, regrouped and intertwined. Rob lay in the middle with his arm around Molly on one side. He tenderly caressed her breast, and pinched the erect nipple that capped it, with the finger and thumb of one hand. Frank lay on Rob's other side, and the woodcutter's son lazily stroked his aristocratic bedmate's flaccid cock and balls, as he coaxed them to relive their harder days.

Now Rob hugged Molly to him and kissed her on the lips. He turned and raised his hand from Frank's sex, in order to stroke Frank's handsome cheek, jaw and manly chin tenderly.

'This man is our lord and master, Moll,' he said to his wife. 'But he's also my dearest friend. He's like a brother to me. Dearer even than a brother, I might say.' Frank looked across as Rob said this with such deep love in his eyes.

The woodcutter continued: 'You don't mind if he comes to warm himself in our bed from time to time, dearest Moll. I love the man so dearly, I can deny him nothing, not even a share of my pretty young wife from time to time.' Here he chucked Molly tenderly under her soft dimpled chin.

'Sweet Rob,' said Moll, and she giggled, and eyed Frank's now swollen cock with avid interest. 'Rest easy.' She patted Rob's hardening pole of flesh seductively, her playful actions seeming to contradict her very words.

'And you, brother Frank, too. Have no qualms about what you do to invade our marriage bed. Indeed, it is no invasion in my reckoning, no.'

She now clambered over Rob's supine form and wriggled in and snuggled down in the space between the two men, before she continued.

'In truth I count it quite the opposite − as a blessing from heaven,' she chuckled. 'For how could a woman complain at finding herself with two men abed when she has such a good appetite for jiggery-pokery as I?' Here she ran one hand over Rob's erect cock to the rear of her and with her other hand she caressed Frank's throbbing cock to the fore.

Now, as if with one unspoken accord, the three of them regrouped once more on the bed. Molly crouched on hands and knees, Frank knelt at her head and she bent her full lips down and took the whole length of his sturdy organ into her mouth, and sucked and slurped on it as if she were feasting on some long and ripe exotic fruit.

Rob knelt behind his bride and guided his cock head into place between her pert arse cheeks. As she felt him there, Moll wiggled and rammed her arse backward on to Rob's cock so that inch by inch his stiff and swollen dick slid up into her back passage.

Once Rob was deeply inside Moll, he began to fuck her arse with strong urgent strokes. And, to mirror his milk brother, Frank responded and fucked Moll's mouth with the same urgency. Moll was in sweet ecstasy as she felt those two mighty manpoles enter her top and tail, and she squirmed with delight and caressed her clitoris with feathery fingerstrokes to heighten her erotic pleasure. Now the two men increased fuck speed and rhythm and began to thrust faster and farther into her, while they gazed all the while across her undulating back at each other. They both loved to fuck Moll like this, to be sure, but, as Rob ran his nails down Moll's quivering flanks to thrill her to the utmost, he winked and grinned across at his 'brother'. Frank knew then, in his heart of hearts, that from time to time he and his beloved Rob would continue to make love together in secret – just the two of them.

IDOL NEW BOOKS

Information correct at time of printing. For up-to-date availability,
please check www.idol-books.co.uk

☐
WORDS MADE FLESH
Thom Wolf

Best-selling novelist Glenn Holden has an appreciation for the rougher side of sex. But when a handsome stranger breaks into his house claiming to be a character from one of Glenn's own thrillers, the author is suddenly thrust into a surreal sexual adventure that goes further than the concoctions of his own dirty mind – a bizarre world full of mysterious men and even wilder sex.

£8.99/$10.95

ISBN 0 352 33544 0

☐
DIVINE MEAT
Edited by David MacMillan

An Idol short-story collection. Gods pleasure themselves with male flesh and vice versa in this astonishing array of tales of human/divine homoeroticism. From Ganymede and Zeus to lustful voodoo deities, sacred genies and the Cerne Abbas giant himself, these stories are hot, horny and (well) hung. *Divine Meat*: where man meets his maker. In more ways than one.

£8.99/$10.95

ISBN 0 352 33587 4

☐
MAN ON!
Turner Kane

Greg Williams of Middleton United is young, talented and handsome, a favourite with both fans and players alike. But when he signs his new football contract with Weston City, and when he starts sleeping with his soon-to-be-wed best friend Matt, things start hotting up, both on and off the pitch.

£8.99/$10.95

ISBN 0 352 33613 7

☐
CUSTOMS OF THE COUNTRY
Rupert Thomas

James Cardell has left school and is looking forward to going to Oxford. That summer of 1924, however, he will spend with his cousins in a tiny village in rural Kent. There he finds he can pursue his love of painting – and begin to explore his obsession with the male physique.

£6.99/$9.95

ISBN 0 352 33246 8

VENETIAN TRADE
Richard Davis

From the deck of the ship that carries him into Venice, Rob Weaver catches his first glimpse of a beautiful but corrupt city where the dark alleys and misty canals hide debauchery and decadence. Here, he must learn to survive among men who would make him a plaything and a slave.

£6.99/$9.95   ISBN 0 352 33323 5

THE LOVE OF OLD EGYPT
Philip Markham

It's 1925 and the deluxe cruiser carrying the young gigolo Jeremy Hessling has docked at Luxor. Jeremy dreams of being dominated by the Pharaohs of old, but quickly becomes involved with someone more accessible – Khalid, a young man of exceptional beauty.

£6.99/$9.95   ISBN 0 352 33354 5

THE BLACK CHAMBER
Jack Gordon

Educated at the court of George II, Calum Monroe finds his native Scotland a dull, damp place. He relieves his boredom by donning a mask and holding up coaches in the guise of the Fox – a dashing highwayman. Chance throws him and neighbouring farmer Fergie McGregor together with Calum's sinister, perverse guardian, James Black.

£6.99/$9.95   ISBN 0 352 33373 1

MAESTRO
Peter Slater

A young Spanish cello player, Ramon, journeys to the castle of cellist Ernesto Cavallo in the hope of masterclasses from the great musician. Ramon's own music is technically perfect, but his playing lacks a certain essence – and so, Maestro Cavallo arranges for Ramon to undergo a number of sexual trials in this darkly erotic, extremely well-written novel.

£8.99/$10.95   ISBN 0 352 33511 4

FELLOWSHIP OF IRON
Jack Stevens

Mike is a gym owner and a successful competitive bodybuilder. He lives the life of the body beautiful and everything seems to be going swimmingly. So when his mentor and former boyfriend Dave dies after using illegal steroids, Mike is determined to find out who supplied his ex with drugs.

£8.99/$10.95   ISBN 0 352 33512 2

THE PHEROMONE BOMB
Edward Ellis

A crack army unit – the Special Marine Corps, consisting of five British and five American soldiers – are on a top-secret mission to investigate, and if necessary eliminate, an illegal private army on a tropical island in the mid-Atlantic. What the tough, hard soldiers realise when they investigate the island is that the enemy doesn't shoot them with bullets. The enemy has discovered a powerful weapon: the pheromone bomb, which produces a gas – and anyone on whom the gas settles is filled with irresistible homoerotic urges.

£8.99/$10.95   ISBN 0 352 33543 2

------- ✂ -------------------------

Please send me the books I have ticked above.

Name   ....

Address   ....

                  ....

                  ....

           .... Post Code ....

Send to: **Cash Sales, Idol Books, Thames Wharf Studios, Rainville Road, London W6 9HA.**

US customers: for prices and details of how to order books for delivery by mail, call 1-800-805-1083.

Please enclose a cheque or postal order, made payable to **Virgin Publishing Ltd**, to the value of the books you have ordered plus postage and packing costs as follows:

    UK and BFPO – £1.00 for the first book, 50p for each subsequent book.

    Overseas (including Republic of Ireland) – £2.00 for the first book, £1.00 for each subsequent book.

We accept all major credit cards, including VISA, ACCESS/MASTER-CARD, DINERS CLUB, AMEX and SWITCH.

Please write your card number and expiry date here:

....

Please allow up to 28 days for delivery.

Signature ....

------- ✂ -------------------------